Life
on
Loan

ALSO BY ASHLEY FARLEY

Only One Life
Home for Wounded Hearts
Nell and Lady
Sweet Tea Tuesdays
Saving Ben

Magnolia Series

Beyond the Garden
Magnolia Nights

Sweeney Sisters Series

Saturdays at Sweeney's
Tangle of Strings
Boots and Bedlam
Lowcountry Stranger
Her Sister's Shoes

Scottie's Adventures

Breaking the Story
Merry Mary

Life on Loan

ASHLEY FARLEY

LAKE UNION
PUBLISHING

Text copyright © 2019 by Ashley Farley
All rights reserved.

Published by Lake Union Publishing, Seattle

www.apub.com

Amazon, the Amazon logo, and Lake Union Publishing are trademarks of Amazon.com, Inc., or its affiliates.

ISBN-13: 9781542043861
ISBN-10: 1542043867

Cover design by Emily Mahon

Printed in the United States of America

To every woman who has ever doubted herself.

CHAPTER ONE

LENA

Lena tapped lightly on her daughter's bedroom door. Kayla had an important interview in less than an hour that she couldn't afford to miss. This job, more than the others she'd applied for, had potential. Four months had passed since her college graduation, and she'd yet to find employment. And Lena had long since run out of patience with the situation.

At the sound of a muffled groan coming from within, Lena reached for the knob. Surprised to find it unlocked, she nudged the door open a crack. Her jaw dropped at the sight of a naked man sprawled out in bed next to her daughter.

Kayla sat bolt upright in bed, her hands covering her bare breasts. "Mom! What the heck!"

Lena stood in the open doorway, paralyzed and speechless.

The man rolled out of bed, landing on his feet. As he scooped his clothes up off the floor, Lena trained her eyes on his body parts from the waist up. His chest was broad and tan, and a tattoo of a bird's feather inscribed with the words *Carpe Diem* adorned his left bicep. A scruffy beard covered his face, and he had more thick wavy hair on his head than Lena's golden retriever had on her entire body.

"Charles! Come quick!" Lena called down the hall to her husband, who was shaving in the master bathroom. "We have a serious problem."

Kayla yanked the covers up over her naked body. "God, Mom!"

Lena glared at the man. "I don't know who you are, but it's clear what you're doing here. If you're not outta my house by the time I count to three, I'm calling the police."

"Chill out, lady," the Golden Casanova said as he pulled on his boxer shorts. "No need to get the police involved."

Lena caught a whiff of booze and cigarettes as he brushed past her. She followed him out into the hall. "And don't you dare show your face around here again!" she yelled at his retreating back.

He took the stairs two at a time on the way down, pausing on the landing to finish getting dressed. He tugged on a paint-splattered T-shirt, but as he was struggling into his jeans, he stumbled, tumbling to the hardwood floor at the bottom of the stairs.

Biscuit, who loved everyone except the mailman, scrambled, with claws against hardwood, to his side, and licked his bearded face with her pink tongue. Shoving the dog off him, Golden Casanova got to his feet and made a dash for the front door. He turned the bolt, and as he threw open the door, he set off the burglar alarm.

When the shrill from the siren pierced the air, Kayla—a sex goddess with blonde hair tousled and bedsheet draped around her body—emerged from her room while her father, with razor in hand and his face covered in shaving cream, appeared in the doorway of the master suite at the opposite end of the hallway.

"What the devil is going on?" Charles shouted above the security system's shrieking.

Lena glared at Kayla. "Your daughter's overnight guest, her *man* friend, set off the alarm."

Charles's brown eyes bulged. "You mean—"

"That's right. Your daughter brought home a strange man last night."

Kayla rolled her eyes. "He's not a stranger. At least not to me. And I don't see what the big deal is. Some of my friends are living with their boyfriends." She spun around, sheet flying about her like a cape, and headed back toward her room.

"Good for them!" Lena yelled seconds before Kayla slammed the door in her face.

When the landline rang in their bedroom, Lena pushed her husband out of the way as she moved to answer it. The woman from the alarm company was abrupt. "This is B-Safe Alarm. Do you have an emergency?"

"No. Sorry. Everything's fine." Lena punched the code on the wall keypad beside the bedroom door, silencing the alarm. "My daughter's friend accidentally set off the alarm."

"Name and password," the woman demanded.

"My name is Lena Browder, and the password is . . ." She searched her memory for the password. "Peanut butter. No, that's not it."

Pressing the receiver to her chest, Lena turned to her husband. "Do you remember the password?"

He threw his free hand in the air and shook his head as though this were somehow Lena's fault.

"Strawberry jam," said Lena.

"Are you sure about that?" the woman asked in a snippy voice.

"Actually, no. I'm not," Lena said, feeling irritated with the woman. Those people were there to protect her, not accuse her. "We haven't set off the alarm in years."

"Have a nice day, Mrs. Browder," the woman said, and ended the call.

Lena returned the receiver to the cradle. "Marmalade! That's it. The password is *marmalade*."

Charles glared at her, the expression on his partially shaved face a mixture of disbelief and disgust. "I can't believe you condone this kind of behavior from *your* daughter."

3

"So she's *my* daughter now?" Lena said, turning to face him.

"I warned you it was a mistake letting her move home after college. Turns out I was right." Gripping his razor, he held it up in front of her face. "Your job was to raise the children, and mine was to provide for the family. I've more than kept my end of the bargain. But you've . . ."

She stared him down. "I've what, Charles?"

"You've become a hermit." His eyes traveled her body, lingering on the muffin top spilling over the waistband of her ratty gym shorts. "You sit around all day reading trashy novels and eating ice cream."

She cringed at the insult. Her metabolism had tanked after she'd turned fifty. She blamed her weight gain on menopause, along with hot flashes and mood swings and other joys associated with being a middle-aged woman. "That's not true. I do stuff."

He rolled his eyes. "Oh right. I forgot. You created a blog that no one ever read."

"There are at least a million cooking blogs on the internet. Do you know how hard it is to stand out?"

"No, and I don't care." He spread his arms wide. "You created this mess, Eileen. And I expect you to fix it."

They stood glaring at each other in the center of their bedroom. Her husband was the only one who'd ever called her Eileen. He insisted her given name was more dignified. But the sound of it on his lips made her skin crawl. She'd never hated him as much as she hated him at that moment. It wasn't a heat-of-the-moment kind of hate, but a deep loathing that had been building over the years, brought on by his dismissive attitude as well as by all the hurtful things he'd said to her.

When she heard Biscuit barking ferociously downstairs, Lena moved to the window and drew back the drapes. A Richmond City police car with blue lights flashing had pulled up in front of the house. An officer got out of the driver's side and approached Golden Casanova, who was hobbling barefoot over gravel on the road at the end of the sidewalk, his bare arms wrapped around his midriff to protect himself against the morning chill.

Lena hurried down the hall to Kayla's room. Despite the chaos around her, Kayla had fallen back asleep and didn't so much as crack an eyelid when Lena retrieved Casanova's flip-flops from under the bed. She flew down the stairs to the front hall, where Biscuit was waiting, tail wagging and leash in mouth, beside the front door. She attached the leash to her collar, and they took off down the sidewalk with Biscuit leading the way.

"Marmalade," she said to the officer. When he narrowed his eyes at her, she explained, "I couldn't remember my password when the alarm company called. But it's marmalade. This young man is a friend of my . . . of the family's. He set the alarm off by accident. There's no intruder. I'm sorry we wasted your valuable time, Officer."

A blue sedan with a dented front fender and Uber logo pasted on the window came to a screeching halt beside them. Lena thrust the flip-flops at Casanova. He slipped them on his feet and jumped into the back seat of the Uber, and they sped off.

Once the sedan rounded the corner out of sight, the officer turned his attention to Lena. "And your name is?" he asked, pen poised above his notepad.

"Lena Browder. I'm the homeowner. Everything is fine here, Officer. Truly."

He scribbled her name on his notepad and returned it to his shirt pocket. "All right, then. I'll be on my way. Have a nice day." He tipped his hat to her and got into his patrol car.

Lena waited on the sidewalk for him to drive away before taking off in the opposite direction. The brisk air made Biscuit frisky, and Lena had to work hard to keep up with her. Autumn was her favorite season, and normally, the sight of brightly colored mums and pumpkins on her neighbors' doorsteps would've boosted her spirits. But not after the scene that had just unfolded in her home. With head bowed, she glued her eyes to the street as she walked behind Biscuit at a feverish pace.

Tears stung Lena's hazel eyes as her husband's words echoed in her mind. *You've become a hermit. You sit around all day reading trashy novels and eating ice cream.* Worst part of all—she knew that what he'd said was true. She'd lost her way. She felt as if she were drowning, and no one cared enough about her to throw her a life jacket. Eating ice cream provided comfort from the loneliness, and reading those so-called *trashy novels* offered an escape from what had become an unbearable life.

Lena had been thrilled when Kayla had moved back home after college. She'd seen it as an opportunity for mother and daughter to reconnect.

"It'll only be for a couple of months," Kayla had promised. "Until I can find a job and a place to live."

Those couple of months had turned into the longest four months of Lena's life. She loved her daughter, but she found her presence in their home a major disruption. Kayla stayed out half the night and slept much of the day. She left dirty dishes in the kitchen sink and wet towels on her bedroom floor. But most exasperating of all was her insolent attitude. And she'd crossed the line by bringing a strange man into their home for sex.

"Not under my roof she won't. Right, Biscuit?"

When Biscuit stopped walking, looking up at her with adoring eyes, Lena reached down and scratched her behind the ears.

She continued on for another block, waving at Gloria, a neighbor from a few streets over, who was jogging in the opposite direction, her tight-fitting exercise pants and tank top showing off her toned body. Gloria reminded Lena of the women at the football tailgate party she'd recently attended with Charles to celebrate homecoming at his alma mater, Hampden-Sydney College. The wives of his classmates had gotten leaner and blonder and less wrinkled. They spoke of bridge lessons, facial treatments, and trips to places she'd never heard of. Feeling self-conscious and having nothing to contribute to the conversation, she'd stood off to the side near the food table.

Lena increased her pace to a jog as she thought about how Charles had chastised her on the ride home, calling her socially awkward and making fun of her for pigging out—such hurtful but true words—on the buffalo chicken dip. In his own way, he'd treated her with the same disrespect as their daughter. He frequently no-showed for dinner without bothering to call. He played golf on the weekends, tennis on Wednesday evenings, and poker every other Thursday night. *I can't even remember the last time he took me out to celebrate my birthday or our anniversary. I'm always cooking and cleaning and shopping for groceries.*

Lena ran until her chest tightened and she experienced a sharp pain in her side. She doubled over as she struggled to catch her breath, dripping sweat on the sidewalk.

She was a doormat. And she was damn tired of her husband and daughter walking all over her. They were vampires, sucking the life out of her. She had to find a way to save herself. She didn't know where she would go or how she would get there. She just knew she had to get out of that house.

CHAPTER TWO
OLIVIA

Olivia parked her suitcase beside the door and circled her one-bedroom, third-floor condominium, lowering the thermostat and checking locks. She stood at the French doors leading to her tiny balcony and looked out over the harbor. She would miss the view. She loved Charleston and hated to be gone for even one day, but she needed to leave town in order to clear her head and distance herself from the Kates.

She'd created her blog, *High Living in the Lowcountry*, known to her followers as *Hi-Low*, to establish a platform for her articles on fashion, food, and events specific to the Charleston area. But she'd gotten caught up in a competition between Kate Baker and Kate Bradford, two young women determined to outdo one another. In their midthirties, they were single, gorgeous, and making careers out of spending their daddies' new money.

Olivia glanced up at her wall clock. She still had twenty minutes before she needed to summon an Uber for her trip to the airport. She brewed herself a fourth cup of coffee—three more than she usually drank—and took it outside to the balcony. She scrolled through her phone's text messages until she found the one she'd sent her daughter three hours earlier. I need to get away from Charleston for a few days. Are you up for a last-minute visit?

The message showed it had been read, but Laura had yet to respond.

Olivia had charged the airline ticket to her mounting credit card debt. But regardless of her ultimate destination, whether she actually went to Seattle or changed her ticket to Houston or Denver or some other city where she could lose herself in the crowd, she would be on a plane at noon, when her blog post went live and holy hell broke loose in Charleston.

Kate Baker would be furious when she read the post, but Olivia had taken measures necessary to preserve her own sanity. She settled back in her lounge chair, propped her feet on the matching ottoman, and sipped her coffee as the events of the previous evening replayed in her mind.

∼

Olivia had made it to the Charleston Harbor Marina just as the hundred-foot special events yacht—the *Eliza Jane*—that Kate Baker had chartered for the evening was preparing to pull away from the dock. She took off her low-heeled wedges and sprinted barefoot past the row of sportfishing boats, calling and waving for the captain to wait for her. A crew member on the stern held his hand out to Olivia, nearly snapping her arm out of its socket as he hoisted her on board. He held her arm until she'd caught her breath and steadied herself before turning her loose.

She took a moment to get her bearings. The party was already in full gear on the open-air deck on the stern of the boat, with guests dancing to rap music blaring from loudspeakers. She spotted Kate at the edge of the crowd and approached her, greeting her with an air-kiss near her cheek. "I'm sorry I'm late. There was traffic on the bridge. It took me over an hour to get to Mount Pleasant from downtown."

"I'm just glad you made it in time. I'm trying out a new caterer. Be sure to let me know what you think. Here." She snagged a champagne flute off the tray of a passing waiter and handed it to Olivia. "Have some champagne and go do your thing." She dismissed Olivia with a sweep of her arm in the direction of the party.

Olivia worked her way to the far side of the deck. As she stood watching the late-September sun begin its descent, the salt air that whipped her strawberry-blonde hair about her face felt cool and invigorating. Thirsty from the physical exertion of running down the dock, she guzzled the expensive champagne as if it were water and placed the empty glass on a nearby table.

Turning to face the partygoers, she leaned back against the side railing and removed her camera from her tattered black leather tote. She took off her lens cap and zoomed in on Kate, whose blonde hair cascaded down her back in perfect waves and curls in spite of the humidity and wind. She wore a black dress so tight it left little to the imagination, ankle-wrap sandals with chunky heels, and a man on her hip who was noticeably younger.

Olivia scanned the crowd with her camera in search of a familiar face. After three years of photographing the same individuals, event after event, she knew most of them by name and reputation. She'd come to think of them as hangers-on, taking advantage of the Kates' hospitality week after week. But in this particular group, she didn't recognize a single person. They were dressed the same—men in skinny jeans and shorts with collared shirts and women in short flowy dresses—but she guessed the median age to be five years younger than the normal crowd. Kate Baker's current boy toy had most likely dictated the guest list.

She focused on a striking couple standing nearby, the woman's dark head tilted back in laughter at something her companion had said.

When Olivia pressed the shutter, the guy spun toward her, his man bun bouncing around on top of his head as he searched for the source of the clicking sound. When he spotted the camera in Olivia's hands, he glared at her from behind aviator sunglasses. "Hey, what d'you think you're doing? I didn't give you permission to take my picture. Erase the image."

"Fine." Olivia was unfazed by the man's rudeness. The younger generation lacked the manners she was accustomed to. She held the camera up for him to watch while she deleted the image.

Man Bun scowled at her. "Who are you, anyway? Some cheesy photographer Kate hired for the night?"

"I'm a journalist." Olivia stared down her nose at him. He was considerably shorter than her five-foot, eight-inch frame, and she wondered if he had a Napoleon complex. "My website, *Hi-Low*, is quite popular with the millennials."

"She's a blogger," Man Bun's date said with a giggle, as if being a blogger were a disreputable profession. Olivia had initially thought the woman attractive, but on closer inspection, her teeth were too big and her makeup too thick.

"I have an extensive following, actually. Most people jump at the chance to be featured in one of my posts." Olivia brought the camera to her face, but as she zoomed in on him, she noticed a trace of white powder under his nose. While she'd suspected the Kates and their friends were into drugs, they respected her enough not to use them in front of her. She lowered the camera. "Or maybe you don't want the public to see that residue under your nose."

"Get lost, Grandma," Man Bun said. "You're way outta your league here."

"Gladly." She pivoted on her wedges, pointing her camera in the opposite direction. As she walked into the crowd away from him, she snapped photographs of a blonde—scantily clad in a halter top and denim miniskirt—dancing provocatively on top of a round teak table. The crowd was edgy, seemingly invigorated by the taste of autumn in the air. They gulped down booze and ignored the platters of appetizing food displayed on a buffet table in the corner of the deck. When Man

Bun dumped a mountain of cocaine on a glass-top table and produced a rolled-up twenty-dollar bill, the partygoers migrated toward him.

Olivia looked around for an exit. She was on a boat in the middle of the harbor at least a mile away from the nearest shoreline. There was no escape, unless she wanted to grab a life jacket, jump overboard, and pray the coast guard rescued her.

She retreated to the edge of the crowd. When a few of the women shed their tops and began dancing on tables and chairs, she turned her back to the party and gazed off into the inky black night.

After a while, thirty minutes or more, she sensed a presence looming behind her. A deep voice near her ear said, "Quite the spectacle, isn't it?"

"That's an understatement. I clearly don't belong with this crowd." With a sideways glance, she caught a glimpse of the man's white double-breasted chef's coat. "And from the looks of it, neither do you." She turned to face him, extending her hand. "It's nice to meet a fellow sore thumb. I'm Olivia Westcoat, sole blogger at *High Living in the Lowcountry*."

Recognition crossed his face as he took her hand in his. "I thought you looked familiar. I'm Oscar Palmer, sole chef at Oscar's Plate. My wife and I wait eagerly for your posts every week. We love the Kate Scapades. Your writing is brilliant."

Brilliant? She'd heard the Kate Scapades column called a lot of things, but *brilliant* wasn't one of them. "Kate mentioned she was trying out a new caterer. I'd love to sample your cuisine, but I'm too afraid to move from this spot."

He offered his arm. "Then allow me to escort you to the food table. Do you like sushi?"

"I happen to love sushi," she said, taking hold of his arm.

He led her through the crowd and into the salon to an untouched food buffet. In addition to the wide assortment of sushi, there were sliders, cocktail shrimp shooters, and meat skewers.

Olivia gasped. "The sushi is too pretty to eat."

"And too delicious to waste, if I say so myself. The other guests are clearly not interested." He handed her a small square plate. "Please help yourself."

Taking the plate from him, Olivia piled it high with an item from every offering. "I never knew there were so many different types of sushi." She took a bite of a salmon roll. "This is delicious."

"I'm glad you like it." He leaned against the table, arms crossed over his chest. "I was intrigued, and not necessarily in a good way, when Kate booked this gig. If you don't mind me asking, how did you get mixed up with those two in the first place?"

She popped the rest of the salmon roll into her mouth. "Totally by coincidence. I met Kate Baker a couple of years ago at a party she was hosting in her tasteful downtown home for one of my now ex-husband's law partners who was getting married. I asked if I could feature the party on my blog, which was in its early stages at the time, and she jumped at the chance. Two days later, when the post went live, *Hi-Low* received more page views than ever before. Within the hour, I received an invitation from Kate Bradford to a formal dinner party she was having the following evening."

"And so you got stuck in the middle of their battle to see who can throw the most outrageous no-expense-spared social function."

"Exactly. The blogosphere's version of reality TV," Olivia said as she bit into a mini mahi-mahi taco.

"I admit I'm totally fascinated by the Kates' scandalous behavior."

"You are not alone, which is why the Scapades has grown so much in popularity. People need celebrity figures to spice up their otherwise mundane lives." Olivia caught herself. "I'm not suggesting your life is mundane."

"Compared to the Kates' it is, and I wouldn't trade anything for it." His expression was one of amusement. "I'm curious, do the Kates ever go to each other's parties?"

"Never. They have some personal vendetta against each other. I have no idea what it is, nor do I care."

His eyebrows shot up. "Do I detect a note of hostility?"

She set her plate down on the table and wiped her mouth with a paper cocktail napkin. "It's my own fault for allowing the Kates to use me as their pawn. I'm trapped in this crazy game they're playing. It's a no-win situation for me. I have a very large following waiting in anticipation for tomorrow's post. No journalist in their right mind would leave them hanging. If I put an end to the Kate Scapades, I'll lose all my followers. But if I continue to feature the parties, I'll tarnish my reputation as a travel and food freelance writer. Not that I haven't already done that."

"When I called your writing brilliant a minute ago, I meant it. I'm sure there are other followers like me who will read anything you write. You're smart and funny, and that personality really shines through in your posts."

She smiled. "Thank you for saying that."

"I'm not just saying that. I mean it. Have you ever thought about writing a novel?"

Olivia laughed, as though she'd never considered the idea when she'd in fact thought of little else recently. She'd once had high aspirations of becoming a published author. "I'd be happy just to take back control of my blog. If only I could figure out a graceful way to exit, to take a break while I regroup."

She stared down at the camera in her hands, her finger on the shutter, itching to photograph something. But what? What was the most exciting thing at this party? *Food!* Oscar's nibbles were the most exciting thing at this party. "Would you consider letting me feature *you* in tomorrow's post? It'll give me the out I've been looking for with the Kates, and you'll get the attention of thousands of readers, ages ranging from thirty to eighty."

A smile spread wide across his face. "That's the best offer I've had since my wife and I moved here last year."

"I'll need photographs, of course." She aimed her camera at a platter of sashimi but lowered it when she realized the lighting was too dim. "Is there somewhere we can go with better lighting?"

"This vessel has a sleek kitchen, and I have a special bottle of Albariño, which pairs nicely with sushi." He grabbed two trays of sushi. "Follow me."

She trailed him up a short flight of stairs and through an informal dining room. The kitchen was all stainless-steel countertops, chrome fixtures, and commercial-grade appliances. And the under-cabinet lighting provided the soft illumination she needed. She began shooting while he poured two glasses.

For the remainder of the voyage, he told her about his life as a chef in a five-star restaurant in Chicago and his dreams back then of starting his own catering company one day. They staged a number of photographs of food and wine and Oscar sautéing onions on the gas range.

She mentally plotted during the shoot, and by the time they arrived back at the marina, she'd worked out her angle for her article. His impressive interview coupled with her phenomenal photographs would make for a dynamite exit post.

Once the boat was secured to the dock, they managed to duck out of the party without Kate seeing her. Oscar walked her to the parking lot, and they exchanged business cards in parting. "I'm going straight home to write my post," Olivia said, eager to get started.

"Now? But it's almost midnight."

She nodded. "Now's the best time, while it's fresh on my mind. I promise to heap praise on your talents, but I'm warning you, Kate will be irate at me for leaving her out. The comments could get ugly. I can censor them to some extent, but there's only so much I can do."

"I trust you to treat me fairly. Besides, they'll be angry at you, not me." He flashed her a grin. "I'm just in it for the publicity."

"You'll definitely get plenty of that," she said, slipping behind the wheel of her tornado-red Volkswagen Beetle convertible. "I only hope it's the right kind of publicity."

Olivia drove back across the bridge and through the nearly deserted streets of downtown Charleston to her condo. She brewed herself a cup of tea and went straight to work. She titled her post: Oscar Palmer: The Area's Next Emeril Lagasse. And the opening remarks read: Last night's cocktail cruise around the harbor on a luxury yacht chartered by Kate Baker would've been unremarkable if not for the exquisite presentation by the area's new renowned caterer, Oscar Palmer of Oscar's Plate. She went on to describe his sushi in detail and to talk about his reputation as a five-star chef. She ended the post with this line: This is the last you'll hear from me for a while as I pause to reflect on the past two years and determine a new direction for the future of Hi-Low.

It was after three in the morning before she signed off her website and began searching the internet for flights to Seattle. Blaming the Kates for her problems was easy, but her urgent desire to leave town was about way more than them. She'd been on the go for two years since her divorce. She'd sold her house and moved into her condo. She'd dined out in restaurants most nights. She'd shopped. God, had she done some shopping. And, of course, she'd spent an absurd amount of time chasing after the ridiculous Kates. She'd convinced herself that staying busy was the best way to keep from being lonely. But the truth was, if she slowed down, if she stopped running for even one minute, she'd be forced to face the reality that the life she'd built with Robert, the man she loved, had come to an abrupt and screeching halt.

CHAPTER THREE

LENA

Lena waited until she was certain Charles had left for work before returning home. She stopped in the kitchen to fill Biscuit's bowls with food and water and then hurried upstairs to pack. Most of her clothes no longer fit, and the ones she could still squeeze into took up only two-thirds of the space in her small rolling suitcase, which left plenty of room for her cosmetics bag. She packed her wallet, a lightweight sweater, and the romance novel she was currently reading in the worn backpack—one of Kayla's castoffs—she occasionally used for overnight trips to her cottage. She zipped her iPad in the front pocket for easy access. Although she'd asked for a laptop computer for Christmas the previous year, Charles had given her an iPad.

Lena quickly showered. Not wanting to waste time on drying her hair or putting on makeup, she slipped on a loose-fitting navy knit dress—one of the ones Charles referred to as a tent.

On her way down the hall, she paused in front of her daughter's closed bedroom door and debated whether to tell Kayla she was leaving. The image of her daughter sleeping peacefully with her mouth wide open and one arm dangling over the side of the mattress, oblivious to the trouble she'd caused, came to mind, and she decided against it. She was done with hand-holding. *Let Kayla figure it out on her own.*

She wheeled her suitcase down the stairs to the family room, where she wrote herself a check for a hefty sum from the household account that she held jointly with Charles. She was leaving the room when she noticed her camera bag in the corner by the bookshelves.

As a photography enthusiast for most of her life, Lena had tried everything—landscapes, macrophotography, action sports shots—but had excelled at none. And so, she'd abandoned her favorite hobby, like everything else she'd given up on. Unable to resist, she lifted the flap on her camera bag and studied the meager contents. She'd purchased her camera body more than ten years ago, a Canon Rebel XS that offered basic features at an affordable price. She owned several lenses, all of them cheap and ineffective with the exception of the Canon zoom—an original 28–80mm she'd bought with her first paycheck after graduating from college. She fastened the lens onto the body and dropped the camera into her backpack along with two memory cards, her battery charger, and an extra battery. *I have no clue where my journey will take me, but with luck, I'll encounter picturesque scenery and interesting people along the way.*

She continued to the kitchen at the back of the house. When Biscuit saw the suitcase, she hurried to her side, staring up at Lena with pleading eyes. Lena dropped to her knees and wrapped her arms around her dog's neck, burying her face in her fur.

"I'm going to miss you, sweet girl. I can't take you with me now, but I'll send for you if it looks like I'll be gone for longer than a few days. You may need to remind them to feed you, but you're good at that. I'll leave a note anyway." Lena got to her feet and, rummaging through the junk drawer, found a pen and notepad. In all caps, she scrawled, *FEED THE DOG!*

She gave the dog one last hug, kissing the tip of her moist nose, and quickly exited the house. She tossed her suitcase into the back of her minivan and climbed in the driver's side, noticing the soft drink stains on the carpet and the upholstery worn thin from years of carpooling Kayla and her friends to school and sporting events. *So many memories. I need to get away from here before I change my mind.*

She drove to her local bank, cashing her check at the drive-through, before getting on the interstate toward the airport. They'd traveled as a family to a few destinations, such as Disney World; Washington, DC; and Gettysburg, Pennsylvania. Most of their vacations consisted of long weekends at their river cottage, and even those had been few and far between of late.

At the airport, Lena parked the van in the long-term garage and wheeled her suitcase across to the terminal. She'd given little thought to where she wanted to go, and without a passport, she knew her travel was limited to the United States. Inside the terminal, she looked around and decided to join the short line of people waiting for service at the Delta Air Lines counter.

When it was her turn, she approached the counter. "I'd like a one-way ticket to San Francisco," she said to the attractive Asian woman wearing a uniform and a nameplate identifying her as Tori.

"Have you booked anything online?"

Lena's eyes filled with tears, and her fingers trembled. "I didn't have time. This is a last-minute trip. I haven't flown in years. Not since my daughter was in middle school and we traveled with a group of families to the Dominican Republic. That seems like so long ago now."

While her lips pressed together in a thin smile, Tori's fingers flew across the keyboard. "The quickest schedule departs Richmond at noon and connects in Atlanta with an hour-and-fifteen-minute layover."

Lena checked her watch. Nine forty. *I've never been to California, and I've never traveled alone. There's a good chance I'll chicken out if I have to wait until noon.* She looked toward the entrance, expecting to see Charles and Kayla entering the terminal, even though she knew it would be hours, if not days, before they figured out she'd left the house. "Do you have anything sooner?"

The ticket agent tapped the keys. "I could put you on the ten thirty out of Richmond, but that would give you a longer layover in Atlanta."

"I'll take it!" Lena said, pulling her wallet out of her purse.

Tori eyed her suitcase. "You can check that for an extra thirty dollars."

Lena stiffened. "Since when are you charging money to check suitcases?"

"Since years ago, ma'am. Your bag is regulation carry-on size if you'd rather take it with you."

"Then I'll take it with me." When Tori told her the fare, Lena thumbed through the bills in her wallet. She thought about paying cash for her ticket but then opted to use her American Express card instead. Why not let Charles pay for it? She couldn't remember the last time she'd bought anything for herself. If her husband checked the online statement, the credit card charge might prompt him to call the airline for information regarding her destination, but she wasn't trying to hide from him—just get away from him. She doubted he cared where she was going anyway.

Tori returned her credit card along with two boarding passes. "Your American Express card will allow you free entry to the Sky Club in Atlanta. Considering your long layover, you might want to take advantage of our comfortable lounge and complimentary refreshments."

Lena thanked the agent and hustled down the terminal toward security. Her heart palpitated as she watched travelers in the line in front of her remove, with practiced expertise, devices from their bags and articles from their bodies. Following their example, she took off her shoes and removed her cell phone from her purse, placing everything in square plastic bins alongside her suitcase on the conveyor belt.

The TSA attendant motioned her through the body scanner and out the other side. She assumed she'd been cleared and was gathering her things off the conveyor belt when another agent pulled her aside. "Ma'am, we have rules about container sizes for carry-on liquids. Open your suitcase, please."

Lena did as she was told, unzipping her cosmetics bag for inspection. Poking around in the cosmetics bag, the agent confiscated her tube of toothpaste and container of cold cream, telling her they were over the limit in size, before sending her on her way. She arrived at the gate as the last passengers were boarding the plane. She located her row, stuffed her rolling bag in the overhead compartment, and wedged herself into the middle seat between two stern-faced businessmen in suits. She didn't remember airplane seats being so small.

She closed her eyes and rested her head against the seat. Two minutes later, when the flight attendant came on the PA system announcing their imminent departure, her eyes shot open and she started to hyperventilate. She gulped in stale air until her breathing steadied. Four hours ago, she'd awoken in her bed on a normal Friday morning, and now she was on an airplane heading first to Atlanta and then to California. She'd left a stack of unpaid bills on her desk. She was running low on coffee creamer and down to the last carton of Kayla's favorite Greek yogurt. Did Biscuit have enough dog food? Who would do the grocery shopping and pick up Charles's shirts from the cleaners? Who would fold the clothes in the dryer and take the trash to the street on Sunday night?

Your daughter, that's who. She doesn't have a job, remember? You're not only doing this for you. You're doing it for them. You need to find yourself, and they need to learn to take care of themselves. Think of it as tough love. You're going to California, Lena. California! Forget about them for once in your life. Focus on yourself.

As the plane taxied out to the runway, Lena removed a scrap of paper from her backpack and jotted a to-do list for Kayla. When her daughter eventually discovered she was gone, she would text Lena. She would forward the list to Kayla then.

Lena closed her eyes as the engines revved and the plane sped down the runway for takeoff. She shoved all thoughts of home and family aside and concentrated on the trip ahead. She would arrive in California around five o'clock Pacific time. She would rent a small car and find a hotel near the airport. She wasn't ready to explore the big city of San Francisco alone. She would start on a smaller scale by venturing down the coast to Monterey and Carmel and whatever points farther south struck her fancy. She would walk the beaches, eat good food, and take pictures of pretty scenes. She would tell anyone who asked that she was . . . What *would* she tell them? Her camera was too outdated for people to believe she was a travel photographer. In order to pass as a blogger, she would need an active website, which she didn't currently have. Perhaps she would tell them she was an artist, doing research on scenes she wanted to paint.

Lena slipped into a light sleep and woke as they were landing in Atlanta. When they reached the gate, she joined the line of passengers exiting the aircraft. She was starving, and her mouth watered as she passed Bojangles', but remembering the ticket agent in Richmond mentioning complimentary snacks, she followed the signs to the nearest Delta Sky Club.

The Delta representative at the reception counter took her boarding pass and American Express card and typed her information into her computer. "Your flight to San Fran is delayed forty-five minutes."

"Delayed?" Lena asked in a tone of alarm. "You mean there's a problem with the engine?"

"Not mechanical," the young woman said with a fixed smile. "This particular delay is weather related. There's a strong storm system moving across the country. You can follow the flight status on the app."

Lena narrowed her eyes. "The app?"

"You know, the Delta Air Lines app." She gestured to the phone in Lena's hand. "You can download it on your phone."

"Oh. Right. Thanks." *Of course there's an app for the airlines. There's an app for everything these days.*

Lena wheeled her suitcase down a short hallway and around a corner. The lounge consisted of a bar, lined with stools and displaying an assortment of liquor bottles, and a comfortable seating area with tables and chairs arranged in front of an expanse of windows. She joined the swarm of travelers waiting at the buffet. When it was her turn, she spooned lettuce and penne pasta into a bowl and topped it with grilled chicken strips and corn salsa.

She circled the room three times before locating a seat by the window. She claimed her chair and settled in for a long wait with her romance book and pasta bowl. Now that she had traveled 470 miles—as the crow flies from Richmond to Atlanta, according to the pilot—the tension had begun to drain from her body. The drama at home was in her rearview mirror, and she was concentrating on the road ahead.

CHAPTER FOUR

OLIVIA

As soon as her plane touched down in Atlanta and began taxiing toward the terminal, Olivia took her phone out of airplane mode. Incoming texts pinged, one after another. Most from Kate Baker. A few from Kate Bradford. One from Oscar. None from her daughter. She clicked on Oscar's text. Stellar job on the feature post. Phone's already ringing off the hook with requests for bookings. I owe you one. She scrolled down to the string of texts from Kate Baker. Are you kidding me right now, Olivia? WTF. I spent a small fortune on that unremarkable cruise. Who cares about Oscar Palmer? Kate Bradford was equally as irate but for a different reason. Are you seriously bailing on me, Olivia? I've planned an over-the-top party for this weekend and you're leaving town? Olivia deleted all the texts from the Kates before blocking their contact information from her phone. In order for her to get a fresh start, she needed to leave all thoughts of the Kates behind.

Wheeling her suitcase behind her, she traipsed up the Jetway to the terminal and fought her way through the crowd to the nearest Sky Club lounge. Her connecting flight to Seattle departed in three hours. She might as well be comfortable while she waited. After checking in with the receptionist while ignoring her grumbling tummy, she bypassed the food buffet and headed straight for the bar. She wasn't celebrating. Running away from her life was plenty of reason to drown her sorrows. But the reality was she needed liquid courage to follow through with her plan.

Pinot grigio in hand, she wandered around the lounge until she spotted a businessman vacating a chair by the window. As she pounced on the empty seat, she spilled a considerable amount of wine on her taupe-colored linen tunic. She wiped at the spill with her balled-up cocktail napkin. "Damn it!"

The woman across from her looked up from her romance novel. The bare-chested sex god on the cover taunted Olivia with his seductive good looks. She had no interest in romance, fiction or otherwise. How could she ever trust a man again after the man she'd trusted with her life for the past twenty-eight years had betrayed her?

"Here you go," the woman said, handing her a stack of napkins.

Olivia took the napkins from her. "Thank you. This blouse is one of my favorites, and now it's ruined for the rest of my trip." She felt the woman's eyes on her as she blotted the stain.

"Olivia? Is that you?"

She stopped wiping and looked up. Her eyes narrowed as she scrutinized the woman, who looked vaguely familiar although she couldn't quite place her. "I'm sorry. Do we know each other?"

"It's me, Lena. Lena Graham. I'm Lena Browder now. Remember Photography 101 at Virginia Commonwealth University?"

Her dark hair had gone gray, but Olivia recognized the once-pretty features of her old friend in the woman's puffy face. "Right! Lena. If my memory serves me correctly, we took more photography classes together than 101."

Lena laughed. "A whole string of them, actually."

"It's hard to believe it's been thirty years since we were at VCU." She abandoned the stain, tossing the soaked napkins on the table between them. "Do you still live in Richmond?"

Lena earmarked her page and closed her book, placing it in her lap. "Home sweet home. Born and raised, and at this rate, I'll die there too."

"We sure spent a lot of time on photo shoots and in the darkroom. How're your parents? Are they still alive?" Olivia had been a regular at Lena's parents' house for Sunday dinners.

Lena shook her head. "They both died three years ago within eight months of one another."

"I'm sorry to hear that. They were such nice people. And both such good cooks. My mouth is watering at the thought of your mother's lasagna and your father's oyster stew."

Lena smiled. "Where are you living now? Didn't you move to South Carolina after college?"

"Right. To Charleston. I'm still there." Olivia spotted a camera strap sticking out of an unzipped section of the backpack at her feet. "Are you still into photography?"

Lena followed her gaze. "Not as much as I'd like to be. I don't have a good excuse. Lack of inspiration, I guess. What about you?"

"I shoot faces, food, and flowers for my blog posts. Although I can't remember the last time I went on an actual photo shoot. I brought my laptop with me but not my camera. I'm more concerned with my inspiration for writing than photography."

With aspirations of becoming a novelist, Olivia had chosen VCU, an urban university in Richmond known for its arts program. She'd majored in English and minored in creative writing. "All those photography classes were electives for me. I can't remember what you studied in college. Were you a film major?"

Lena shook her head. "Photography was a hobby for me as well. I majored in art history."

"That's right. Did you pursue a career in art?" Olivia asked.

"I worked for several years at the VMFA—the Virginia Museum of Fine Arts—in their collections management department. After my daughter was born, I quit my job and became a stay-at-home mom."

Their phones pinged simultaneously on the table with texts from Delta announcing delays in their flights. "Great," Olivia said. "My flight to Seattle is delayed two hours."

"Mine too, to San Francisco. I guess it's the storms."

"What storms?" Olivia asked.

"The woman at the reception desk mentioned something about a line of storms causing travel delays."

"In that case, since I spilled most of my first, I'm going to the bar for another drink." Olivia drained the remainder of her wine and stood. "Can I get something for you?"

"Why not? After all, I'm on vacation. White, please. Chardonnay, if they have it."

While Olivia waited in the line at the bar, she eavesdropped on conversations around her. The majority of flights to destinations west of Tennessee were delayed indefinitely due to an outbreak of dangerous thunderstorms in the country's midsection.

The man in front of Olivia turned to face her. "Looks like I'm stuck here for a while. What about you, gorgeous? Is your flight delayed?"

She glared at him as she elbowed her way to the bar. She was used to strange men making passes at her. Olivia's bartender friends in Charleston affectionately referred to her as the Ice Queen. They often placed bets on how long it would take Olivia to give the cold stare to whatever poor sap decided to hit on her.

Returning to her seat, she handed Lena a glass of chardonnay. "We might be here awhile. Sounds like the storms are pretty bad."

Lena furrowed her brow. "Maybe I should change my ticket and go somewhere else."

"But you already have your trip planned to California. Where else would you go?" Lena's expression became guarded, and Olivia added, "I'm sorry. I didn't mean to pry."

Lifting a trembling glass to her lips, she took several big gulps of wine. "This is actually a spur-of-the-moment trip. I'm running away from home, however ridiculous that may sound coming from a fifty-four-year-old woman."

"What a coincidence! I'm doing the exact same thing." A mischievous smile tugged at Olivia's lips. "I'll tell you mine if you'll tell me yours."

Lena hesitated before giving in. "Only if you go first."

Olivia settled back in her chair and crossed her legs. "Deal."

As they sipped their way through two glasses of wine, Olivia told Lena a little about her divorce and a lot about the Kates, and Lena spoke of the events of her morning and how she was fed up with her daughter and husband taking advantage of her.

"I was mad as the devil this morning," Lena said. "I wanted to be anywhere except home. But now that I've calmed down, the idea of traveling alone to California terrifies me. I wish there was somewhere I could hide out for a month."

"Like where?"

"Somewhere less intimidating than California." Lena set her empty wineglass on the table. "Will you still go to Seattle if you don't hear back from Laura?"

Olivia shrugged. "Why not? I've already purchased the ticket, and I love the Pacific Northwest. I have a bucket list of places I'd like to visit." The hassle of renting a car, staying in hotels, and eating out every night suddenly exhausted her. Not to mention the expense. "Although now that I think about it, I'd rather not spend the money."

Lena nodded. "I know what you mean."

"I can't promise you a month, but you're welcome to hide out in my condo while I'm gone. It's on the waterfront in downtown Charleston."

Lena's hazel eyes grew wide. "That sounds heavenly. I could offer you my river cottage in exchange. It's charming this time of year. The area, not the house. The house needs a lot of work. There's no internet."

Olivia's ears perked up. "No internet? That sounds perfect. Where is this river house?"

"In the Northern Neck, about ninety minutes from Richmond in a little town called Irvington."

"I remember hearing people talk about the Northern Neck when I lived in Virginia. I always thought it was a funny name, but I never understood exactly where that was."

Lena smiled. "It is a funny name when you think about it. The peninsula between the Potomac and Rappahannock Rivers is known as the Northern Neck. By water, my cottage is located on Carters Creek, which is off the Rappahannock River, which is off the Chesapeake Bay. I have a dock with a kayak and paddleboard but no boat or pool."

Olivia's hopes soared. Lena's river cottage sounded like the ideal place to clear one's head and reset one's life. "What about your husband and daughter? Won't they be using your cottage on the weekends?"

Lena shook her head. "The cottage belongs to me. I inherited it from my parents. We spent a lot of time there when Kayla was a child, but neither of them wants to go anymore. Kayla says it's boring, and Charles is always too busy playing golf."

"I don't understand, Lena. Your river cottage sounds like the perfect place to hide out. Why aren't you there now instead of here, waiting to catch a plane to California?"

Lena shifted her gaze away from Olivia, staring through the window at the long line of airplanes connected to the terminal by gangways. "It's hard to explain. I have such wonderful memories of the river, of happy times from my own childhood with my parents as well as when Kayla was coming along." A faraway expression settled on her face. "Charles and I used to take carloads of her friends down for long weekends. We'd pull the girls tubing during the day and roast hot dogs on bonfires at night. But instead of comforting me, especially now that my parents are gone, those memories make me feel even more lonely than I already am."

Lena emitted an aura of sadness that made Olivia feel awkward. She wasn't good at offering consolation.

"Tell me about Irvington," Olivia said. "Is there much to do there?"

Lena snickered. "Not really. There's a handful of businesses, including a café—owned by my best friend from childhood and next-door neighbor, Alistair—where you can go for internet. And there's the Tides Inn, which is always a hubbub of activity. There's a lot of history associated with that old hotel. You'd enjoy going there for dinner."

When Lena's phone pinged with another incoming text, Olivia said, "Delta again?"

Lena picked up her phone and read the text. "No. It's Kayla. She wants to know if I'm at the grocery store. We're out of her favorite yogurt. Not one word of apology about what happened this morning."

Olivia snorted.

Lena thumbed off a text and set her phone down.

"What'd you tell her?"

"To buy her own yogurt. That I've left town and won't be home for a month."

Olivia sat up straight in her chair. "So we're gonna do it? We're actually gonna swap houses for a month?"

Lena's lips parted in a smile that transformed her face into the pretty young woman she'd once been. "Why not? For the next thirty days, the month of October, you'll stay in my cottage in the Northern Neck and I'll stay in your waterfront condo in Charleston. We'll indulge ourselves—eat whatever we want, sleep late, and leave our beds unmade if so desired. We'll follow our hearts to wherever they may lead us."

"Damn straight, girlfriend! A month of discovery. We'll reset our lives and rediscover our passion for whatever it is that inspires us."

Lena lifted her backpack onto her lap and rummaged through it for a set of keys. "My car's in long-term parking at the airport—south deck, row B, slot sixteen." She handed Olivia the keys. "And the key to the cottage is under the planter beside the front door."

"And you can use my car. The keys are in the tray on the chest by the door, and the car is parked in the building's garage. Unless it rains, you won't need to drive anywhere except the grocery store. Charleston is a walking city, and the weather this time of year is pleasantly mild."

They discussed logistics, exchanging not only cell numbers and addresses but idiosyncrasies about their residences relating to appliances, climate control, and neighbors.

"Feel free to use my desktop computer," Olivia said. "I'll text you the password."

"Alistair is right next door if you need him," Lena said. "You can trust him. I've known him all my life. I'll give him a call in the morning to let him know you're coming."

Olivia's phone pinged with a text from her daughter. Timing's not great. Working on a big project. You're welcome to stay in my apartment.

"Well, then. Looks like everything is working out as it was meant to be. Laura is working on something big, and it isn't really a good time for me to visit her." She stood, smoothing out the wrinkles in her linen tunic. "Let's go talk to the Delta agent about changing our flights."

Lena gathered her belongings and followed Olivia through the crowded lounge to the reception desk.

"We should book our return now," she said as they waited in line for assistance. "That way we have an end date set in stone."

"That makes sense." Lena consulted the calendar on her phone. "Today is Friday, September twenty-eighth. What about Halloween? Although that's technically more than a month."

"What's a few extra days? How about November first? Charlestonians go all out for Halloween. I'd hate for you to miss it."

"November first it is," Lena said with a definitive nod.

"We need a selfie to commemorate the moment." Olivia leaned in close to Lena, holding her phone out in front of them. "We'll take another one when we meet back here in November. Before and after shots of the old and new us."

CHAPTER FIVE

ALISTAIR

Alistair sat alone, nursing a draft beer at the bar in the Chesapeake Restaurant at the Tides Inn. A semicircle of windows overlooking the inn's small marina served as the focus for the two-tiered restaurant, with the bar on the upper level and the dining area below. The tables were occupied, and a crowd of weekend vacationers waited near the bar and on the terrace. Even though Alistair didn't recognize anyone, the presence of the strangers offered him comfort.

The bartender, Roy, a heavyset man with a deep belly laugh, performed multiple tasks at once, pouring wine and mixing cocktails. Alistair and Roy had been friends for years. They'd met as teenagers during their first summer working at the Tides Inn—Alistair as an instructor for the sailing camp and Roy serving drinks to guests lounging by the pool.

"Ready for another?" Roy asked Alistair in passing.

Alistair lifted his half-empty glass. "I'm good. I'm waiting for business to slow down so you'll talk to me."

"It's Friday night, dude. I hope you're prepared to wait awhile."

"I have all the time in the world," Alistair mumbled as he gazed at the amber liquid in his glass.

God, he missed Mary Anne so much—his girl next door with the sun-kissed cheeks. He closed his eyes and tried to summon her image—those baby blues and kilowatt smile, her boyish figure that looked better in jeans and cable-knit sweaters than in sequined dresses. She'd been different from other women he knew. She preferred playing tennis to shopping. Hot tea to cappuccinos. Dinner and a movie at home to an evening out. How he yearned to hold her in his arms again, to place his hands on her slim hips. Her memory grew fainter by the day, even though he worked hard to keep it alive by leaving her clothes in their walk-in closet and displaying her photographs in key positions around the house.

Alistair was just finishing his second beer when the crowd in the Chesapeake Restaurant finally thinned around ten o'clock. Roy set two empty tumblers and a bottle of Bowman Brothers Virginia Bourbon in front of Alistair and came around the bar, collapsing onto the high-backed chair beside him.

"What a night! I thought summers were hard, but these fall week-ends are killing me." Pouring two fingers of bourbon into each of the glasses, he downed his in one gulp and refilled it. "I've said this before, Alistair, and I'm going to say it again. You need to see a therapist. There's nothing wrong with getting professional help when you lose someone you love."

Alistair gave him a weak smile. "Why do I need a therapist when I have you?"

Roy leaned into the bar. "Because I don't know what else to say to you. I've been counseling you for two years now. Clearly, I'm not get-ting through to you."

"I don't need anyone to get through to me. I just need someone to listen. Mary Anne was my first and my only. Her death left a void in my life that I don't know how to fill." Alistair felt the sting of tears. He was tired of crying. It was not unusual for him to be working in the yard or driving down the road and not realize he had tears streaming down his face.

"You can start by spending time with the people you love. You've pushed everyone who cares about you away. You wouldn't be sitting here with me now if the Tides wasn't so conveniently located near your house. What about the boys? I know you last saw them at Christmas. When's the last time you talked to them?"

Alistair shrugged. He couldn't remember when he'd last spoken to his sons.

"Do you even know how they're coping with their grief? They loved Mary Anne, too, you know."

"They have each other," Alistair said. "They don't need me. Besides, they're in New York City. They have full lives with busy careers."

"Plenty to occupy their time and take their mind off their grief."

Alistair glared at Roy. "If you're suggesting I have nothing to occupy my time, you're wrong. I stay plenty busy."

"Doing what? Mowing your grass? Going fishing by yourself?"

"Among other things." Alistair thought about how he stayed in constant motion, always searching for his next chore or project, terrified that if he stopped moving those dreaded feelings of loss would catch up with him.

"What about Lena?" Roy asked. "I haven't heard you mention her in a while. The two of you used to be tight."

"Lena doesn't spend as much time here as she used to."

"Come on, man." Roy jabbed Alistair's arm with his elbow. "She lives in Richmond. That's right up the road from here. Why don't you go see her?"

"Because her husband's a prick."

Tossing his hands in the air, Roy fell back in his chair. "You're making excuses. You've pushed her away, too, haven't you?"

"I need some air." Alistair drank the rest of his bourbon, slammed his glass down, and pushed his chair back from the bar. Exiting the

Chesapeake Restaurant, he cut across the terrace and down the brick steps leading out to the dock.

The light from the moon cast a dim glow over the assortment of cabin cruisers tied up at the marina. Boat owners enjoyed nightcaps on their open-air sterns with waves gently lapping against their hulls.

Alistair sat with his feet dangling over the edge of the dock. He expected Roy to join him momentarily. This was their place, where they used to sneak cigarettes and drink beer late at night after their shifts ended.

Everything his friend had said was true. Alistair had let Mary Anne down. He'd made a deathbed promise to her that he would keep their family close, but he'd retreated into his own world with thoughts only of himself.

He'd been too busy working his high-pressure job to spend much time with his boys when they were growing up. To compensate for his absence, Mary Anne had made Mike and Josh her top priority. And that had continued when they went away to college. As a result, she'd been their go-to person when they were working through problems or had exciting news to share. She'd known what questions to ask—about girl-friends, fraternity activities, academics, and athletics. While he'd grown closer to Mike and Josh during his wife's illness, an awkwardness had settled between them since her death. Because he struggled to communicate with his sons, he found it easier to avoid phone conversations unless he had something important to discuss.

"I brought the bottle." Roy handed Alistair the bourbon and removed two cigarettes from his shirt pocket. "And these from the stash I keep behind the bar for nicotine-craving customers."

Leaning against the same piling with knees bent and feet on the dock, they smoked cigarettes as they passed the bottle back and forth.

"I can't remember when I last smoked a cigarette," Alistair said. "But it sure tastes good."

"That it does," Roy said, taking a deep drag. "You won't like what I'm gonna say, but you need to hear it. I think you should consider moving back to New York. You can resume your life where you left off when Mary Anne got sick. And being near the boys would be good for both you and them."

"Nah, man," Alistair said, feeling dizzy from the nicotine. "My New York days are long gone."

"Then move somewhere else. Start over somewhere new. I'd miss you like hell, but moping around an empty house day in and day out is only making things worse for you."

Alistair stubbed his cigarette butt out on the piling. "You're right, man. I appreciate your concern. You've given me a lot to think about."

He'd come to the Tides seeking sympathy. He'd gotten a lecture about moving on with his life instead. Roy was a true friend. He had Alistair's best interests at heart. But while he meant well, Roy didn't understand that without Mary Anne, Alistair had no life to move on with. Alistair would get through his days as best he could. Alone. He hadn't pushed the boys and Lena away on purpose. He'd been avoiding them in an effort to spare them the burden of his grief. The same was true with Roy. It was unfair of him to dump his problems in Roy's lap. From now on, when he came to the Tides for a drink, he'd be sure to leave his problems at home.

CHAPTER SIX

LENA

It was after midnight by the time Lena Ubered into town from the airport, familiarized herself with Olivia's condo, and made room for her meager belongings in the custom built-in wardrobe in the master bedroom. She fell into a deep slumber and slept soundly until after eight the next morning.

Rolling out of bed, she plodded on bare feet to the window and threw open the plantation shutters. In the bright light of the new morning, she realized what a bold move she'd made in leaving her family so abruptly. She'd set a drastic change in motion, one she couldn't reverse even if she wanted to. And the part of her that was terrified of change desperately wanted to jump on an airplane back to Virginia and beg Charles to forgive her for her lapse in judgment in making such a hasty departure. But she couldn't throw away her big chance—the chance she hadn't known she wanted but now realized she desperately needed to save herself from her miserable life.

Olivia's condo was appointed like a luxury boutique hotel with high ceilings, hardwood floors, and French doors leading from the main living area to a balcony overlooking the harbor. She found coffee in Olivia's pantry but not much else.

"Oh my, Biscuit, does this woman not eat?" Lena asked, and then remembered Biscuit wasn't in her usual place at her feet.

She brewed a cup of coffee and took it out onto the balcony. The salt-tinged air was damp and cool, reminding Lena of autumn mornings in the Northern Neck. Her thoughts drifted to Alistair. He'd been so despondent since his wife's death. And understandably so. Mary Anne was a special person. She'd been like a sister to Lena, one of the few close friends she'd ever had.

Lena made a mental note to call Alistair later, to ask him to be on the lookout for Olivia. Maybe having a pretty woman next door would lift his spirits.

She watched the pedestrians moving about in the park below, which according to the GPS on her phone was called Waterfront Park. She wondered about their lives. The man with the sweat-soaked T-shirt jogging on the path near the marsh. Was his wife at home waiting with breakfast for him? What about the young couple with golden retrievers on leashes and disposable cups of coffee in hand? Were they newlyweds? Were those dogs his and hers from a previous life before they married? And the woman walking at a clipped pace. Was she in a hurry to meet someone or late to work? Lena envied the woman her purpose. Thirty-three days stretched out ahead of Lena. She had no one to see and no place to be. Nothing had changed in her life aside from her location.

Lena caught sight of a woman wearing a pink baseball cap sitting on a park bench reading a novel. She strained her eyes to see the book's cover. Was it a romance? She yearned to sit down next to the woman and strike up a conversation about the types of books she liked to read. But Lena was a stranger to the woman. To all the people in the park. She didn't belong in this community of Charlestonians. She was an outsider, a visitor here on an extended stay. This life, Olivia's condo and her car, all of it was on loan to her for the month of October. On November 2, she would return to her real life, the one she'd grown to despise. And then what?

Her phone pinged with an incoming text, followed immediately by two more. All three were from Kayla. The lack of punctuation gave her pause, and she had to study each one to understand its meaning.

enough with the melodrama already when are you coming home

dad wants to know what we're supposed to do for food

where are you anyway at the river

Alarmed, Lena quickly responded. A friend of mine from college is using the river house. Do NOT bother her. I'm staying at her place in Charleston until the end of the month. Tell your father to find a grocery store and learn to cook. She pressed send and, as an afterthought, tapped out another text: BTW, you need to have found a job by the time I come home.

She read Kayla's texts again as she finished her coffee: dad wants to know what we're supposed to do for food. Lena was surprised Charles had not called or texted her when he'd discovered she'd left home. Was he unconcerned about her traveling alone? Wasn't he curious about what had driven her to leave town so abruptly? Was she nothing more to him than a cook and grocery shopper?

Her stomach rumbled. *Speaking of food.* Returning to the kitchen, she found that Olivia's refrigerator was as empty as her pantry. According to Siri, the nearest grocery store was only a half mile away. Straight up East Bay Street. No chance of getting lost.

She dressed in exercise clothes, located Olivia's car keys, and went to the garage. The sight of the red convertible Volkswagen Beetle parked in the space assigned to Olivia's condo inspired a victory dance. "Look out, Charleston, here I come!"

On the drive to Harris Teeter, she noticed numerous tourists strolling the sidewalks, and she longed to join them.

What's stopping you? Get out and explore this romantic city you've heard so much about but never visited.

With only herself to shop for, she loaded up on fruits and salad greens. On her way to the checkout, she made the mistake of turning down the freezer aisle. Despite her resolve to eat healthier, she couldn't resist adding a carton of Haagen-Dazs Bourbon Praline Pecan ice cream to her cart.

She was so famished by the time she returned to the condo, she went straight for the ice cream instead of having a yogurt with fresh fruit and granola as she'd planned. She sat down at Olivia's computer with the carton of ice cream and the journal she'd purchased on a whim in the Atlanta airport to document her month of discovery. The carton of ice cream was empty by the time she'd made her lists of popular restaurants and places of interest she wanted to visit in Charleston.

Your choice, Lena. You can either be a hermit in Olivia's condo like you've been at home in Richmond, or you can do something about it. Start slow by taking a walk around the neighboring blocks to familiarize yourself with the area.

She threw the empty carton of ice cream in the trash can and went to the bedroom to get ready for her outing. She stayed in the hot shower for longer than usual, trying out Olivia's shower gels and salon shampoo. Wrapping a towel around her body, she entered Olivia's dressing room—a rectangular walk-in closet divided into sections for hanging clothes and shoes. She ran her hand along the row of dresses, which offered choices for every occasion—casual, church, cocktail, and black-tie parties. She removed a silver sequined dress from its hanger and held it up to her body in front of the full-length mirror. She would never borrow Olivia's clothes without asking. Not that any of them would fit. But she didn't see any harm in trying on this one dress.

She let her towel fall to the floor and slipped the dress over her head. But she couldn't get the zipper to zip even a fraction of an inch. She tugged the dress off and stood naked in front of the mirror. She took a good hard look at herself, and she didn't like what she saw. Returning to the bathroom, she stepped on Olivia's scale and gasped at the number on the digital display.

The diet starts today, Lena. And one of the key ingredients to weight loss is exercise.

She dressed in comfortable clothes, grabbed her backpack, and left the condo. The weather was pleasant, with partly cloudy skies and a cool breeze. Slinging the backpack over her shoulder, with the GPS on her phone to guide her, she headed south toward the Battery. She recognized the row of brightly painted buildings she passed from photographs she'd seen of the famous Rainbow Row. At the seawall, she strolled down the promenade, sucking in big gulps of salty air, before venturing into the park across the street, where she studied the monuments and statues and Civil War cannons. She wandered through the neighboring streets, snapping photographs of the historic homes, luscious gardens, and window boxes.

Changing direction, she walked north on Meeting Street to the historic City Market—a narrow brick building lined with archways that stretched three blocks to East Bay Street. The market was mobbed with tourists buying clothing and locally made treats and art, including various shapes and sizes of sweetgrass baskets handwoven from bulrush, a strong yet supple marsh grass that thrives in the Lowcountry's sandy soil. As she inched her way through the crowd, she shopped the goods, purchasing several packages of stone-ground grits to give neighbors back home for Christmas.

She was perusing an exhibit of hand-painted watercolors of scenes from the Lowcountry when she heard a voice say, "I can make you a good deal on a sweetgrass basket. I have the widest variety to choose from in the market."

Lena looked up to see a woman wearing a floppy sun hat over her gray curls and grinning from ear to ear. She was seated in a stadium chair, her hands expertly weaving the small oval-shaped basket in her lap.

Lena moved closer to the table and examined her goods. The woman did, in fact, have the largest variety of sweetgrass baskets she'd seen so far in the market—big, small, round, oval, some with lids, others with handles. "These are exquisite, like works of art. Did you make all of them yourself?"

"Yes, ma'am. Every last one of them. I been making baskets since I was a girl." Setting her basket aside, she rose from her chair slowly as if the effort caused her pain. "Is this your first visit to Charleston?"

Lena smiled sheepishly. "How can you tell? Is the word *tourist* written all over my forehead?"

She laughed. "After thirty years, I can just tell."

"I love them all. I don't know how I'll ever decide which basket to buy."

The woman came to stand beside Lena, leaning in as if to tell her a secret. "I ain't like my competitors. They'll tell you whatever they think you want to hear to make a sale. I pride myself on customer satisfaction. How long you in town for?"

"Until the first of November."

Her brown eyes got big. "A whole month? That ain't a vacation. That's an extended stay. And plenty of time to figure out which basket you wanna take home with you. My name's Bessie, and I'm here every day. If you stop by to visit me from time to time, when your month's up you'll know which basket you like the most."

"I'm Lena. And I like your way of thinking. Do you mind if I take your picture?"

Bessie hesitated. "I ain't much for having my picture took. But I'll tell you what, when you come back at the end of the month, if you buy a basket from me, I'll let you take my picture then."

Lena nodded. "Fair enough. By the time I leave Charleston, I suspect you and I will be old friends."

She carried on similar conversations with several different vendors as she worked her way up and down the aisles of the market. The friendly folks of Charleston made her feel welcome. She felt so at home, she ventured to the rooftop bar at the Market Pavilion Hotel, where she sat at the bar and ordered a cucumber martini. As much time as she'd spent by herself, she'd never dared to go to a restaurant alone. Glancing around, she noticed that everyone was too engrossed in their own conversations to pay any attention to her. The feeling of anonymity that washed over her offered a sense of relief. She could be anybody she wanted to be while in Charleston. And now, with a month all to herself, she was determined to make the most of it.

She took her martini to the railing to watch the sunset. Feeling the first pangs of hunger, she realized she hadn't eaten since polishing off the pint of ice cream. The health app on her phone indicated she'd walked close to five miles that afternoon, but she'd been too enchanted by her surroundings for it to feel like exercise.

She left the Market Pavilion Hotel and walked a block south to the Amen Street restaurant where, once again, she took a seat at the bar and ordered the raw bar sampler and a glass of the South African chenin blanc. Her first day in Charleston ended on a more upbeat note than it had started, and she could hardly wait to see what Sunday would bring. For the first time in forever, she felt a tinge of excitement about her future.

CHAPTER SEVEN

OLIVIA

Olivia spent her first night in Virginia at The Jefferson Hotel in Richmond—the grand historic hotel where her parents had always stayed for parents' weekends when she was in college. She slept past nine on Saturday morning and lounged for another hour, reading the *Richmond Times-Dispatch* and sipping coffee in the fuzzy bathrobe supplied by the hotel. After checking out at eleven, she drove through the city in Lena's beat-up minivan, amazed at how the VCU campus had taken over the downtown area.

She drove west on Monument Avenue, admiring the lovely Civil War monuments—Robert E. Lee, Jefferson Davis, Stonewall Jackson, J. E. B. Stuart. Dismissing the concern that Lena's husband or daughter might recognize Lena's minivan, Olivia ventured farther west to the area near the University of Richmond.

After eating a salad for lunch at The Continental, she visited the shops on Grove Avenue. She admired the window display at Peter-Blair, the popular upscale men's clothing store, before crossing the street to Levys, where she purchased two cashmere sweaters and a pair of jeans. She experienced buyer's remorse as she signed the credit card slip. She really needed to get a handle on her spending. As the wife of a successful corporate attorney, she'd never had to worry about budgeting. She'd seldom even balanced her checkbook. Robert had been extremely generous in her divorce settlement, but once that was gone, she would be faced with earning her own living. Although she'd monetized her website, the proceeds from ads, sponsored posts, and affiliate income didn't earn nearly enough. And she hadn't a clue how to go about doing that.

It was almost two o'clock by the time she returned to the van. She pondered driving to one of the area's two outdoor malls, but then she realized she was procrastinating about what she needed to do. Sorting through her emotions once she arrived at Lena's river house, she admitted, would be soul wrenching.

It's time, Liv. Stop running away and start running toward.

She got on the interstate heading southeast in the direction of the coast, the first leg of her ninety-minute drive to Irvington. At Lena's suggestion, she stopped for groceries at the Food Lion in Saluda before continuing on toward the Rappahannock River bridge. Lena had not mentioned the narrow lanes and low guardrails on the bridge. White-knuckling the steering wheel, she was nearly paralyzed with fear as she crossed the river. She would be certain to take a Xanax before driving over the bridge on her way home. Lena had hinted that Irvington was small but had not warned her she could miss it if she blinked while driving through. Aside from the par-three golf course, she couldn't see much of the Tides Inn from the road. She would treat herself to Sunday brunch in the hotel's restaurant the following day.

Lena's cottage was set back from the road a quarter mile and shared a driveway with her next-door neighbor, who was cutting his grass on his riding lawnmower as she drove by. She veered off to the left and continued the short distance to the cottage. With gray siding, black shutters, and a yellow front door, the cottage was quaint and inviting, and for the first time since boarding the plane to Richmond, Olivia felt confident she'd made the right decision in coming here.

She turned off the engine and popped the tailgate. She was rounding the back of the van when she noticed the neighbor coming toward her.

He stopped in his tracks. "You're not Lena."

"No," Olivia said. "I'm definitely not Lena."

He closed the distance between them.

"I'm Olivia Westcoat, a friend of Lena's from college. We swapped houses for the month. She's staying at my place in Charleston. I guess she forgot to call and tell you I was coming."

"Hmm. That's strange. I haven't heard from her. At least I don't think I have. She may have tried while I was cutting the grass." He removed his phone from the pocket of his khaki shorts. "Yep. I missed two calls from her." He stuffed his phone back in his pocket. "I'm Alistair Hoffman, next-door neighbor. Is Lena alone or with her family?"

"Alone. We both needed some time to ourselves."

"Wait," Alistair said, shaking his head as if he'd heard her wrong. "Are we talking about the same woman—gray hair, slightly overweight, big heart?"

"She's the one. Why is that so shocking to you?"

"I've known her all my life, and I feel as though I'm entitled to say this. In fact, I've said as much to her face. It's about damn time Lena did something for herself." He smiled, his brown eyes warming. "Good for her." He grabbed as many plastic grocery bags as he could carry. "I wish I'd known you were coming. I would've freshened up the cottage for you."

"No worries. I don't want to be any trouble to you."

He strode toward the cottage, and as she followed him up the sidewalk with her suitcase, she noticed his navy T-shirt, soaked with perspiration, stretching taut across his muscular back. His dark hair was graying at the temples, and he wore a scruffy beard on his oval-shaped face. He had the rugged good looks of a man who spent much of his time outdoors.

He set the grocery bags down on the slate surface of the small front porch and removed a silver key from beneath a planter of dead geraniums. "The lock's a little tricky. You have to pull the door toward you and jiggle the key."

She racked her brain but couldn't remember whether Lena had said if Alistair was married. As he fumbled with the lock and her eyes traveled to his left hand, she experienced an unexpected sinking feeling at the sight of the platinum wedding band on his ring finger. Just as well. The purpose of her hiatus was to clear her head, not complicate her life.

He pushed the door open and stepped out of the way for her to enter. It was stuffy inside as though it had been closed up for some time. Leaving her suitcase at the foot of the stairs in the entryway, Olivia walked through to the adjacent sitting room. "This is lovely." The room was light and airy, more a summer vacation home than a cozy winter retreat, with white walls and furniture upholstered in pastel colors. Just beyond the small dining area, a granite counter separated the sitting room from the kitchen.

"I'm sorry it's so hot in here. I've told Lena a thousand times to turn the air conditioner up instead of turning it off completely when she leaves." Depositing the grocery bags on the dining table, Alistair adjusted the thermostat and opened the sliding glass doors.

Olivia went to stand beside him in the open doorway, staring out at the houses dotting the opposite shoreline of Carters Creek. "It's more like a small river than a creek."

He nodded. "The name is deceiving. Carters Creek is a tributary of the Rappahannock River, the mouth of which is just around the bend."

Olivia stayed in the doorway, the fresh air cool on her face, while Alistair zipped around the room, fluffing up pillows and organizing the magazines on the coffee table into stacks.

"Let me give you the nickel tour. The downstairs has the kitchen, living areas, and master bedroom. There's another bedroom and bath and small study on the second floor. The view is stunning from up there. I prefer the upstairs. You might want to check it out before you settle in the master suite."

He transferred the grocery bags to the kitchen and began unpacking items onto the counter. "Phew! Something smells rotten in here." He turned on the hot water, poured dishwashing liquid down the drain, and flipped on the disposal. The disposal whirled and the drain gurgled. After a minute, he turned off the disposal and sniffed. "Still stinks."

Olivia joined him, and together they sniffed around the kitchen, like a pair of bloodhounds, until their noses landed simultaneously on the vintage 1970s avocado-colored refrigerator.

"Lena's had the repairman out to work on this clunker too many times to count. I warned her it would give out at an inconvenient time." When he opened the refrigerator door, the same but now intensified foul odor assaulted her nose.

She stepped back, pinching her nostrils. "That's rancid."

This is not a good omen, she thought. *No telling what else is broken around here. I should drive straight back to the airport and get on the next plane to Seattle.*

"What am I supposed to do without a refrigerator?" she said in a nasal tone, her fingers still on her nostrils.

"We'll get you a refrigerator." He tugged his cell phone out of the pocket of his khaki shorts. "A friend of mine is the appliance dealer in Kilmarnock."

She narrowed her eyes. "Killmarnie who?"

"Kilmarnock. It's the next town over." He tapped on the screen and lifted the phone to his ear.

"Is Kilmarnock a real town?"

He chuckled. "Unlike Irvington, you mean? You'll be happy to know that Kilmarnock has grocery stores and restaurants, doctors, and a hospital. They even have a Walmart."

When his friend came on the line, Alistair angled his body away from her. "Rich, buddy, are you running any specials on refrigerators? Lena's fridge finally died, and she has a friend staying in her cottage."

Alistair listened for a minute. "That could work. How much is it?" More listening. "Sold. How soon can you deliver it?" His face fell. "All right, then. If that's the best you can do." He reached for his back pocket. "My wallet's at home. I'll call you back in a few minutes with my credit card information."

"I gather he can't deliver it today?" Olivia said when he ended the call.

"It's too late in the day, and his driver is already out on a delivery. They're closed tomorrow, but he promised to have it here first thing on Monday morning."

"What am I supposed to do with all these groceries?" she asked, spreading her arms wide at the plastic bags lining the counter.

"I have a cooler you can use." He withdrew a black trash bag from the drawer beside the sink and began throwing away the contents of the refrigerator—a chunk of moldy cheese, several containers of Greek yogurt, a carton of eggs, and the salad dressings and condiments from the door. "Disgusting! Lena hasn't been down in a couple of months, but when I checked on things a week or ten days ago, the refrigerator was still running and there was no smell."

He tied a knot in the bag. "I'll take this to the trash and grab the cooler. I'll be back in a few minutes," he said, already on his way out the door.

Olivia had grown tired from watching him. The man was a steam engine.

After conducting a brief tour of the master suite, she climbed the stairs to the second-floor bedroom. While the decor was too country for her taste, she found the yellow walls, patchwork quilt, and white iron bed inviting. She passed through the bathroom, which was small but clean with gleaming white tiles and a walk-in shower, to the adjoining room, a second bedroom that had been converted into a study. Bookshelves lined one wall, while a worn blue velvet chair with matching ottoman occupied the opposite corner. The moment Olivia sat down at the oak desk in front of the window, her mind began to whir. *This desk, this setting, feels so conducive to writing. I can see myself finding inspiration and a new direction here.* Encouraged by what lay ahead, she pushed away from the desk and went downstairs to get her suitcase.

Through the storm door, she spotted Alistair driving up the sidewalk in a golf cart. He hoisted a large rectangular Igloo cooler off the back of the golf cart and carried it into the kitchen. "This should be big enough," he said, opening the cooler.

Crushed ice filled the bottom third of the cooler. "Where'd you get the ice?"

"I have a commercial ice maker. Comes in handy to ice down all the fish I catch." When he grinned, Olivia caught a glimpse of the mischievous little boy he must have been.

Olivia laughed. "So you're one of those," she said, recalling her father, who'd been an avid fisherman. The one time he'd invited her to go fishing with him, she'd squirmed and complained and gotten a hook stuck in her finger. "Does your wife like to fish?"

"She used to. She passed away two years ago."

Her face fell. "I'm so sorry. I didn't know."

His eyes darted around the kitchen, as though he was suddenly anxious to escape. "I should leave you to get settled. I'm right next door if you need anything."

She walked him to the door. "Thanks, but I should be fine. You've done enough already."

She couldn't help noticing his muscular calves as she watched him go. *So what if he's single. He's off-limits to you. A man is the last thing you need right now.*

She locked the storm door behind him and returned to the kitchen. After loading the cooler with groceries, she dragged her suitcase upstairs and unpacked her clothes into the empty dresser drawers. Opening the single-paned door, she stepped out onto the narrow wooden balcony and leaned against the railing. She regretted not bringing her camera. Maybe she could find a suitable point-and-shoot at the Walmart in Kill-whatever.

She stretched out on one of two lounge chairs and closed her eyes, feeling the warmth of the late-day sun on her face. *This is it, Liv. You've finally stopped running. Time to face your demons. Revisiting the day your world fell apart seems like as good a place to start as any.*

CHAPTER EIGHT

OLIVIA

September 17, 2016
The occasion of her twenty-eighth wedding anniversary

Olivia placed the hotel brochures in the gift box along with the sexy black teddy she'd ordered from Victoria's Secret, one of her countless attempts to spice up their love life. Robert was the ideal husband in every other way. He was easygoing, fun to be with, and a generous provider. And he had a wonderful relationship with their daughter. Olivia could forgive him his awkwardness when it came to making love. But that didn't mean she had to give up trying.

She took meticulous care in wrapping the box with the paper she'd selected for the occasion—silver foil covered in pastel hearts. She and Robert always exchanged anniversary gifts, some years with gifts more elaborate than others. He almost never missed with her. To ensure he'd get it right this year, she'd dropped several heavy hints about the purse she'd been admiring in the Louis Vuitton window on King Street. Her tattered black leather tote had run its course, and he was as tired of it as she was. For her gift to him, she'd planned the fall foliage trip to New England they'd been talking about forever. They were empty nesters, and his career as a corporate attorney was finally slowing down. They could lead the life they'd been working toward for years.

She'd set the table on the patio with floral linens and their fine wedding china—the Herend Chinese Bouquet in blue that she'd always loved. A bottle of Veuve Clicquot was chilling in the refrigerator, and she'd purchased the ingredients to make shrimp pad Thai, their favorite Thai dinner. In addition to outdoor sports and time on the water, cooking was another of the many activities they enjoyed together.

At six thirty, she was in the kitchen cutting up chicken for the satay appetizer when she heard the front door open and close, followed by footsteps on the wooden front stairs. Ten minutes later, Robert came bounding down the back stairs in khaki slacks and a bright green golf shirt. After nearly three decades, his blond good looks still stole her breath. She smelled his mint and lavender cologne when he bent down to kiss her cheek.

"Oh good! We're having Thai tonight." When he opened the refrigerator and saw the bottle of Veuve Clicquot, he said, "Champagne? What's the occasion?"

Olivia's hand stilled, the knife poised above the chicken breast. Robert never *ever* forgot a birthday or anniversary. He typically showed up with his arms full of elaborate bouquets of flowers and ornately wrapped packages. "It's our anniversary."

The color drained from his face. "I'm so sorry, sweetheart. I forgot. I'm so preoccupied with this big case."

She wasn't aware he'd been working on a big case. She set the knife down and rinsed her hands, wiping them on a piece of paper towel. "Don't worry about it! You're entitled to be less than perfect every now and then." She stood on her tiptoes and pressed her lips against his. "I got you a present." She handed him her gift. "It's really for both of us."

He unwrapped the package, folding the paper neatly in half, before opening the box and removing the brochures.

"I've booked our dream trip to New England," she said, taking one of the brochures from him. "Seven nights in four different luxury hotels."

"Great," he said without much enthusiasm.

She nodded her head at the box. "There's something else."

He lifted back the tissue paper and peered at the black teddy for a minute before looking away. Resignation crossed his face followed by sadness.

Dread settled over Olivia. "What is it, Robert?" She knew something was terribly wrong. *Does he have cancer? Has something happened at the firm? Are we in financial trouble?* She had faith that their marriage was strong enough to overcome any of the above, but she was in no way prepared for his confession.

"I can't live like this anymore," he said, lowering himself to a nearby barstool. "I love you so much, my darling. You're my very best friend in the whole entire world, and I can't imagine what my life will be like without you. But I'm in love with someone else. A man. I'm in love with a man, Liv. I'm gay."

She gaped at him, completely and utterly dumbfounded. "You're discovering this now? After twenty-eight years of marriage?"

"Of course not. I've tried so desperately to live a fulfilled life as a heterosexual man. But I can't deny my sexual orientation any longer."

Her mind traveled back over the years. She realized with a jolt that their problems in the bedroom stemmed not from Olivia's lack of sensuality as she'd suspected but from his attraction to other men. Bitter bile burned her throat at the image of her husband, *her* Robert, having sex with a man.

Turning her back on him, she went to the window and gazed out at the table she'd set on the patio. Their anniversary dinner was ruined, not that she'd ever be able to stomach food again. What did this mean for their future? Would he leave and go live with his man? Would he tell their friends he was gay?

So this is what being blindsided felt like. He'd left for work that morning like it was any other day and come home that evening and blown their world to smithereens.

He came to stand behind her. "If it's any consolation, I've been faithful to you until recently. I can't explain it. I woke up one morning, looked at my reflection in the mirror, and decided I couldn't lie to myself anymore. Or to you."

"And so what? You found a gay man to have sex with and now you're in love?" Her tone was harsh, but she didn't care.

"The man is Adam," he said in a voice so meek it was almost inaudible. "And yes, we're in love."

The second blow hit her like a punch in the nose. Adam was one of his law partners who'd come out of the closet and divorced his wife a couple of years back.

Olivia spun around to face him. "That's just great, Robert. I'll be sure to consult with his ex-wife about best practices for moving on with your life when your husband discovers he's gay."

"I know you're upset, honey. But once you've had a chance to calm down, you'll see—"

"I'll see what, Robert? That our life together—our marriage, our home, our family—was all a fraud? And speaking of family, I'll let you be the one to explain this to Laura." Olivia didn't envy him that task. Laura worshipped her father. This would be as much of a shock to their daughter as it was to Olivia.

"You didn't let me finish. You'll see, Liv, in the long run, we'll both be better off. You'll find a man who loves you the way you deserve to be loved." He moved to take her in his arms, but she pushed him away.

"I already had that man, Robert. You were that man. Until today, you've been the best husband a woman could ever ask for. What about all our plans? We were going to travel, enjoy our golden years together." The fog suddenly cleared, and she realized the conversations about trips to Provence and South Africa and buying a beach cottage on Sullivan's

Island had all been one sided. "You were never planning to grow old with me, were you? All this time, you've been planning for a future with Adam. Or someone like Adam. And I'll be left to grow old alone. I deserve better than this, Robert. I've been a good wife to you."

"I know you do, sweetheart." Once again he moved toward her, but she stopped him in his tracks with her death glare.

"I want you out of this house." Her arm shot out, finger pointed at the door. "I can't stand the sight of you for another minute. I hope you find what you're looking for with Adam. But I warn you, Robert. You're going to pay for what you've done to me."

"I'll make sure you're taken care of." He kissed the tips of his fingers and touched them to her cheek. "Don't ever question my feelings for you. I have loved you with my whole heart."

She brushed his hand away. "Just not your whole body."

With chin lowered to his chest, he crossed the kitchen toward the stairs.

"Happy anniversary," she said to his retreating back. "Twenty-eight years, down the drain in a blink of an eye."

CHAPTER NINE

LENA

At the crack of dawn on Sunday, Lena stood on the end of the fishing pier in Waterfront Park, watching in awe as the sky transitioned from pink to yellow beyond the Cooper River bridge. The cable-stayed bridge was like a majestic sailboat, with dual masts and triangular sails, suspended high above the Cooper River. She removed her camera from the backpack and adjusted the aperture, shutter speed, and ISO settings. Peering through the viewfinder, she pressed the shutter release, but when she previewed the image on the LCD display, she experienced the same disappointment she always felt with her photography. She was rarely able to capture the true beauty of a scene as viewed with her naked eye.

A woman materialized on the pier beside Lena, her sundress flowing softly about her willowy frame as she proceeded to set up a tripod with camera and wide-angle lens. Although she appeared to be in her fifties, she glided around her camera with the agility of a much younger woman. Lena watched with curiosity as she attached a square apparatus with tinted glass to the front of her lens and a cabled remote control to the side of the camera's body. The breeze whipped her long auburn curls around her face as she took a step back and pressed the button on her remote. A minute passed, maybe longer, before Lena heard the shutter click.

She inched toward the woman. "I apologize for the intrusion, but do you mind if I inquire about your equipment?"

The woman shifted her gaze from the camera to Lena. "Not at all. What would you like to know?"

"Anything you're willing to share. I'm frustrated with my photography. My images never turn out the way I see them in real life. For example, this scene is breathtaking with the bridge and the sunrise, but the photograph I took is blah." Lena held her camera out to the woman, showing her the image on her viewfinder.

"Try giving more consideration to your composition," the woman said. "Regardless of how beautiful the sky, we're too far away from the bridge. You need to get closer and shoot at an angle. Use the bridge as your backdrop with another element, like marsh grass, in the foreground as your focus. If you google images of the Cooper River bridge, you'll see what I'm talking about."

Lena frowned. "How is your composition any different than mine? We're standing on the same pier with the same choppy water between us and the bridge."

"My focus is not the bridge but the clouds and the sky and the water. I'm using a neutral density filter in order to get a long exposure, which will give me a motion blur effect on the water."

"So you're using a slow shutter speed. Can I do that with my camera?"

"May I see it?" The woman took Lena's camera and fidgeted with the controls. "Your maximum shutter speed is thirty seconds, which is good, but you'd still need a neutral density filter and a tripod to avoid camera shake."

Disappointment crossed Lena's face. "Obviously, I have a lot to learn."

The woman smiled. "I'm a professional, and I still have a lot to learn."

Lena's eyes became saucers. By *professional*, did the woman mean she worked for a publication like *National Geographic*? "I'm terribly sorry. I didn't mean to interfere with your work."

"You didn't. I'm always happy to offer advice to budding photographers." The woman looked up at the sky. The pinky glow had faded to pale yellow. "The moment of opportunity has come and gone." She dismantled her equipment and returned it to her camera bag. "I have a while before I need to be home. Would you like to go for coffee? We can get one at The Vendue hotel just up the road."

Lena was taken aback at the unexpected invitation. "I'd like that." What harm was there in making a new friend, considering she knew not another soul in town aside from Bessie?

The woman leaned over and zipped up her camera bag, threading her tripod through the straps on the side, and then straightened. "I'm Jade, by the way. Jade Dowdy."

Lena thought the name exotic and very fitting for a creative type. "Nice to meet you, Jade. I'm Lena."

"I should clarify that I'm a wedding and portrait photographer," Jade said as they walked up the pier together. "I'm little more than an amateur when it comes to landscape photography."

"You certainly know a lot for an amateur. Is your business here in Charleston?"

"Actually, my business is in Nashville, Tennessee, where I've lived for the past twenty-five years. But I'm originally from Charleston. I moved back home six months ago to take care of my aging mother."

Lena offered a sympathetic smile. "I've been down that road. I know how difficult it can be. Is your mother ill?"

"She has age-related macular degeneration. Otherwise she's perfectly healthy."

"I'm sorry to hear that. I imagine that's hard on her."

"Hard on all of us," Jade mumbled.

They reached the end of the pier and continued on through the park, past a large fountain that Jade referred to as a splash pad where kids cooled off on hot days. They walked up Vendue Range and entered The Vendue hotel. The lobby was empty aside from a few uniformed employees scurrying about.

Following Jade's lead, Lena helped herself to a cup of coffee from urns set up on a banquet table for the benefit of hotel guests. "Shouldn't we pay for this?" Lena asked as she stirred cream and sugar into her coffee.

"No need. They owe me. I took some photographs pro bono from their rooftop bar for their website."

Regardless of the circumstances, drinking their coffee without paying for it didn't seem right to Lena. But who was she to argue with someone as savvy as Jade?

The world came alive around them as they sipped their coffee at a table by a sunny window in the corner of the lobby. A nearby elevator deposited sleepy-eyed vacationers in search of caffeine while locals passed by on the sidewalk outside the window in exercise clothes or casual weekend attire.

"Tell me about yourself, Lena. Are you from Charleston?"

"No. I'm from Richmond, Virginia. I've never been to Charleston before, believe it or not. I'm staying at a friend's condo, right here on the park." Without sharing too many details, she explained how she and Olivia had swapped houses for the month of October.

"Lucky you! A whole month to yourself. Do you have plans?"

Lena avoided her gaze. "However cliché this might sound, and ridiculous for a woman my age, I'm hoping to find myself."

Jade pursed her lips in thought. "Wouldn't it help to determine how you got lost?"

Lena laughed. "I'm well aware of how that happened. Marriage. Raising a child. Being a stay-at-home mom."

Jade gathered her curls at the nape of her neck and secured them with an elastic band. "I wouldn't understand any of that. I never married or had children. I've spent all of my adult life chasing my own dreams. Selfish, my mother calls me. I prefer to think of myself as driven."

Lena examined the woman's face. Her deep blue eyes gave little away. "At least you have plenty to show for your efforts."

"I'm not so sure about that. Being successful often comes with a price. I've employed dozens of photographers over the years, not one of whom I ever thought of as a friend."

Lena sensed a loneliness she could relate to in the woman.

"How old are you, Lena?"

"Fifty-four. And you?"

"I'm fifty-six. If you ask me, we have a lot of life left to live." Jade lifted her Styrofoam cup to toast. "Here's to living it."

Lena touched her cup to Jade's. "If only someone would be so kind as to tell me how to go about doing that."

Jade snickered. "I'm no life coach, but I can certainly help with your photography."

Lena moved to the edge of her chair. "Are you serious? That would be so wonderful."

"I don't see why not. I can always use another set of hands when I go on shoots." Jade checked the time on her phone. "I should be getting home to Mom. Would you like to come over for dinner tonight?"

"Sure! I'd love that."

Jade removed a business card from her camera bag and scribbled an address on the back. "We can talk more about photography," she said, handing the card to Lena. "The first step is to upgrade your equipment. I have a closet full of bodies and lenses I'm not using that you're welcome to try out." She stood to go. "Does six thirty work for you?"

"That sounds perfect." Lena stood until Jade had made her departure and then sat back down to finish her coffee.

She conducted a Google search for Jade Dowdy on her phone. From what she read, Lena deduced that Jade's wedding photography company in Nashville was secondary to her real work as a portrait photographer. She'd photographed some of the most famous actors, musicians, and politicians of all time. And now, with this golden opportunity to be Jade's protégé and use her professional equipment, Lena knew she would need to brush up on her photography skills.

Tossing her empty cup into a nearby trash can, she exited the building onto East Bay Street and set off for another day of exploration.

CHAPTER TEN

OLIVIA

Olivia woke early on Sunday morning, pulled on a sweatshirt and shorts over her bathing suit, and hurried down to the water without stopping for coffee. She discovered a kayak and paddleboard, along with life jackets and paddles, in a rickety wooden shed near the dock. Slipping on a life jacket, she tucked a paddle under her arm and dragged the kayak down to the floating dock. Sliding the kayak into the water, she climbed in, shoved off, and paddled across the creek.

The air was still and the temperature mild, an indication of the eighty-five-degree afternoon high the forecasters were predicting. Carters Creek was peaceful in the early-morning hours, aside from the clanging masts of anchored sailboats and murmured voices from porches as she paddled near their docks. Her arms burned and her mind was blissfully clear as she rowed in and around the coves of Carters Creek. She spotted wildlife—herons and ospreys, fish and blue crabs— and admired the towering pine and oak trees gracing the landscape. She ventured farther than she realized, and by the time she made her way home two hours later, it was going on ten o'clock.

Olivia hauled the kayak out of the water onto the floating dock and climbed the hill to the house. She showered, dressed in jeans and a sleeveless coral-colored blouse, and set off on foot to the Tides Inn. Fifteen minutes later, hunger pangs gnawed at her stomach as she made her way up the long driveway. The hotel sat high up on the banks of the main body of Carters Creek, just around the bend from Lena's cottage. In addition to the main building, the property featured a pool, marina, and several outbuildings all meticulously landscaped with seagrasses, lush green shrubs, and brightly colored perennials.

As she entered the lobby, the clerk at the front desk greeted her with a smile and pointed her down the hall in the direction of the Chesapeake Restaurant, where she was shown to a table on the terrace overlooking the marina. Her waitress, an older woman with freckles dotting her caramel cheeks, arrived within minutes to take her order.

"The chef has outdone himself today, if you're interested in the buffet," the waitress said.

"In that case, I'll have the buffet and a mimosa."

Olivia loaded her plate with scrambled eggs, French toast, sausage, grits, and fresh fruit. Her mimosa was waiting for her when she returned to the table. The atmosphere was enchanting and the food delicious. She knew the waitstaff in most of her favorite restaurants in Charleston and had grown accustomed to dining alone. But here, in the Northern Neck where she knew no one, she had a heightened awareness of the couples gathered at the surrounding tables—her own age and older, paired with other couples, laughing and sipping brunch cocktails. *Are they on their second marriages, or have they been together for decades? And what about their sex lives? Are they still intimate, or has their passion for each other died down over time?*

She wasn't interested in commitment, but did that mean she had to go through life alone? She ignored advances from men—some she'd known for years and others she'd only just met—all the time. Why not accept their dinner invitations? What was so wrong with spending time with a man she found interesting?

The three attractive couples at the table beside her grew rowdy. Suddenly, an afternoon alone sunbathing on Lena's dock seemed more appealing, and she signaled the waitress for the check. After paying her bill, she spent a few minutes in the hotel's gift shop, where she selected a house gift for Lena—a bottle of lavender hand soap. She was shocked when her debit card was declined.

"There must be something wrong," Olivia said to the clerk. "I just used that card to pay for my meal in the Chesapeake Restaurant. Do you mind trying again?"

The clerk tried three more times with the same result. "I'm sorry, ma'am. Do you have another card?"

"I'll just pay cash," Olivia said in a snippy tone as she pulled out her last two crisp twenty-dollar bills.

Standing outside the gift shop, she signed into her banking app and transferred $200 from her savings to her checking. The rate she was burning through money had spiraled out of control, and as she retraced her steps down the long drive toward the main road, she vowed to be more frugal about her spending.

She'd gone a short distance on King Carter Road when Alistair pulled up alongside her in his silver pickup truck. He tooted his horn and rolled down the passenger window. "Can I offer you a lift?"

Olivia hesitated. "I should walk off some calories from my brunch at the Tides Inn."

"Are you sure? It's pretty warm out today. I couldn't live with myself if I allowed Lena's houseguest to suffer a heatstroke."

A trickle of sweat ran down her back as she contemplated his offer. "Why not. It's warmer than I thought."

She climbed into the truck, and he drove off down the road.

"What'd you think of the Tides?" he asked.

"Charming. Brunch was delicious." She eyed his navy sport coat and striped tie. "I take it you're coming from church."

"I try not to miss a Sunday. Except, of course, when the rockfish are biting." He flashed his boyish grin, and she burst out laughing.

"I gather the rockfish aren't biting today."

"Nah. The fishing's been off this week. But I'm going out in the boat anyway. I may bring my rod along just for kicks, but I don't plan on doing any hard-core fishing." He rested one hand casually on the steering wheel. "Would you care to join me? I could show you around, help you get acclimated to the area by water."

Olivia never turned down an invitation to go out in a boat, especially on such a warm autumn day, even if she considered the man dangerous territory. "I'd like that. As long as you don't expect me to hold the fishing rod."

"Deal." Pulling into their shared driveway, he stopped at the fork to let her out. "I'll change clothes, grab a sandwich, and meet you on my dock in thirty minutes."

Olivia debated over what to wear as she let herself in the front door. Despite the warmth from the sun, it would likely be chilly out on the water. She finally decided on rustic-red Bermuda shorts and a pale blue tee. She stuffed a gray cashmere sweater, navy baseball cap, and tube of sunscreen inside a beach bag she found in the master bedroom closet downstairs.

When she moseyed down to the dock, Alistair was already on his boat, cramming the last of a sandwich in his mouth as he peeled the canvas cover off the center console. The sight of his manly legs in navy fishing shorts awakened parts of her body that had been asleep for what seemed like decades.

"Welcome aboard." He took her bag and held her hand as she stepped onto the boat. After stowing the bag in a covered compartment on the bow, he started the dual outboard motors, untied the boat, and pushed off from the dock. As they idled out into the creek, he said, "I thought we'd ride out to the mouth of the Chesapeake Bay. We might drop a line in this one spot, just in case the fish are biting."

She gave his arm a playful slap. "You're so bad."

He appeared wounded. "I'm merely looking out for your best interests. I want you to get the full Northern Neck experience, and you can't do that without catching at least one rockfish."

"Don't hold your breath. I have a lot of talents, but I assure you, fishing isn't one of them."

When they reached the jetties at the mouth of the creek, he sped up and they cut through the calm waters of the Rappahannock River, under the bridge, and all the way out to where the river met the Chesapeake Bay. She sat beside him on the leaning post, doing her best to ignore the tingling sensations in her body when their arms touched. They rounded a spit of land with a shoreline of rocks, docks, and sandy beaches that Alistair referred to as Mosquito Point. They traveled a little farther to a tiny uninhabited island. He killed the engines, then raised the propellers out of the water before gliding in close to the grassy bank.

Olivia moved to the side of the boat, staring down into the water. "I can see the bottom."

"If you look closely, you'll see more than the bottom."

When she shielded her eyes from the sun, she could see minnows swimming in schools and blue crabs scuttling across the sandy bottom.

Alistair cast his fishing rod over their heads, his bait landing in the water with a splash. With short jerking movements, he reeled the line back in and repeated the process. The third time, he got a bite.

"Oh baby!" The reel made a fast-paced whining noise as the fish took off with the line. "He's a big'un. Here."

When Alistair tried to give her the rod, Olivia shrank away from it. "Don't give that thing to me. I'll lose the fish for sure."

"You won't if you do what I tell you. Turn around with your back to me."

Olivia followed his instructions. Wrapping his arms around her from behind, he placed his right hand above hers on the rod and his left over hers on the reel handle. When the fish slowed and the line went slack, with his body pressed against hers, they began to reel together. They'd only made a little progress when the fish took off with the line again.

"Ugh!" Olivia exclaimed. "What'd I do wrong?"

"Not a thing," he said, his breath close to her ear. "Don't get discouraged. This is the fun part. You've got a red drum on the line. It'll take time and patience to bring him in."

Olivia peered over the top of her sunglasses, but all she could see was water. "How can you tell what kind of fish it is?"

"Experience. You'll be able to see him when we get him closer to the boat."

For the next twenty minutes, they fought the fish together, gaining line and losing line, waltzing between the bow and the stern as the fish swam around the boat. Finally, they were able to get him close enough for Alistair to catch him in his net.

"He's a beauty." With the fishing line wrapped around his right hand, Alistair gripped the handle of the net with his left. "We can try for a picture of you holding him, but you'll smell like fish for the rest of the day."

She peered over the side of the boat. The fish had shiny reddish-gold scales and appeared bigger than both her thighs put together. "I wouldn't be able to hold him. I'll take a picture of him from here."

She removed her phone from her pocket, snapped a half dozen photographs of the fish, and collapsed on the bow seat in giddy laughter. "That was insane. I never knew fishing could be so exhilarating."

Alistair removed the hook, turned the fish loose, and stowed his net in the compartment beneath the gunwale—the upper edge of the side of the boat. "You're a natural. Wanna try for another?" he asked, holding the rod out to her.

"No way," she said, shaking her head with vehemence. "I'm exhausted."

He smiled. "As you should be. That was quite a fight."

"But don't let me stop you if you want to keep fishing."

"I'm good. That was plenty of excitement for one day." He turned on the engines. "Where to now?"

"You're the captain." She returned to her seat beside him, and they sped off in the same direction they'd come, the wind and noise of the motors making it impossible for them to carry on a conversation. When they passed the entrance to Carters Creek, she hollered, "Where're we going?"

"I thought we'd ride over to Urbanna, which is across the river and down a ways." He pointed and her gaze followed his finger, but they were too far from the opposite shore to see anything except the line of trees that made up the horizon.

Fifteen minutes later, he slowed the engines, and they passed a row of houses on their right opposite a narrow spit of land with a sandy beach on their left. "If you'd like to see the town, it's only a short walk from the city marina."

"Sure! Why not?" Her calendar for the afternoon was free.

He tied up at the marina's main dock, and they got off the boat. Alistair stuck his head in the marina store and called to the young woman behind the counter. "Afternoon, Sally. I won't be more than an hour."

Sally waved at him. "No problem, Alistair. Take all the time you need."

"You must come here often," Olivia said as they began walking up Oyster Road toward town.

"Every now and then when I'm over this way. Do you fancy a chocolate milkshake? Marshall's Drug Store still has their original soda fountain."

When was the last time she'd indulged in something as decadent as a milkshake? "I'm still stuffed from brunch, but you go ahead."

He gave a shrug of indifference. "We'll see how crowded they are."

"I gather you grew up around here," Olivia said as they trudged up the hill toward town.

"I'm actually from Alexandria, but I spent summers and Thanksgivings here as a child."

"But you live here permanently now?"

He smiled over at her. "Correct. After college, I took a job on Wall Street and moved to New York. Four years later, I married my high school sweetheart. Our sons were born within fifteen months of each other, and when our apartment got too small with two rambunctious boys running around, we bought a house in Connecticut, and I commuted to work."

Something inside him shifted, and his expression grew grim. "Our perspective on life changed when Mary Anne got sick. I'd saved enough for an early retirement, and we moved down here where the pace is slower and the air cleaner. It made even more sense because both boys, at the time, were in college at UVA."

"How long did you say your wife has been gone?"

"Going on two years," Alistair said.

"That's how long it's been since my divorce. Although my situation can't compare, I understand what it's like to lose your spouse when it's not your choice." *Dang it, Liv! Why'd you bring up the divorce when you know you're not ready to talk about it?* "Lena mentioned that you own a café."

He nodded. "The Jumpstart Café. It fell into my lap about a year after we moved here. A friend of mine who wanted to start a new business venture in Richmond offered to sell his café to me at a steal. I figured, heck, why not? Sherry, the manager of the Jumpstart, basically runs the place. And it does quite well. Not only do we offer free Wi-Fi, but the lattes and mochas are the best in town."

Raising her brows, she looked at him over the top of her sunglasses. "Aren't they the only lattes and mochas in town?"

"Ha ha. I guess that's true."

They came to an intersection with a two-story white clapboard building on one corner and the Virginia Street Café opposite it. "Is this the town?"

"Yep, pretty much. Small-town USA. There are a lot of really nice folks who live in Urbanna. Their annual Oyster Festival is a ton of fun. Maybe you'll still be here. It's being held November second and third this year."

"I'm leaving on November first," Olivia said, disappointed.

"That's too bad." Alistair placed a hand at the small of her back and guided her across and down the street. "I'm parched. Let's go find us a cold drink."

Olivia stepped back in time when she entered the old pharmacy. Rows of shelves packed with everything from night-lights to enemas made up half the store, and the lunch counter the other half, where hungry patrons currently occupied every round stool there. Alistair managed to get a harried waitress's attention long enough to order two limeades.

He paid for their drinks, and they left the pharmacy. At the intersection, he said, "There's a dress shop just down the road, if you're interested. My wife always enjoyed shopping there."

Although Olivia rarely passed up an opportunity to shop, she reminded herself she could no longer afford to buy expensive clothes. "Thanks, but I'm not in the mood to shop today."

"Then we'll head back to the boat." They turned right toward the marina. "Tell me about your life in Charleston. You mentioned a divorce. Do you have any children?"

"I have one daughter, Laura. She works for Google in Seattle."

Olivia hadn't seen Laura since her visit to Seattle for Thanksgiving two years ago. An awkward tension had crept into their relationship since the divorce. Olivia suspected that Laura was having a difficult time coming to terms with her father being gay—as if that were somehow Olivia's fault.

"That sounds like a fascinating career," Alistair said. "How about you? What do you do for a living?"

"I'm a freelance writer. Or I was. It's a long story. Suffice it to say, I'm looking for new direction in my writing."

CHAPTER ELEVEN

LENA

Lena couldn't remember when she'd last taken the time to blow-dry her hair and apply makeup, but she felt pretty and feminine. After donning a linen dress the color of the summer sky, she slipped her feet into her comfortable sandals for the half-mile walk to Jade's house. Removing the bottle of chardonnay she'd purchased at the Harris Teeter from the refrigerator, she placed it in her backpack along with her camera, iPad, and wallet.

The days were getting shorter, and when she left the condo a few minutes before six, the sun had already begun its descent. Strolling down Queen Street, she rounded the corner onto Church Street as the bells of Saint Philip's Church struck the six o'clock hour. She paused for a moment to listen before continuing south on Church Street. Horses clomped past, leading a carriage packed with tourists, followed by a chauffeur-driven convertible Mustang with bride and groom waving to passersby from the back seat. Throngs of vacationers loitered about on the crowded sidewalks, exuding a festive mood as they hopped from one lively bar or restaurant to another.

When Lena arrived at Jade's house—a three-story taupe-colored colonial with black shutters—Jade came to the door wearing an apron along with a gooey substance dripping from her left hand.

"Come on in. I'm in the kitchen making crab cakes." She motioned for Lena to follow her as she left the parlor and disappeared into the adjacent room.

Lena entered the house, closing the door behind her. She noticed an elderly woman—presumably Jade's mother—reclined with her eyes closed in a leather chair while a television in front of her broadcast the evening news. Quietly, so as not to disturb the sleeping woman, Lena started toward the back of the house.

"Who's there?" the woman called out.

Lena did an about-face and crossed the room to greet her. "You must be Jade's mother. I'm Lena."

Although the woman looked straight at her with aqua-colored eyes, Lena couldn't tell whether or not she could actually see her. "And I'm Phyllis. It's very nice to meet you, Lena. That's a lovely name. Where are you from?"

"I'm from Richmond, Virginia."

"I visited Richmond once. But that's been eons ago. I had a friend who lived on the street with all the monuments."

Lena smiled. "That would be Monument Avenue."

"Lena! Are you coming?" called out Jade from the kitchen. "I could really use your help."

"Be right there," Lena answered. "Can I get you something, Phyllis?"

"If it's not too much trouble, I'd love a glass of white wine."

Lena placed a hand on the backpack dangling at her side. "It just so happens I brought a bottle of chardonnay with me. I'll go find us some glasses."

She walked through the dining room and down the short flight of steps to the kitchen where Jade was scooping slices of avocado into a bowl of salad greens. Lena wandered around the spacious room, dragging her fingertips across the worn pine table. While the kitchen was overdue for a renovation, the random-width oak floors and natural light spilling in through the bank of windows along the back wall made up for the outdated appliances and cheap paneled cabinets.

"What a lovely spot," Lena said, looking out at the manicured courtyard garden. "I'm sure your mother enjoys spending time out there."

"Actually, she sits in front of the television most of the day."

"Can she see anything at all?" Lena asked.

Jade, focusing on dicing tomatoes for the salad, said, "Mom's is the wet form, the worst kind, of age-related macular degeneration. She has a significant blind spot in the center of her vision."

"Poor thing. That's horrible."

Jade shrugged. "At least she's not totally blind. She has a sliver of peripheral vision."

Lena could think of nothing worse. Such an impairment would affect her ability to read. And she couldn't bring herself to think about a life without books.

Turning her back to the window, Lena pulled the bottle of wine from her backpack. "Tell me where you keep your glasses, and I'll open this bottle of wine."

"The cabinet to the right of the refrigerator."

Lena removed three wineglasses from the cabinet, lining them up on the counter.

Jade eyed the glasses. "Who's the third one for?"

"Your mother," Lena said, removing the screw cap. "She asked for some. I hope that's okay."

Jade snatched one of the glasses, returning it to the cabinet. "She can't have wine."

"I'm sorry. I didn't know." Lena remembered how much her own mother, even in her last months of life, had enjoyed a glass of wine in the evenings. "Is she on a medication that prohibits it?"

"She's legally blind and ninety years old," Jade said. "She has a high risk of falling even when she's sober."

Even though she understood the logic, Lena still felt sorry for the poor old woman. "Can I get her some sweet tea then?"

"She's fine for now," Jade snapped. "She can have some tea with her supper." She poured olive oil into an iron skillet on the stove for the crab cakes. "I should've thought to ask you if you have a seafood allergy."

"No allergies. I love all kinds of seafood."

While Jade sautéed the crab cakes, Lena searched through the drawers for placemats and silverware, setting the table for three. But once the meal was ready, Jade fixed a separate tray for her mother. "I'll just take this in to Mom. She likes to eat in front of the TV."

"I'd enjoy her company if she'd like to dine with us," Lena said.

"She's fine. We have photography business to discuss anyway," Jade said, and departed the kitchen with her mother's tray.

Lena transferred the remaining two plates to the table and sat down, placing her cotton napkin in her lap. She salivated at the sight of the crab cakes, cheese grits, buttermilk biscuits, and green salad. She was beginning to understand that the best way to remain committed to her diet in a foodie town like Charleston was to eat in moderation.

When Jade returned, she sat next to Lena at the table. "First thing we need to do is go over the schedule for the next few days. I hope you're an early riser."

"The earlier the better for me. Sunrise is the golden hour for photographers."

"It is indeed." Jade forked off a bite of crab cake and stuffed it in her mouth, chewing while she talked. "We'll start tomorrow in Mount Pleasant. I've been wanting to photograph the shrimp boats docked at Shem Creek. Tuesday, we'll go to Sullivan's Island, and depending on the weather, we'll shoot Saint Philip's Church on Wednesday."

"I walked by Saint Philip's on the way here," Lena said. "It's a stunning church. I'm surprised you haven't already photographed it."

Jade paused midchew. "Oh, I have. At least a thousand times. But I'm striving for perfection. I won't stop until I get the one that wows me."

Lena nibbled at her food, savoring each bite, as they discussed the photography-worthy scenes in and around the city. Removing her iPad from her backpack, she accessed her photos app and slid the tablet in front of Jade. "I took these during my walks around town. I'd love your feedback."

Jade swiped through the photographs, pausing briefly on each one. "These are okay. But as I told you this morning, your composition needs improvement. As your audience, I need to feel what you felt when you were shooting them. Take this image, for example." She spun the iPad around to face Lena. "No one will argue that it's a lovely garden. But what specifically inspires you about this garden? The iron gate, the lily pond, or the roses?"

Lena swallowed past the lump in her throat. She reminded herself that this woman wasn't her husband. That, unlike Charles, Jade intended her criticism to be constructive. She would have to toughen up if she was going to work with a professional. She scrutinized the image displayed on the iPad. "The lily pond, of course."

"You say 'of course' as if it's obvious to me. But it's not. You understand the rule of thirds, right?"

Lena nodded, even though she only vaguely remembered the concept from her college days. "What would you have done differently?"

"Focused my lens and adjusted my aperture so that the lily pond is to the right in the foreground with the roses blurry in the background."

Lena envisioned the scenario. "That makes sense." She made a mental note to google the rule of thirds when she got home. In order to improve her skills, she would have to learn from her mistakes.

Jade returned her attention to her meal. "It's better if it happens in camera, but oftentimes you can crop an image to get the desired effect. I assume you're shooting in raw."

Lena hesitated. "I've heard of that, but I'm not sure what it means."

Jade's hand shot out. "Let me see your camera," she said in an exasperated tone.

Lena removed her camera from her backpack and handed it to Jade, who powered it on and thumbed through the controls.

"Now it's set to raw." She gave Lena back the camera. "Raw is a type of file that saves all the data recorded by your camera's sensor, which enables you to produce the highest-quality images. Your homework assignment for tonight is to research why you should be shooting in raw."

"Got it," Lena said, returning the camera to her backpack.

"What editing software do you use?"

"Apple's editing software, whatever that program is called. Photos, I think."

Jade glared at her. "Please tell me you've at least heard of Photoshop."

"I'm no expert, but I've used Photoshop before to create graphics for my blog."

Jade pounded her fist on the table. "Now we're getting somewhere."

Lena felt relieved, a shred of her confidence restored.

"Is this blog of yours a photo blog?"

The way she'd abandoned her blog months ago when she'd failed to identify a purpose for communicating with potential readers popped into Lena's mind. "I haven't decided what direction I want to take with it. I'm still learning the ins and outs of WordPress."

"That's a start." Jade shoveled the last spoonful of grits into her mouth and got up from the table, taking her plate and Lena's to the sink. "I use Photoshop for more complicated editing. But mostly I use another Adobe product called Lightroom. Which leads me to the second part of your homework assignment for tonight. I want you to download Lightroom to your computer. You do have a computer, right?"

"I'm using my friend's at the condo where I'm staying." Lena left the table and stood at the counter beside Jade as she cut three slices from a store-bought Key lime pie.

"I'll take this to your mother." Instead of taking one slice of pie, Lena took two plates into the parlor.

"I brought you some pie, Phyllis." She removed the old woman's dinner plate from her tray, setting it on the coffee table and replacing it with the pie. "Do you mind if I join you for dessert?"

"Mind?" Phyllis said. "I'd love it."

Lena sat down at the end of the sofa nearest Phyllis. Jade appeared a few minutes later, looking perplexed and none too pleased. Instead of taking a seat, she leaned against the doorjamb as she ate her pie.

"Do I detect a hint of a British accent?" Lena asked Phyllis.

"Why yes, dear, as a matter of fact, you do. I was born and raised in London. I met Jade's father while he was serving as US ambassador to Great Britain."

Lena moved to the edge of the sofa. "Tell me what that was like, being married to such an important government official."

While she ate her pie—every last morsel of it without dropping a crumb—Phyllis spoke of glamorous balls and state dinners and going to Buckingham Palace to meet Queen Elizabeth. "We traveled extensively and to exotic places," she said, a dreamy expression on her face. "Africa. Asia. India."

Lena found the woman's life fascinating and was disappointed when Jade sent her to bed.

"It's time for you to head up, Mom." Taking her mother's plate, she helped Phyllis to her feet. "I'll come check on you in a minute."

Gripping the arms of her chair, Phyllis rose to her feet. "It was a pleasure speaking with you, Lena."

"The pleasure was all mine," Lena said. "I loved hearing about your life. I hope you'll tell me more sometime."

Phyllis made her way to the stairs, using the furniture as landmarks for guidance.

Following Jade into the kitchen, Lena shooed her out of the way of the sink. "I'll take care of the dishes while you get your mother settled."

"It won't take long." Jade set the plates on the counter by the sink. "When I come back, we'll have a look in my equipment closet."

Lena rinsed the plates, arranging them in the dishwasher, and was scrubbing the grits pot when Jade returned less than ten minutes later.

"Leave this. I'll finish cleaning up later." She took the scrub brush from Lena and turned off the faucet. "I have a camera and lens I think will work nicely for you. Come, let me show you."

Lena followed Jade down a narrow hallway behind the kitchen to a paneled study whose furnishings consisted of a worn plaid couch and a small desk with an oversized computer monitor.

Jade opened a closet door, revealing shelves packed with photography equipment. She removed a camera body and lens and took them over to her desk. "This camera is an older version of a model that remains a top seller, and the lens, a 24–70mm with 2.8 aperture, is from Canon's top-of-the-line L series." She attached the lens to the body and handed the camera to Lena. "Try it out for a couple of days. If you like it, I'll give you a good deal on it."

Lena inspected the camera in her hands. "Are you not using it anymore?"

"I just upgraded to the new mirrorless Canon. Cost me a fortune, but so far, it's been worth it." She went back to her closet. "As you can see, I have more equipment than I need." She removed a messenger-style camera bag and tripod. "Here. You'll need both of these as well."

"This is very kind of you. Thank you so much. I promise to be careful with them." Lena placed the camera in the bag and slung it over her shoulder.

"You're not leaving so soon, are you?" Jade asked in a disappointed tone.

"I don't want to overstay my welcome." Lena flashed her a smile. "And I need to get on those homework assignments."

"Oh, come on." Jade opened a door leading to a porch that housed a bench swing and several rocking chairs. "We can't let the evening go to waste. It's so nice out. Feel that cool autumn air."

Lena didn't relish the idea of going home to an empty condo, even one as nice as Olivia's. "Maybe for a little while."

They settled into the rocking chairs and listened to the sound of jazz music drifting toward them from a nearby party. "I'm grateful for this opportunity," Lena said. "But why are you being so nice to me?"

"Because you seem so sad, like you need a friend. And because you and I have something in common. We're both searching for something."

"That surprises me," Lena said. "You seem so put together."

"I'm a good faker," Jade said with a little chuckle. "The truth is, my inspiration for portrait photography has run its course. I've been toying with the idea of selling my business and focusing on landscape photography. I want to travel, to photograph the world."

Lena shifted slightly toward Jade. "What's stopping you?"

"The timing's all wrong. I'm stuck here with Mom. I can't very well leave her alone in her condition."

Jade's voice took on a vulnerable quality. One Lena had not picked up on before from Jade, but one she recognized all too well. "Do you have other siblings?"

"I have a younger sister, Marie, who lives in Boston. But she has a family and a medical practice—she's an orthopedic surgeon—that make it difficult for her to help out much."

"Nursing an aging parent is a heavy burden to bear alone. I'm an only child. I spent every waking hour of my mother's last months at her bedside. Being on call 24-7, not being able to escape the illness, wears on you after a while. What about an assisted living facility? Phyllis is so vibrant for a woman her age. I would think she'd love making new friends."

"She won't consider it. She refuses to leave her house."

In spite of the uneasy feeling that crept over her, Lena decided that any skeletons in Jade's closet were none of her business. She wasn't interested in making long-term relationships. But having a friend to pal around with during her month in Charleston was more than she'd hoped for. It was certainly more than she'd had at home in Richmond.

CHAPTER TWELVE

ALISTAIR

Alistair hated for his outing with Olivia to come to an end. He couldn't remember when he'd last enjoyed the companionship of a person other than Mary Anne.

"We could stay out longer if I didn't have so much yard work to finish," he said as he maneuvered the boat alongside his dock.

"Duty calls," Olivia said. "But thank you. I enjoyed myself immensely."

"Next time, we'll ride over to Fishing Bay, which is off the Piankatank River, the river just south of the Rappahannock."

Olivia removed her beach bag from the bow's storage compartment. "I'd like that."

After securing his lines to the cleats, he held on to her bag while she stepped off the boat onto the dock. "One thing irritates me about being single. You can never buy just one chicken breast. Would you like to come to dinner? I'd hate for the extra breast to go to waste."

She squeezed his bicep. "Strong man like you can't eat two chicken breasts?"

His face heated. "Truth is, I'd appreciate the company. It's hard to get excited about cooking on the grill by myself."

Her plump rosy lips parted in a sympathetic smile. "I'd love to join you, as long as you let me bring a salad and some wine."

"Salad and wine would be great." They started up the dock together. "By the way, has the ice in the cooler melted?"

"I'll find out when I make the salad. I heated up a can of soup for dinner last night, and since I ate brunch at the Tides Inn this morning, I haven't had reason to open the cooler."

"If you find it needs replenishing, give me a holler, and I'll bring some over."

"Will do," she said, casting a brilliant smile at him as they parted.

Alistair spent the next three hours trimming hedges and raking the top layer of old mulch out of his flower beds. Inviting Olivia to dinner had seemed like a friendly gesture to an out-of-towner at the time, but as he rushed around, vacuuming and cleaning the powder room and setting the table on the patio, he felt as though he was preparing the house for a date. And he was definitely not ready for dating. Nor was he in the mood to entertain. He wanted to drink a few beers, watch a little football, and go to bed early. But he perked up the minute he saw her crossing the yard from Lena's, looking elegant in a white sleeveless top, a black skirt that swished around her shapely legs, and a pink sweater tied around her neck.

He walked out into the yard to greet her. "Thank you for bringing the salad," he said, taking the bowl from her.

"You're welcome." She held up a bottle of wine. "I hope you like red."

"Red is perfect. We'll save it for dinner. Unless, of course, you'd like a glass now. I'm having a beer to start. But you may want something harder. I have vodka, whiskey, scotch, gin. Or you may prefer white wine. And I have that too. Both chardonnay and pinot grigio." He realized he was babbling. "I'll stop talking now."

She laughed. "I'm fine with beer. It's a beer kinda night."

"I like your way of thinking. It is a beer kinda night, isn't it? Being outside. Autumn chill in the air."

"And football on the TV." She entered the house through the open sliding glass doors and into the family room, where she stood in front of the wall-mounted flat-screen showing the Giants playing the Saints.

Alistair didn't know many women who liked football. Although she'd tolerated his obsession with the sport, Mary Anne had never known one team from another. He went to stand beside her. "I take it you're a football fan?"

"Absolutely! The Saints are my team. I'm originally from New Orleans."

"You don't say. How did you end up in Charleston?"

"By way of Virginia, actually. I attended college in the arts program at VCU. After graduation, I took a job writing copy for an advertising agency in Charleston. I met my husband at a cocktail party six month later."

"And your parents, are they still in New Orleans?"

With a sad smile, she said, "They've been dead for years."

"I'm sorry to hear that. You mentioned a divorce earlier. Are you still on amicable terms?"

"We're friendly enough, I guess. I'd rather not talk about it."

I can relate. I have a few off-limits subjects of my own.

They stood in silence, watching two more plays until the Saints were forced to punt the ball to the Giants.

Turning her back to the television, Olivia looked around the room. "Your home is so warm and cozy, so inviting."

Alistair smiled. He, too, found the room cozy with its stone fireplace, seagrass rug, and leather-upholstered furniture. "I have to give Mary Anne all the credit for the decor." Tears blurred his vision at the mention of his late wife, and he waited a minute for the emotion to pass. "I don't know about you, but I'm ready for that beer."

Olivia followed him into the kitchen, setting the bottle of wine beside the platter of chicken marinating on the counter. He removed two Stellas from the refrigerator, then popped the caps and handed a bottle to Olivia. "Shall we start the grill? We can watch the game from the deck while I cook."

"Sounds like a plan. What can I do to help?"

"If you'll slide the mac and cheese in the oven, I'll get this." He grabbed the tray he'd prepared with the platter of chicken and cooking utensils, and they exited the kitchen through the sliding glass doors that mirrored the ones in the family room.

As they watched the end of the game, Alistair was impressed by Olivia's apparent knowledge of football. She was full of surprises, a study in contrasts, sophisticated yet down-to-earth, an intoxicating combination of femininity and tomboy.

He'd just put the chicken on the grill when she shivered. "Brrr! It suddenly got cold." She untied her sweater from around her neck and slipped it on.

"Warm days and cool nights are typical for Virginia this time of year. This should help you warm up." He used a BIC lighter with a long metal wand to start the small fire he'd set earlier in his built-in firepit.

Moving closer to the pit, she wrapped her arms around her midsection and tilted her head back, staring at the night sky. "I'm amazed at the number of stars out tonight. The night sky in Charleston isn't nearly as brilliant."

"The Northern Neck isn't for everyone, and sometimes it takes a while to grow on you. But it's really a special place. I suspect you won't want to leave come November first."

"I like what I've seen so far. I'm just worried I might get . . ." Her voice trailed off.

"Bored?"

She smiled. "*Stir-crazy* is the word that comes to mind. The nearest gourmet grocery store is in Richmond, for crying out loud. I like to eat in good restaurants, and I need to be around people." Her expression grew serious. "Although I could definitely do without the people I've been hanging out with lately."

"I'm intrigued." He transferred the chicken from the grill to a clean plate on the tray, which he lifted. "You'll have to tell me about them while we eat."

"I'll spare you the indigestion," she mumbled.

In the kitchen, she served helpings of salad, chicken, and macaroni and cheese onto two plates while he opened the bottle of red wine and poured two glasses. They took their plates and wine back out to the patio and sat down at the table.

He raised his glass to her. "To a perfect autumn day."

Repeating his words, Olivia clinked her glass to his and took a sip of wine. "I can't believe you did all this," she said about the linen placemats and napkins and lit candles in hurricane globes.

"When my wife was alive, setting the table was one of my assigned chores."

"How did your wife die?" Olivia asked and then reddened. "I'm sorry. I understand if you don't want to talk about it."

"I don't mind," he said, toying with his noodles. "Mary Anne had ovarian cancer."

"That must've been really hard on your family."

He nodded, stuffing a forkful of salad in his mouth and gulping it down with wine. "At first, everything happened so fast. The diagnosis. Surgery. Resigning from the firm and moving down here. And then the next eighteen months crept by. The chemo made her so sick. It broke my heart to watch her suffer. And to see my boys so devastated."

Olivia watched her wine spinning as she twirled her glass. "You mentioned earlier that your sons were at UVA at the time. Where are they now?"

"They're both in New York." He changed the subject before she asked questions about Mike and Josh he couldn't answer. Despite Roy's insistence that he reach out to his sons, Alistair had made every excuse in the book not to call them. "Tell me about these people, the ones you've been hanging out with lately that you could definitely do without."

She waved her fork in a dismissive gesture. "You don't want to hear about them."

"Actually, I do."

"Okay, but don't say I didn't warn you." She sat back in her chair with her arms crossed over her chest, wineglass in hand.

The flames from the nearby fire cast her in a warm glow. She was a woman of classic good taste, poised and stylish and so damn gorgeous with her strawberry-blonde hair and dazzling green eyes. He never planned to remarry. Couldn't risk having his heart broken again. But he didn't see anything wrong with admiring an attractive woman from afar, especially since she would be staying in Lena's cottage for only a few weeks.

He struggled to keep a straight face as she told her story about getting caught in the middle of a catfight between two young women. She was clearly upset about the situation, but Alistair thought it was the most ludicrous thing he'd ever heard and had a difficult time summoning much sympathy.

"You think I'm ridiculous," she said when she'd finished her story. "It's written all over your face."

Alistair broke into laughter, and once he started, it took him several minutes to regain control. "I'm sorry. I promise I'm not laughing at you. It's just . . . well . . . I'm a simple man. I lead a simple life. Those women . . . the whole thing is so absurd, it's beyond my realm of comprehension. After watching my wife die from cancer, it makes me angry that people are so frivolous."

Her eyes glistened with tears. *Oh boy! I've done it now.* He had no experience with crying women. He had no daughters, of course, and Mary Anne had never been a crier. He scooted his chair close to hers. "I didn't mean to make you cry."

"I feel like such an idiot for falling into their trap." She dried her eyes with her napkin. "And now I'm the laughingstock of Charleston."

"You're not the laughingstock of anything, Olivia. You're the victim in this situation. And you put the Kates in their places. What kind of response have you received on your Chef Oscar post?"

She shook her head. "I've been avoiding my laptop since I left Charleston."

"You just need some time to yourself to put things into perspective. And you've come to the right place. The salt air has the ability to help us see things clearer." Once upon a time, he'd believed that was true. All he ever saw anymore was fog.

Holding his gaze, she brought her hand to his cheek. "You're a kind man, Alistair." She leaned into him, brushing her lips against his.

"Whoa!" He jerked his head back as if he'd been shocked by an electrical current. "Where did that come from?"

Horror crossed her face. "Oh God! I don't know what got into me. I've never done anything like that in my life." She sprang to her feet, snatched her plate off the table, and entered the house, returning seconds later with Lena's salad bowl.

He walked her to the edge of the patio. "Come on, Olivia. Don't leave like this. You surprised me is all."

As she stormed off, Alistair debated whether to go after her. Had he inadvertently given her the impression he was interested in a romance? He decided it was best to let her calm down before explaining that friendship was all he could handle at the moment. With Mary Anne as his one and only, he lacked experience when it came to romantic relationships. He didn't know how to be with a smoking-hot woman like Olivia even if he wanted to, which he definitely did not. He was content with his life as a bachelor.

Alistair watched Olivia until she was safely inside before taking his plate to the kitchen. He cleaned up from dinner, refilled his glass with wine, and returned to the patio, plopping down in a chair near the fire.

Light beamed through the second-floor window next door, from the bedroom that had belonged to Lena as a child. On long-ago summer nights, he used to shimmy up the maple tree and climb onto the balcony. He and Lena would stretch out on the wooden floor and stare at the sky while sharing their deepest secrets and dreams for the future. She had always been an important part of his life, and he'd been overjoyed when she and Mary Anne had become close friends. He owed Lena an apology for being so standoffish toward her. Why couldn't he shake his depression? While his mood had improved since those dismal days immediately following Mary Anne's death, he still felt some shade of blue most of the time.

Alistair was draining the last of his wine when his cell phone rang from an area code he didn't recognize. He'd barely spoken *hello* when a female voice, young and panicked, filled the line. "Mr. Hoffman, this is Stacy, Michael's girlfriend."

Stacy? Alistair wasn't aware his youngest son had a girlfriend.

She continued in a breathy tone, "Mike and I were in an accident tonight. Our Uber driver ran a red light and hit a city bus. I'm fine, but the doctor says Mike needs surgery."

Alistair's heart hammered in his chest. "Do you know the nature or extent of his injuries?"

"No!" she sobbed. "They won't tell me anything. I'm so scared, Mr. Hoffman."

"I know you are, Stacy. Let me think for a minute." He glanced at his watch. It was already after nine, way too late to get a flight out of Richmond. That late at night, he should make good time on the highway. "I'll have to drive. Depending on traffic, I can be there in seven hours, tops. Please call with updates as you get them. Which hospital is he in?"

"Mount Sinai West. We were on our way home from dinner at a restaurant on the Upper West Side." They discussed logistics for a minute more before hanging up.

Alistair switched into crisis mode. With his mind on autopilot, he stuffed clothes and toiletries into a duffel bag, made a cup of coffee for the road, and locked up the house, tossing the trash from the kitchen in the outdoor trash can on the way to his truck. He drove off toward town, his headlights bright on the dark country road.

The realization that he could lose his youngest son, that Mike might die, brought about an ache in his chest that made it difficult for him to breathe. He retrieved his cell phone from the cupholder and placed a call to Josh.

CHAPTER THIRTEEN
OLIVIA

Loud banging on the front door and pounding of the brass knocker jolted Olivia from the depths of sleep on Monday morning. *Alistair! Who else could it be?* How could she possibly face him? She'd tossed and turned half the night, the shame of her impetuous kiss at the forefront of her mind, before finally taking an Ambien around three.

More loud door banging drove her from the comfort of the bed with its high-thread-count sheets, mountain of feather pillows, and warm duvet. While the rest of the house was in a state of semi-disrepair, the bed linens were comparable to a five-star hotel.

Throwing on her robe, she padded barefoot down the stairs and onto the hardwood floors. She prepared herself to face Alistair—chin up and head held high—but when she swung open the door, she was surprised and a little disappointed to find two appliance deliverymen on the front porch.

"Morning, ma'am." They tipped their caps in unison. Based on her observations, the shorter of the two men, with bulging biceps, was strong as a mule, while the tall, skinny guy with the sunken chest appeared too weak to lift a bag of sugar—let alone a refrigerator.

"We're with Northern Neck Appliance," Muscle Man said. "We have a refrigerator delivery for you."

She wrapped her robe tighter and ran her fingers through her hair. "I forgot you were coming today. Please come in." As she stepped out of their way, she stole a glance across the yard in the direction of Alistair's house. His driveway was empty, his truck gone. He owned a café. Wouldn't he need to be there to serve the breakfast crowd? Then again, he'd mentioned that his manager ran the business for him.

She showed the deliverymen to the kitchen and supervised the exchange of refrigerators. "I thought we were getting a scratch-and-dent model," she said, marveling at the new stainless-steel KitchenAid refrigerator with water and ice dispensers.

Muscle Man said, "Yes, ma'am. You got yourself a good deal on this beauty."

Thin Man said, "She's in mint condition, aside from the small ding in the freezer door near the bottom."

"I know the homeowner will be pleased," Olivia said.

Muscle Man ran his hand down the side of the old refrigerator. "And this old clunker is headed for the appliance graveyard."

Olivia watched as they strapped the fridge onto a commercial-size dolly and wrestled it out the front door. Once they were gone, she opened Alistair's cooler. The ice had melted, and the contents—containers of yogurt, a carton of coffee cream, and deli baggies of sliced turkey and low-fat mozzarella—floated on top. Through the kitchen window, she kept an eye on Alistair's driveway while she dried each item with a dish towel and placed them in the new refrigerator. With some effort, she dragged the cooler across the sitting room floor and out the sliding glass doors to the edge of the deck, where she removed the plug, allowing the water to drain.

She tilted her head back, feeling the warmth of the sun on her face. According to her weather app, another summerlike day was on tap. On impulse, she dashed inside and up the stairs to her bedroom, quickly changing into her bathing suit before heading back outside toward the dock.

She dragged the paddleboard from the shed down to the floating dock and set off in the direction opposite from where she'd explored in the kayak the day before. As she glided through the water, her mind drifted back to the previous night. She couldn't believe she'd kissed him. Had her sex deprivation driven her to making passes at men? Or had she simply gotten caught up in the moment—the fire and candlelit dinner and chill in the air?

She hoped she hadn't blown the friendship that was developing between them. She would apologize by making him something, perhaps an apple crisp in celebration of the season.

She spent most of the morning on the water, returning to the dock around eleven thirty to find that Alistair had not yet come home. She showered, ate half a turkey sandwich for lunch, and set off for Kilmarnock.

As Alistair had promised, the town was of ample size with several quaint-looking boutiques on Main Street that tempted her. Exercising willpower, she drove toward the grocery store. When she spotted a large produce stand about a mile down the road, she pulled into the dirt parking lot and got out of the minivan.

Large umbrellas covered two wooden carts offering pumpkins and mums in addition to seasonal fruits and vegetables.

A midthirties woman in cutoff jean shorts greeted her. "Afternoon, ma'am. Are you looking for anything in particular?"

"Apples," Olivia said, surveying their offerings.

"All our apples are grown in Virginia. Do you have your heart set on a specific variety? We have Gala, Golden Delicious, Granny Smith."

Olivia decided on the Gala apples and selected eight—six for the crisp she would make for Alistair, and two for herself.

The woman bagged and handed the apples to Olivia, saying, "If you're interested, I'm offering a good deal on pumpkins today—three for the price of two." She gestured at the display.

"I'll take the deal. And throw in a mum as well." She picked out three fat, round pumpkins—one green, one white, and one orange—and a large yellow mum full of blooms.

She paid with her debit card and then stored the items in the back of the van. She went on to the grocery store, where she purchased the remaining ingredients for the apple crisp and enough groceries to last her the week.

Alistair was still not home when she arrived back at the cottage, nor had he returned by the time she finished baking the apple crisp around three. Her concern mounting, she tried to remember if he'd mentioned a trip. *You're being ridiculous, Olivia. You hardly know the man. He doesn't have to report his whereabouts to you.*

She opened the Halloween card she'd picked up at the grocery store and jotted a quick note.

Dear Alistair,

Thank you for a lovely dinner. Please accept my sincere apology for my improper behavior. I hope we can still be friends.

Best regards,
Olivia

She placed the note alongside the warm crisp in the cooler and dragged it around the side of Alistair's house, leaving it at his front door.

Back at the cottage, she stood staring out across Carters Creek, contemplating the long hours until bedtime. There was always something to do in Charleston—yoga or meditation classes, strolls along the seawall, shopping on King Street. But here, in this peaceful countryside, she felt cut off from the rest of the world. She missed the noise—sirens blasting and the whir of truck engines. She wasn't sure she could handle the silence.

What choice do you have, Liv? You made a deal with Lena. You can't very well go home, and an expensive plane ticket to Seattle is out of the question. Embrace this time alone. Allow yourself the luxury of leisure. Focus on your goals—clearing your head and finding your inspiration. Search for a new direction for your writing. You owe it to yourself to at least give it a few more days.

Olivia climbed the stairs to the study, opened the window to the afternoon breeze, and settled in behind the desk. Powering on her laptop, she created a blank document and then stared at it for thirty minutes without a single idea of what to write. Suffering from writer's block was a first for her. She snapped the laptop closed and gazed out the window, watching a cluster of Sunfish sailboats zigzagging across the creek.

What now? she asked herself. *Television? A nap?* She spotted a rope hammock nestled in the middle of two pine trees between the house and the dock shed. *Read a book? Hmm, yes, that's just what I need—an escape into the land of fiction.*

Retrieving her e-reader from her bedroom, she scrolled through the titles. Not even one unread book in her library captured her interest. Without Wi-Fi, she couldn't download anything new. She would have to settle for one of Lena's romance novels.

Grabbing a lightweight sweater from her room, she hurried downstairs to the sitting room. She scrutinized the paperbacks lined in neat rows on the bookshelves before settling on a relatively new release by Catherine Bybee. Not only did she find the dark-haired woman on the cover attractive, but she could totally relate to the title, *Not Quite Crazy*.

She hesitated. Olivia considered herself a literary snob. Commercial fiction had never appealed to her. Since she was old enough to appreciate the classics, she'd aspired to become a modern-day equivalent of Jane Austen or Charlotte Brontë. *Are you seriously going to read a romance novel?* she asked herself and answered, *Why not? If ever there was a time to try something new, this is it.*

Olivia took several pillows from the sofa and went outside to the hammock, making herself comfortable. Hooked from the first sentence, she read until the sky grew too dark to see the words. She went inside to the kitchen, making herself a salad and pouring a glass of wine. She read while she ate, so engrossed in the novel that she no longer cared whether Alistair had returned home. After dinner, she turned on the gas logs and read by the fire until she finished the novel a few minutes past midnight.

She stood and stretched. She'd never read an entire novel in one sitting, let alone a romance. But she couldn't get enough. She wanted more. She returned *Not Quite Crazy* to the bookshelves, exchanging it for another novel by the same author.

With the paperback tucked under her arm, she went upstairs, changed into her pajamas, washed her face, and brushed her teeth before climbing into bed. Midway through the second chapter, she fell asleep with her reading glasses on and the book spread open on her chest. She slept peacefully, dreaming of a woman named Leesa who was searching for romance.

CHAPTER FOURTEEN

ALISTAIR

Alistair was sleeping so soundly he failed to hear Josh leave for work on Monday morning. He showered and dressed and was scrambling eggs in the galley kitchen of his sons' apartment when Mike stumbled out of his room around ten.

"How're you feeling?" Alistair asked as he scooped eggs onto two plates and added several slices of bacon to each.

Mike collapsed on a chair at the small round dining table. "Like I got hit by a bus. Oh wait. I did get hit by a bus."

Alistair placed one of the plates in front of his son. "You're lucky you weren't killed." He poured two glasses of orange juice and joined Mike at the table.

"You're right about that," Mike said, gripping his fork with his good hand as he shoveled eggs into his mouth.

To Alistair's enormous relief, his youngest son's injuries had turned out to be non-life-threatening. While he needed surgery to pin his broken collarbone, the outpatient procedure would take place sometime later in the week.

"Did they give you a prescription for pain meds?"

"I told them I didn't want one. Narcotics are addictive. I'm gonna suck it up and stick with ibuprofen."

Recalling Mary Anne's illness and all he had learned about pain management, Alistair didn't think Mike would survive the pain after surgery without narcotics. "Let's consult with the doctor. Some meds are more addictive than others. When is your surgery?"

"I'm not sure. I have to see the orthopedist first. Speaking of which, what time is it?" Mike's eyes traveled to the clock on the stove. "Jeez, it's after ten already. My appointment's at eleven. I need to get in the shower." He pushed his plate away and slowly rose to his feet, struggling to get the sling over his head as he strode across the room.

Alistair followed him into his bedroom. "Here, son, let me help you with that."

Mike stopped fighting with the sling long enough for Alistair to ease the strap over his head. "Do you think we'll be able to get a taxi, or is everyone in Manhattan using Uber nowadays?" Alistair asked.

"Getting a taxi shouldn't be a problem this time of day. But seriously, Dad, you don't have to go with me. I can handle this myself."

"Humor me, son. I'm already here. I'd like to see you through the surgery."

"Okay, Dad. I'd like that."

"But if I'm cramping your style by sleeping on your couch, say the word and I'll stay in a hotel."

"Don't you dare. Josh and I want you to stay with us."

"Good! That's settled." He gave Mike a gentle nudge toward the bathroom. "If you don't hurry, you'll be late for your appointment."

Alistair cleaned up from breakfast while Mike showered and dressed. He'd been so out of touch with his sons, he didn't know they'd ditched their roommates and moved in together last spring. Their apartment was on the sixth floor of a restored historic building in Gramercy Park. Two bedrooms shared a bath, and the main room—which served as living, dining, and kitchen—was tastefully decorated with heavy furniture, leather upholstery, and a geometric-patterned rug on the floor. Even the contemporary artwork adorning the walls was to Alistair's liking, although not necessarily his taste.

He felt a stab of envy when Mike emerged from his room wearing a dark gray suit and striped tie. He remembered all too well what it was like to be young, living and working in Manhattan. While the boys had their mother's sandy hair and bright blue eyes, they possessed Alistair's drive and determination. When he'd first seen them at the emergency room the night before, he'd marveled at how much they'd matured since Christmas. They were no longer boys but young men. Not only had they changed physically—their faces were fuller, and they'd lost the fifteen pounds they'd put on in college from drinking beer—they'd become self-sufficient, determined to make it on their own.

"Do you always dress up for your doctors' appointments?" Alistair asked.

"Aren't you the wise guy," Mike said with a fake laugh. "I'm going to work after my appointment. And don't try to talk me out of it."

"I wouldn't dream of it." Alistair smiled to himself. He'd been equally committed to his job at Mike's age.

He waited until they were in a taxi speeding up Madison Avenue before asking, "Is your relationship with Stacy serious?"

Alistair had been less than impressed with Mike's current girlfriend when they'd met at the hospital the previous evening. She was a blonde bombshell, a fashion model in the making, but she appeared to lack any common sense whatsoever.

Mike rubbed the stubble on his chin. "I'm not sure what we are. We're definitely not serious. *Convenient* is a better way to describe our relationship. I'm sure you noticed that she's a ditz. She's a ton of fun to hang out with. And the sex is amazing."

Alistair's hand shot out. "Too much information."

Mike laughed. "Bottom line—Stacy is not marriage material, not that I'm even thinking about marriage at this age."

"Unfortunately, we have no control over when, where, or how we fall in love. Take your mother and me, for example. As you know, she and I met our freshman year in high school." Alistair placed a hand on Mike's thigh. "The thing is, son, you never know when the right girl will come along. It could be very *inconvenient* if you're in a relationship with someone else."

"That's true," Mike said with a sigh.

The taxi pulled up in front of an all-glass skyscraper. Alistair paid the driver, and they got out. "How'd you find this orthopedist?" Alistair asked as they rode the elevator to the tenth floor.

"Emily, one of the nurses in the ER last night, recommended him. She's the orthopedist's daughter." When Alistair gave him a skeptical look, Mike added, "I know what you're thinking, but Josh checked him out, and he's supposed to be the best in town. I wouldn't have gotten the appointment if not for Emily. She was totally into me. And hot too. Come to think of it, she could be marriage material."

Alistair bumped elbows with Mike's good arm. "But you blew it because she thinks you're in a relationship with Stacy."

"All right, Dad. You've made your point. No sense in driving it home."

The doors parted, and they exited the elevator. The doctor's office was crowded, but after filling out the necessary paperwork, they were immediately shown to an examination room, leading Alistair to wonder exactly what Emily had said to her father about Mike.

He guessed Dr. Davidson to be in his sixties with a head of gray hair and a friendly manner that undoubtedly made him popular with his patients. After examining the X-rays the hospital had sent over, Davidson discussed with Alistair and Mike the best course of action—a minimally invasive procedure to insert a pin into the broken collarbone.

"It'll provide immediate stability and a speedier recovery," Davidson said. "You'll need to have the pin surgically removed at some point down the road, but we can worry about that later. My next surgery day is Wednesday. You can schedule that at the front desk on your way out. If you need me in the meantime, you can call this number and have me paged." He handed Mike a business card and exited the room.

Mike and Alistair retraced their steps through the maze of hallways to the lobby. Mike was speaking to one of the receptionists about his surgery when Alistair spotted an old friend and colleague, Henry Warner, entering the waiting room. Henry was small in stature, barely five feet five, but a dynamo in the financial industry. Aside from a few lines etched deeper around his eyes, he hadn't changed a bit since Alistair last saw him at Mary Anne's funeral.

"I don't believe my eyes," Henry said when Alistair went to greet him. "It's Alistair Hoffman in the flesh. How the hell are you, man?" Henry extended his hand to Alistair and then pulled him in for what the younger generation referred to as a bro hug.

Alistair clapped him on the back. "Better now that I'm seeing you, old buddy."

"What brings you to the big city?" Henry asked.

Alistair gestured across the room at his son. "Mike was in a car accident last night. His Uber driver ran a red light and hit a city bus. He's having surgery to pin a broken collarbone on Wednesday."

"Damn! He's lucky it was only his shoulder. But he's in good hands with Davidson. He's the best. He repaired my rotator cuff when I tore it playing golf last summer."

"That's good to know," Alistair said. "I feel better hearing the recommendation from you."

They moved together to the reception desk. "How long are you in town for?"

"I'm not sure," Alistair said. "A lot depends on how the surgery goes on Wednesday."

"I'd love to get together while you're here," Henry said as he signed the register, logging himself in for his appointment. "Why don't we plan on lunch on Friday? Twelve o'clock at our usual place. If something happens and you can't make it, text me. You have my number."

Alistair smiled as he thought back to the many Friday lunches they'd shared over the years in the warm atmosphere of Felidia, a converted brownstone. "I'll do my best to make it."

"A word of warning," Henry said, "I'm going to try to talk you into coming back to work for us."

Alistair chuckled. "And I'm warning you, you'll be wasting your breath."

Mike finished with the receptionist and turned to face them. "Mr. Warner, it's nice to see you. Are you a patient of Dr. Davidson's?"

Henry repeated what he'd told Alistair about his torn rotator cuff and what a great job Davidson had done repairing it. As they said goodbye, Alistair realized how much he was looking forward to having lunch with his old friend on Friday.

Alistair and Mike rode to the lobby in the elevator before parting ways in front of the building. Mike headed north to catch the subway for work, and Alistair took off on foot toward Central Park.

The park was crowded with people wearing shorts and flip-flops, enjoying the unseasonably warm seventy-degree weather. He strolled for hours as he assessed his life and contemplated his future. What if Henry offered him a job? Would moving back to New York be such a bad thing? He appreciated his simple life in the Northern Neck. But was he ready for retirement? He was only fifty-four years old. He had a lot left to offer the world.

He hadn't realized how much he missed the energy of a big city. The sounds of sirens and car horns. The smells of fresh bagels and coffee wafting out from cafés on his way to work in the mornings. Walking in Central Park after a heavy snow. The Yankees and the Giants. Attending theater openings and strolling through Times Square. Even more so, he missed his job as the managing director of an investment banking firm, wining and dining clients, the adrenaline rush from closing high-powered deals. Even after he moved his family to Connecticut, he'd spent his days in the city and, when work dictated, many nights in the company apartment as well. He'd gladly given it all up and moved to Virginia when Mary Anne got sick. But why had he stayed in the Northern Neck after she died? Was he even happy there? He was lonely. He knew that much. Alistair had not only lost his wife, he'd lost his life as well.

On the way back to the apartment, he stopped in at Whole Foods, where he purchased a container of chicken salad for his lunch and the ingredients to make lasagna and a salad for dinner.

Alistair spent the remainder of the day cooking and cleaning, domestic chores he'd never minded doing even when he'd been the sole breadwinner. At six thirty that evening, with the salad made and the lasagna warming in the oven, he poured himself a glass of pinot noir and turned on the national news. Exhausted from lack of sleep the night before, he dozed off within minutes, sitting straight up on the sofa with his head resting against the cushions. The boys woke him when they arrived home around seven fifteen. Alistair noticed the fatigue in their slumped postures and dark circles under their eyes.

"Dinner's ready, boys." He motioned them to the table. "Sit down. I'll get the lasagna."

"Thanks, Dad. This is nice," Josh said, observing the table Alistair had set with placemats and a candle he'd found at the back of one of the kitchen cabinets.

"Let's hope it's edible." Alistair brought the casserole dish to the table and served a heaping portion of lasagna on each of their plates before returning to the kitchen for the salad bowl and bread basket.

"How's your pain?" he asked Mike when he joined them.

Mike lifted his good shoulder in a shrug. "Bearable."

Alistair understood his son's reluctance to take pain meds. Watching his wife become addicted to morphine had broken Alistair's heart. But sometimes narcotics are necessary. In his wife's case, there had been no other course of action.

They bowed their heads while Alistair blessed their food, the simple "God is Great" blessing they'd said at family dinners when the boys were growing up.

"Amen," they said in unison and lifted their forks.

Alistair smiled to himself as he watched Mike and Josh attack their food with little consideration for manners, just as they'd done when they'd come home ravenous from sports practices in high school. He passed the basket of warm chunks of French bread to Josh on his right. "I owe you both an apology," he began. "I haven't been a very good father lately."

"What're you talking about?" Josh said, taking the basket from him. "You've been a fine father. A little distant, maybe. But we understood you were going through some heavy stuff. Mike and I talked about it on the way home tonight. We're the ones who should be apologizing to you. We've been avoiding you lately. Not because we didn't want to see you or talk to you, but because you seemed like you wanted to be left alone."

"And I'm sorry for that," Alistair said. "I let my grief come between us. I promised your mother I would keep our family close, but I failed her. And I failed you."

Mike stabbed at his salad. "You didn't fail us, Dad. We've failed you. Josh and I have helped each other through our worst days. We had each other, but you had nobody."

Alistair smiled. "I needed this time alone, son. Everyone grieves in their own way. I'm glad you've had each other." He lowered his head, staring at his plate as he forked off a bite of lasagna. "Anyway, I just wanted you to know I'm planning to be a better father from now on."

"We don't want a better father," Mike said. "We just want our old father back."

"I'm taking as many steps backward as I am forward, but I'm trying to come out of my funk."

"It doesn't matter how many steps it takes as long as you eventually get where you want to be," Mike said.

Josh lifted his glass of wine. "Welcome back, Dad. We've missed you."

"Does this mean we can spend more time together?" Alistair asked, clinking Josh's glass.

"That's the other thing we wanted to talk to you about," Mike said. "We're hoping you'll come to New York for the holidays. It's not easy for us to get away. And . . . well, we think the Northern Neck is kinda boring, especially this time of year."

Alistair laughed. "The Northern Neck is what you make of it. But I can see where someone your age might find it boring." He buttered a chunk of bread. "I'd like come to New York for the holidays. At least for one of them. I have wonderful memories of the Christmases we spent here together when you boys were young."

Josh set his fork down and wiped his mouth with his napkin. "You know, Dad, you're not the only one who made Mom a promise."

"We promised her that when the time was right we'd make sure you moved on with your life," Mike said.

Alistair looked from one boy to the other. They were tag-teaming him. He knew the tactic well. He and Mary Anne had used it on the boys all the time.

It was Josh's turn. "What we're trying to say is, Mom didn't want you to be alone. She knew how hard it would be for you to find someone else."

"And you're never gonna find someone in Irvington," Mike said.

Josh's smile was full of mischief. "But there's a woman in my office. She's pretty hot for someone her age. Your age. If you come for Christmas, we thought maybe you could stay a few extra days . . . so, you know, you could take her out."

"This is not the conversation I thought we'd be having tonight." Alistair's gaze traveled to the window, and silence settled over the table as he stared out at the lit skyline. A long minute passed before he shifted his gaze back to his sons. "Wouldn't you find it strange to see me with someone other than your mom?"

Mike frowned as he contemplated the question. "A little, maybe."

Josh added, "But we'll get used to it. You're still young, Dad. We want you to be happy. It makes us sad to think of you all alone."

Alistair let out a sigh of resignation. "I'm not sure I'm ready for dating, but I'll give it some thought."

He'd been unable to get Olivia off his mind since leaving Virginia, and now his thoughts once again turned to her. His sons, and indirectly his wife, had given him permission to move on with his life. This permission—which he'd been waiting to hear—sparked inside him a glimmer of hope about his future.

CHAPTER FIFTEEN

LENA

In working with Jade, Lena began to recall the basic skills of photography she'd learned in college. She also discovered many new techniques brought about by the advent of the digital camera. The Canon she'd borrowed from Jade was a high-tech machine, capable of rendering beautiful photographs and enabling the photographer to get the desired image even when the elements weren't ideal.

Much to Lena's disappointment, Jade lacked the patience to be a great teacher. When Lena made a mistake, Jade barked orders and criticized her with harsh words, not unlike the way Charles spoke to her. But Lena thought the verbal abuse was a small price to pay for the knowledge and experience she was gaining. Jade was a professional who expected competence from her assistants. Any aspiring photographer would sell their soul to have such an internship. And despite Jade's brusque attitude toward her, the quality of her images was improving every day.

Lena hid her lack of knowledge of photography well. During their morning shoots, she made mental notes of the terminology and techniques she would research in the afternoon when she was alone at Olivia's computer.

Her life soon fell into a routine. Awake well before dawn. On location for the day's shoot by the time the sun broke the horizon. Return to Jade's study midmorning for editing. Lena learned a lot from watching Jade bring her photographs to life in Lightroom. Her images were nearly perfect right out of camera, but she was hypercritical of her work. Even though she spent hours editing them, she never seemed totally satisfied with the result.

During her visits to the house, Lena made a point of spending at least a few minutes with Phyllis. She'd grown fond of the old woman and her stories. Lena didn't mind at all when, on her first Wednesday in Charleston, Jade asked if she would stay with Phyllis while she ran to the grocery store.

"I won't be gone long," Jade said. "An hour max."

"I don't have to be anywhere," Lena said. "Take as long as you need." She waited for Jade to leave before asking Phyllis if she'd like to sit in the garden.

"I would love that." Phyllis was out of her chair, onto her feet, in an instant. "I can't remember the last time I went outside."

Lena's frustration at Jade for keeping her mother cooped up in the house mounted. "The fresh air will do you good."

Even though Phyllis didn't need the support, Lena braced her elbow anyway as she made her way down the short flight of steps to the kitchen and out the back door. A wall of old Charleston bricks surrounded the garden, offering privacy from the neighbors and creating a charming backdrop for the boxwoods, flowering shrubs, and rosebushes.

Lena continued to hold on to her arm as Phyllis lowered herself to the antique wrought-iron bench. "Can I get you anything?" she asked.

"Not a thing. I'm perfectly content." Phyllis tilted her head back. "It's nice to feel the sun on my face."

Lena wondered just how long it had been since she'd ventured outdoors. The leaves had yet to change, and even though the weather was warmer than usual for that time of year, the air was clean and clear with a hint of autumn.

Phyllis inhaled a deep breath. "I can smell the roses. Tell me, dear, how do they look? My daughter is not much of a gardener."

Lena inspected the row of hot-pink tea roses along the wall. "They're gorgeous." She fingered one of the leaves. "And perfectly healthy."

"Come and sit a spell." Phyllis patted the bench beside her. "Tell me how you're liking Charleston."

"How do I like Charleston? It's hard for me to express my feelings for your wonderful city," Lena said as she sat down next to Phyllis. "Do you think it's possible to fall in love with a city? Because I've fallen head over heels for Charleston. I'm totally infatuated with the sights and smells and food."

Phyllis stroked Lena's arm. "I know exactly what you mean, dear. I've felt that way every single day of the forty-three years I've lived here. What restaurants have you discovered?"

Lena thought of the restaurants she'd tried so far and the three pounds she'd lost by selecting healthy options from their menus. She also credited the weight loss to all the walking she'd been doing and the ice cream she'd been denying herself.

"I haven't eaten a bad meal yet, but if I had to choose, I'd say 167 Raw has been my favorite so far. Their ceviche is the best I've ever had." She angled her body toward Phyllis. "It's totally out of character for me. At home, in Richmond, I would never have considered dining alone in a restaurant, let alone sitting at the bar or a community table. But I've struck up conversations with some of the nicest people. In my research on the Lowcountry, I discovered that Charleston has received accolades for being the friendliest city in America as well as the most polite and hospitable. And I believe it. Southern hospitality is alive and well in Charleston."

They spoke for a few minutes about the gracious people of South Carolina and the wonderful restaurants the city had to offer, which led to an even longer conversation about the virtues of old-fashioned home cooking.

"My most cherished recipes are the ones my grandmother gave me," Phyllis said. "You're welcome to look through my recipe box anytime. I keep it in the cabinet to the right of the stove."

"I would love to read some of your recipes." Lena's stomach rumbled. She hadn't eaten since seven o'clock the previous evening. She glanced at her watch. Twelve thirty. Jade had already been gone an hour. "All this talk about food is making me hungry. Why don't I fix us lunch? I noticed some pretty tomatoes on the kitchen counter. If you have any bacon, I could make us BLTs."

Phyllis curled her upper lip. "We have bacon, if you call that turkey stuff Jade buys bacon. My daughter is liable to be a while. When Jade says she'll only be gone for an hour, she usually means three or four."

Lena's skin prickled. "Does she leave you here by yourself when she's gone?"

"Sometimes. Although she usually runs her errands in the afternoons when I'm napping." Phyllis gripped the arm of the bench as she slowly rose to her feet. "I'm not an invalid, dear. If not for my impaired vision, I'd be totally fine on my own."

"I think you do exceptionally well," Lena said, managing to hover near the elderly woman until she was seated at the round pine table in the kitchen.

Lena removed a package of turkey bacon, a head of iceberg lettuce, and a jar of Duke's mayonnaise from the refrigerator. While she nuked the bacon and toasted the bread, Phyllis chatted on about the many ways her disability had affected her once-carefree lifestyle. "I miss reading the most. I tried learning braille, but I got frustrated."

"What about audiobooks?" Lena asked as she slathered mayonnaise on the toasted bread.

"I've thought about that, but I wouldn't begin to know how to listen to an audiobook."

Lena pressed her lips into a thin line. Why hadn't Jade taken the time to set her mother up with audiobooks?

Lena placed the sandwiches on plates, and after cutting up a pear, she added several slices to each plate and poured two tall glasses of sweet tea. "There are a number of different ways to listen to audiobooks." She transferred the plates and glasses to the table. "The easiest way I know of is on an Apple device like an iPhone or an iPad."

Phyllis broke into a smile that made her appear ten years younger. "I have an iPad. I haven't charged it in a while. Marie, my younger daughter who lives in Boston, gave it to me for Christmas several years ago before my eyesight started to fail."

"Why don't we get it out and charge it up?" Lena suggested. "I'll help you download the necessary apps. You can either purchase audiobooks from an online retailer or you can reserve them from your library."

An expression of amazement crossed Phyllis's face. "Is that possible?"

"As long as you have a library card. I assume you have one for your local library."

Her amazement morphed into excitement. "Yes! Of course. Will you get my iPad for me, please? It's in the drawer of the table beside my chair in the other room. The charger should be there as well."

Lena retrieved the old-model iPad and said a silent prayer that it would hold a charge as she plugged it into an outlet near the table. As soon as she was seated, she said, "It'll take a few minutes at least. Let's have our sandwiches and talk while we're waiting. I'd like to hear about the kind of books you like to read."

"Historical fiction and mysteries mostly, but I never turn down a good love story as long as it's clean."

"Those are popular genres. You should have plenty to choose from," Lena said, and listed several recent releases that she knew of from each category.

By the time they'd finished eating and Lena had straightened the kitchen, the iPad was charged enough to power on.

"My library card's in my wallet in my room upstairs. If you can find my purse in all that mess." Phyllis pointed at the ceiling. "Top of the stairs, first door on the right."

Lena had never been to the second floor of their house, and she was discouraged to find Phyllis's bed unmade, articles of clothing strewn about, and a basket of laundry—presumably clean but unfolded—on the floor at the foot of the four-poster bed. She picked up the basket and placed it on top of the bureau where Phyllis wouldn't trip over it.

Lena found Phyllis's purse dangling from the arm of a nearby rocking chair. She removed her wallet and left the room, taking a moment to snoop around the other rooms. There were three more bedrooms, all smaller than Phyllis's but equally as messy. A tiny bathroom with outdated tile and filthy rings around the tub and toilet was located off the center of the hall.

Shame on Jade for allowing her poor mother to live in such a pigsty.

She rejoined Phyllis at the table in the kitchen, and they spent an hour installing the OverDrive app, downloading two historical fiction novels, and adding titles to her waitlist.

"This is like Christmas." Phyllis's blue eyes were bright as she slipped the earbuds Lena had found in Jade's desk drawer into her ears.

Lena smiled. "Thanks to your library, it's Christmas all year long."

Phyllis listened to her audiobook for a few minutes before her eyelids began to droop. Tugging off the earbuds, she said, "I don't know how to thank you, Lena. This will make a big difference in my life. But all this excitement has exhausted me. It's time for my nap. Jade should be back by now."

Lena checked the clock on the stove. It was almost two, and Jade had been gone since eleven thirty. "Would you like to take your iPad up to your room for a rest? I can help you get settled."

"No need. I can manage on my own."

Lena would never forgive herself if something happened to Phyllis on her watch. "Let me at least carry your wallet and iPad for you."

"All right. I'm too tired to argue." Stuffing her hands in the pockets of her worn brown cardigan, Phyllis shuffled to the front of the house.

Insisting Phyllis go ahead of her up the stairs, Lena stayed close behind, ready to catch her should she fall. While Lena gathered the discarded clothes from the floor and hung them in the closet, Phyllis felt her way around her bedroom, searching for the seersucker bathrobe she eventually found hanging on a hook on the closet door.

Phyllis had taken off her cotton dress and was slipping into her bathrobe when Lena noticed four purple bruises the size of finger pads on her right upper arm.

"Where'd you get those bruises?" Lena asked, running her fingertips lightly over the bruises. "Did you hurt yourself?"

"I'm an old woman, Lena," she said, pulling the robe tighter around her. "Thin skin bruises easily."

Lena knew this to be true from her experience with her own parents. Certain medications, like blood thinners and ibuprofen, also caused bruising. For fear of upsetting the elderly woman, she decided it best not to press the issue. She helped Phyllis into bed with her iPad, placing the earbuds in her ears. As she tucked the blanket under her chin, Phyllis closed her eyes and a contented smile spread across her lips as she drifted off into the world of fiction.

Lena paced the worn Oriental rug in the parlor, speculating about the bruises on Phyllis's arm. Someone had obviously been manhandling her. As far as Lena knew, Jade was her mother's only caretaker. Maybe Jade had gripped Phyllis's arm too hard when helping her out of the tub. Or perhaps Phyllis had tripped over the edge of a rug and Jade had grabbed her by the arm to prevent her from falling. It wasn't out of the realm of possibility that Jade, God forbid, had been abusing her mother. She would mention the bruises to Jade, if for no other reason than to let her know someone was watching. And watch she would. Lena would stay close to the family until she was certain Phyllis was not in any danger.

Jade finally returned home an hour later with a square Styrofoam container—the kind restaurants use for leftovers—but no grocery bags. By then, Lena had lost her nerve to talk to Jade about her mother's bruises. Instead, she resorted to her usual passive-aggressive approach reserved for handling unpleasant situations. She spent the next several days stewing about it.

CHAPTER SIXTEEN

OLIVIA

Around noontime on Tuesday, when Alistair failed to return home, Olivia rode Lena's bike to the Jumpstart Café, hoping to learn something of his whereabouts. She found the atmosphere cozy as soon as she entered. A handful of small round tables occupied the center of the room, while a row of barstools stood at a counter in front of the single large window overlooking Irvington Road. An oversized chalkboard, listing the large assortment of drink and food offerings, hung high on the wall behind the service bar that boasted a display case of homemade treats.

"I don't think I've seen you in here before," one of two pretty young waitresses said to Olivia. "Are you new to the area?"

"I'm a writer. I'm here doing research on a novel I'm working on," said Olivia, surprised at how easily the words slipped from her tongue.

"Cool!" The waitress leaned across the counter, her yellow-green eyes wide and halo of blonde corkscrews bouncing about her head. "I love to read. Have you written anything I may have read?"

Olivia's face heated. "I haven't actually published anything yet," she confessed, and busied herself with removing her debit card from her wallet to pay for her pumpkin spice latte.

Olivia hadn't actually written anything yet, either, although the woman from her previous night's dream had occupied her thoughts all morning. She imagined Leesa in different scenarios, just as a real author might when contemplating potential plots for a new novel. And because the Jumpstart was the ideal place to people watch, to study the habits and mannerisms of the steady stream of customers who came and went, she became a fixture at the window counter over the course of the next couple of days.

She spent her mornings paddling around the creek in the kayak or on the paddleboard and her midday hours at the Jumpstart, not only people watching but taking advantage of the free Wi-Fi to read articles related to the craft of writing a novel. She sampled the items on the lunch menu that appealed to her—arugula and pear salad with grilled chicken breast, grilled cheese with three kinds of cheese on sourdough bread, and creamy tomato bisque. And she grew to know the friendly staff on a first-name basis—Jess and Jasmine, the two waitresses, and Sherry, their manager, an average-looking woman with mousy brown hair who popped in and out of the café but never seemed to stay for longer than a few minutes at a time. She heard the cook's name mentioned, Johnny, but she never saw him come out of the kitchen.

Olivia's ears perked up when she heard Sherry and Jasmine talking on Wednesday afternoon. "It's not like Alistair to leave town without letting me know," Sherry said. "He's not answering my calls or returning his texts."

"Hmm," Jasmine said. "I hope he's not sick, poor man with no wife to care for him."

Olivia wanted to tell them that she, too, was terribly worried about Alistair, but she thought better of it. They would think her a stalker if she suddenly admitted that she was Alistair's temporary neighbor and that she hadn't seen him since making a pass at him on Sunday night.

That afternoon, before paying her tab, she checked the balance on her checking account and discovered that it had once again grown low.

When she clicked on her savings account to transfer money, she was horrified to find that she only had enough money left from her divorce settlement to last until January. And that was only if she was careful. She'd known for some time that she would sooner or later have to find a way to earn a living. That *later* was now *sooner*. Time to get serious about writing her novel. She'd created her character; the challenge she now faced was to identify, develop, and work through Leesa's situation.

In high school and college, when she dreamed every night of becoming an author, she'd started half a dozen different novels, but she'd never finished any of them. She'd set her expectations too high by trying to mimic the style of her favorite authors, like Pat Conroy with his long, flowing sentences and descriptive phrases that read like poetry. In contrast, commercial romance novels seemed fairly straightforward, with simple plots about intriguing characters falling in love. Having a happy ending was a key element for romance novels. And Olivia was all about happy endings.

She spent some time studying the romance novels on the current bestseller lists and stalking the websites of the authors who wrote them. She researched freelance editors, cover designers, and best practices for self-publishing. Through her blog, *Hi-Low*, she'd built a respectable social media following from which to launch her first novel. *Now, Liv, all you have to do is write it.*

After leaving the coffee shop, she stopped by Alistair's to retrieve the apple crisp she'd left in the cooler at his front door. Chucking the crisp in the trash, she settled into the hammock with a stack of pillows and the romance novels of Lena's that she'd recently read. For the remainder of the afternoon, she skimmed through the books as she studied the author's writing techniques. She took a break for dinner—a mixed green salad and glass of red wine on the deck while watching the sunset— before continuing with her work until past midnight.

Olivia fell into a deep sleep but then woke up abruptly three hours later. She'd been dreaming about a woman in a kayak being chased by her husband on a paddleboard. No matter how hard the woman paddled, she couldn't make the kayak go forward. When she risked a glance behind her, the woman saw that her husband wasn't chasing her after all. He was paddling in the opposite direction toward his lover. Another man.

When her heart stopped pounding and she could once again think straight, she understood that the woman in the dream wasn't Olivia, rather a woman in her forties with silky black hair and golden eyes. *Leesa.*

Knowing that sleep would not be forthcoming, she brewed a cup of ginger tea in the kitchen and took it to the desk in the upstairs study. The words traveled from her brain to her fingertips at rapid speed as she wrote an opening scene certain to grab any reader's attention. Leesa, still reeling from discovering her husband was gay, met a dashing single man on a ferry en route to a small island in the Pacific Northwest.

Once she started writing, she couldn't stop. Writing Leesa's story offered Olivia a bird's-eye view into her own marriage. With crystal clarity, she was able to see how much Robert had sacrificed to have a wife and family. While the sex had never fulfilled either of them, their relationship was based on the mutual respect of a beautiful and rare friendship. She felt a sense of peace as she opened her heart to the possibility of forgiveness.

By the time the sky turned pink over the horizon of trees on the other side of the creek, she'd written two thousand words, the first chapter in a novel she'd already come to think of as *Marriage of Lies.*

Olivia took a break for breakfast and a brisk five-mile walk. The fresh air cleared her mind, enabling her to mentally plot subsequent chapters. When she got home, without bothering to shower, she returned to her desk and worked on her manuscript for the rest of the day and well into the evening.

"How's the novel coming?" Jasmine asked, greeting Olivia with a smile when she entered the café at noon on Friday.

Jasmine had asked her the same question every day that week, but today, Olivia was able to give an honest answer. "Great." Four chapters in twenty-four hours. She was well on her way. She'd come to the café for food only because there was nothing to eat in the cottage.

"Tell me about your book," Jasmine said in an eager tone.

Olivia beamed, feeling like a real author. "I'm not ready to talk about it just yet. Maybe soon."

She ordered a bowl of tomato bisque and set her computer up in her usual place by the window. She was slurping her first spoonful of soup when a conversation between Jasmine and Sherry caught her attention. They were standing behind the service counter near the cash register.

"I finally heard from Alistair," Sherry said. "Come to find out, his son was in a bad car accident in New York on Sunday night."

Olivia set her spoon down and, without being obvious, angled her body toward them to allow for more effective eavesdropping.

"Oh no!" Jasmine said, hand on mouth. "Josh or Mike?"

"I'm not sure," Sherry said. "The younger of the two."

"That would be Mike," Jasmine said. "Was he badly hurt?"

"Alistair thought so at first, which is why he left town so suddenly. But it was only a broken collarbone." Sherry sounded disappointed. "Although he had to have surgery, so it must have been pretty bad. Anyway, Alistair's coming home sometime this weekend. We'll find out more then."

So that's why he left in such a hurry.

Sometime this weekend could mean as early as tomorrow. Olivia's heart fluttered at the thought of seeing Alistair again. But what about her vow to stay away from men? She thought about Leesa, who'd allowed herself to be vulnerable to the possibility of loving again. If Leesa could do it, why couldn't she?

CHAPTER SEVENTEEN

LENA

Lena was sitting at the computer, reading through the *High Living in the Lowcountry* blog posts, when Olivia called. She'd stumbled upon the website during her internet search of things to do in Charleston. She thought the Kate Scapades column was well written and showcased Olivia's talent as a writer, but she was disgusted by the content—not only the young people's behavior and the language used in the comments, but most of all, the magnitude to which the Kates had taken advantage of Olivia.

"How do you like Charleston?" Olivia asked.

"I love it. I have to remind myself daily that this life is on loan from you. You're gonna have a hard time getting rid of me come November first. How are things in the Northern Neck?"

Olivia snickered. "Quiet. But just what the doctor ordered. I had no idea how much I needed a change of pace."

Lena said, "I assume you've met Alistair. How is he?"

"Alistair is the reason I'm calling, actually. Earlier in the week, he left town without telling me where he was going. Not that he's obligated to tell me his whereabouts. We barely know each other. But your houses are so close together, it's hard not to notice when someone's coming and going."

Panic gripped Lena's chest. "And you have no idea where he went?"

"I do now. I overheard the waitresses at the coffee shop talking. Apparently, his son Mike was in a car accident in New York. He broke his collarbone and needed surgery, but otherwise he's okay."

"Poor Mike. I've known those boys since birth. My daughter grew up with them. I'll give Alistair a call. Do you have any idea when he's coming home?"

"Sometime this weekend. I thought I'd make him a treat to welcome him home. Do you have a key to his house? I'd like to leave it on his kitchen counter."

A treat, huh? Was it possible that Olivia was sweet on Alistair? Lena smiled to herself at the thought of the handsome couple they would make. Olivia might be just the person to rescue him from his grief. "I'm sure he would appreciate that. His house key is in the junk drawer in the kitchen, second to the left of the sink. It's the one on the yellow key chain."

When the computer screen in front of her went dark, Lena hit the trackpad, bringing it back to life. "While I've got you on the phone . . . I was reading through some of your blog posts when you called. Aside from the Kates—what a pain they are—your website is attractive and informative. You have some great articles about shopping and dining that visitors to the area might find helpful."

"Maybe I'll take the blog page down and maintain what I already have on the website."

"Or you could refocus the blog," Lena suggested. "You're off to a good start with your feature on Chef Oscar. The response in the comments was positive."

"Really?" Olivia sounded surprised.

Lena summoned the nerve to present her idea. "Would you consider turning your blog over to me for the remainder of my stay? I'd like to start a journal. *An Outsider's Look at Charleston.* I was thinking I could post some of my photographs along with short write-ups from a tourist's perspective."

"Have at it," Olivia said. "The readers will love it. I'll send you the sign-on credentials."

They talked awhile longer, comparing experiences in Charleston and the Northern Neck, before hanging up.

Lena tapped on Alistair's number. When the call went straight to voice mail, she left him a concerned message about Mike, asking him to call her back when he got a free minute.

She accessed the Lightroom app and scrolled through her photographs, not the landscapes she'd taken on her shoots with Jade but the images she'd captured on her late-afternoon walks around town, during the golden hour when the sun was beginning its descent. Her favorites were candids of strangers—an older couple holding hands while strolling through the market, a bride and groom departing the sanctuary of Saint Michael's Church after their wedding ceremony. She couldn't post photos of real people without their permission, but she imagined most people would be flattered at the opportunity to appear on a popular website. She cropped out the faces of the bride and groom, leaving only their torsos showing, her white dress pressed against his black tuxedo, a lovely bouquet of lavender roses between them. She would accompany the images with an article about Charleston being a popular destination for weddings.

Excitement mounted as Lena mulled over ideas for posts. For trendy restaurants, in addition to featuring the cuisine, she would photograph the staff performing their various duties and the patrons enjoying a delicious meal and good time with friends over bottles of wine. She would spotlight some of the vendors at the market, including Bessie, whom she visited nearly every day. She would stop tourists on the streets, questioning them about their experiences in Charleston. In Richmond, she would never have conversed with strangers or called restaurants to request interviews. But she was finding that she could be herself in Charleston, away from her husband's constant scrutiny.

She got up from the desk, stretched, and walked to the kitchen to refill her water bottle. She'd discovered that drinking lots of water was vital to weight loss. Much to her delight, her clothes fit looser, and she felt more energized than she had in years. She walked out onto the terrace, breathing in the humid salty air she'd become acclimated to. Leaning against the railing, she watched a cruise ship make its way across the harbor toward Union Pier.

Lena, gripping her phone while waiting for Alistair to return her call, was surprised when it pinged with an incoming text from her daughter. She'd had no communication with Kayla since her first morning in Charleston.

Hi mom. How r things in Charleston? I miss you

Lena started and erased three sarcastic remarks, settling on: It's nice to be missed. How're things at home?

Horrible. Dad's so mean.

Of course he is! Her husband wasn't happy unless he had someone to bully. With Lena gone, Kayla would be in his direct line of fire. But Kayla was a grown woman now. She would have to learn to take up for herself. Try not to let him get to you.

Kayla: K. I had a job interview today. It didn't go well but at least I'm trying. Meg asked me to get an apartment with her.

A wave of relief swept over Lena at the mention of Meg, Kayla's best friend from high school and a positive influence on her daughter.

Lena: You need to get a job first.

Kayla: Duh. I'm not even sure I want to live in Richmond.

Not live in Richmond? Since when? Lena: That's an abrupt about-face. What happened?

Kayla: IDK. I'm not sure what I want to do with my life. Why did you let me major in business administration?

Lena laughed out loud. As if she'd had any say in any aspect of her daughter's life since she'd turned eighteen and gone off to college. Lena: You'll figure it out in due time. Maybe you should consider graduate school.

Kayla: No way! No more school for me. I wanna do something fun like work in a hotel.

Lena: Why don't you see if any of the better hotels are hiring?

Kayla: No one will hire me without a degree in hospitality. Good chatting with you.

Kayla ended her text with a heart emoji.

Lena's heart swelled with love for her only child. Perhaps Kayla's heart was growing fonder of Lena in her absence. As much as she wanted to have a healthy relationship with her daughter, she also wanted Kayla to find some direction, even if it meant getting a job as a clerk in a hotel. Kayla had interviewed for countless positions, everything from managing a cycling studio to working in a trendy women's boutique. She'd been offered several jobs but had turned them down for various reasons. Was it any wonder her daughter was floundering with Lena as her role model?

As she looked blankly at the screen, her phone rang with the anticipated call from Alistair.

"How's Mike?" she said by way of greeting. "I was sorry to hear about his accident."

Alistair chuckled. "He's one resilient kid. He went back to work today." He paused. "I thought you were in Charleston. How'd you hear about his accident?"

"Olivia heard about it at the café and called me. She knew I'd want to know. When're you going home?"

"I'm hoping to leave early tomorrow morning to beat the traffic. How are you, Lena? Are you finding yourself down there in South Carolina?"

Lena was relieved to hear the upbeat quality that had been absent in his voice since Mary Anne's death. "As a matter of fact, I am. I should've run away from home years ago. What about you, Alistair? You sound more like yourself than you have in years."

"I'm sorry it took Mike's accident for me to come to New York, but this trip has helped me put things in perspective. I've been barely functioning, moving through the motions of life. I'm finally ready to get back to the business of living."

"I'm thrilled to hear you say it. That's what Mary Anne would've wanted."

Lena settled into a nearby chair with her feet on the matching ottoman. She couldn't remember the last time they'd had a heart-to-heart talk. The years fell away, and they were on her balcony in the Northern Neck, confiding in each other their deepest feelings as well as their hopes and dreams for the future.

Alistair had a special way of making her believe in herself, and when they finally hung up thirty minutes later, she felt prepared to conquer the world. She grabbed her camera and went out for her afternoon walk. Her spirits were high. Her life had a new purpose. She had a job of sorts. Olivia's blog already had a large audience. She just needed to engage with them by consistently providing fresh content. With no expectations of where it might lead, she viewed the opportunity as a stepping stone to a midlife career. *Think about it, Lena. A midlife career.* She found the mere idea of such a thing hard to believe. Only a week ago, she'd run away from her reclusive life with a man she'd grown to despise. Now she was going after life with gusto—reinventing herself. She was Lena Graham, reborn.

She would officially change her name back to Graham, her maiden name, after she divorced Charles. Lena stopped dead in her tracks.

Divorce? She'd never thought ending her marriage was possible. She was tethered to Charles like a horse to a hitching post. She had no clue how to go about living on her own. As she stood in the middle of the sidewalk, while pedestrians walked around her, Lena thought about the potential ripple effects of divorce. Richmond was her home. She'd never lived anywhere else. And what about Kayla? How could she possibly leave her daughter now, if they were, in fact, forging a new relationship? Who would maintain her cottage in the Northern Neck? And how would she pay her bills without Charles's financial support? Then again, he would give her a divorce settlement, which would enable her to start fresh and be free of him.

She continued onward, staring down at the sidewalk in front of her, as the reality that she was stuck in her loveless marriage hit home.

CHAPTER EIGHTEEN

ALISTAIR

Alistair left New York before daybreak on Saturday morning. He was as sad to leave his boys as he was impatient to return home to his solitude. He'd enjoyed being in the hustle and bustle of the city again, although at the same time he'd missed the tranquility of the Northern Neck's rural setting.

He'd taken Mike and Josh out for a farewell dinner at Gramercy Tavern on Friday night, where he told them about Henry's offer.

"That'd be cool," Josh had said. "I'd love to have you around."

"Me too, Dad," Mike had added. "I really miss you."

After a long discussion, they agreed the boys would come to the Northern Neck for two days at Thanksgiving and Alistair would spend Christmas and New Year's in New York. He planned to book a suite at The Ritz-Carlton on Central Park. He didn't mind the expense, and having Christmas in Manhattan with his boys seemed as good a time as any to splurge.

During the long drive home to Virginia, Alistair contemplated his time with Henry. Their lunch at Felidia had lasted well into the afternoon. They'd ordered the strip steak, even though both men were more health conscious than they'd been in younger days.

"You can write your own ticket," Henry had said when the subject of Alistair returning to work at his investment banking firm came up. "We're willing to do whatever it takes to get you back."

"But I've been retired now for five years," Alistair had argued. "You're better off hiring someone younger, right out of an MBA program."

Henry had shaken his head. "A younger person lacks your experience. You're one of the most brilliant negotiators I've ever known, Alistair Hoffman. You have much to give, not only to our clients but to the young associates at the firm."

In parting, when Henry told him to take all the time he needed to think about it, Alistair had promised him an answer by the end of the year.

He'd debated whether to tell Lena about Henry's offer. They rarely kept secrets from each other, and he valued her opinion, but in the end, he'd decided not to mention it. A part of him felt foolish for even considering the offer, while another part of him wanted to move back to New York so bad he could taste it.

When he arrived home around two o'clock, he stood inside the front door with his duffel bag at his feet. The solitude he'd been so eager to return to felt more like desolation. Having stopped only once on the other side of DC for gas and a package of peanuts, he left his bag in the entry hall and went to the kitchen. He was pleasantly surprised to see on the counter one of Lena's baking dishes with an envelope taped to the foil. He tore open the envelope and read the note from Olivia, apologizing for her forward behavior and expressing her concern for his son.

He removed a fork from the silverware drawer and peeled back the foil. Even cold, the crisp was delicious with all the flavors of autumn—apples and cinnamon and cloves. Suddenly ravenous, he was shoveling in heaping forkfuls when, through the window, he caught sight of Olivia reading in Lena's hammock. He took one last bite and secured the foil on the dish, placing it in the refrigerator.

Exiting through the sliding glass doors, he cut across his grass—which he noticed was in desperate need of mowing—to Lena's yard.

"Alistair!" she said, struggling to sit up. "I didn't hear you. When did you get back?"

"A few minutes ago." A smirk tugged at his lips. "Looks to me like boredom suits you."

"Ha. I've been spending way too much of my time in this hammock." She swung her legs over the side of the hammock and stood to face him. "How's Mike?"

"On the mend. Thanks for asking. And thank you for the apple treat. I was in such a rush to get home, I didn't take time to stop for lunch."

She lowered her gaze. "It was nothing, really."

An awkwardness from *the kiss* hung in the air between them. Alistair considered mentioning her apology letter, but he didn't want to embarrass her. He gestured toward his yard. "I need to mow the grass, obviously, but I'm hoping to get out on the water later. I'd love it if you'd join me. We can take a sunset cruise around the creek, then go to the Tides for dinner on the terrace." He held his breath as he waited for her response and realized how much he wanted her to say yes.

She smiled. "I'd like that very much."

"Great! Shall we meet down on the dock at five thirty? Or is that too early?"

She shook her head. "Not too early at all."

Taking this alluring woman on a date made him feel like skipping back across the yard to his house. He had no idea whether anything would come of it. He only knew he enjoyed her company. And for him, that was a start.

~

After spending the afternoon doing laundry and yard work, he was waiting with the engine idling when she sauntered down to the dock at precisely five thirty.

"I wasn't sure what to wear. Is this okay?" she asked of her black silk top and denim jeans.

"You look wonderful." His khaki slacks and blue-and-white-striped polo paired nicely with her outfit. When he gave her a peck on the cheek, he caught a whiff of her perfume that smelled both sweet and seductive.

"Thank you." She took off her wedges, stuffed them in her bag, and stepped barefoot onto the boat.

He helped her stow her bag in the front compartment, then handed her a Yeti tumbler. "I took the liberty of making us a roadie. I hope you like Mount Gay rum and tonic."

"Mount Gay rum is one of my favorites," she said, taking the tumbler from him.

He pushed the throttles forward, putting the dual motors in gear, and they glided away from the dock. Sunset was still an hour away, but the sky had already begun to turn yellow. He gulped in a deep breath of salt air, exhaling slowly as the tension of the past week exited his body.

"Tell me what you've been up to in my absence," he said.

"Well, let's see." She furrowed her brow. "I made my way through your menu offerings at the Jumpstart Café. I felt compelled to try every last item in exchange for all the free Wi-Fi I sucked up. Jess and Jasmine are now my besties, although I haven't told them that I know you."

"Have you made any headway on finding new direction for your writing career?"

Her expression became guarded. "I'm working on something. But I'm not ready to talk about it just yet."

"Fair enough." Whatever she was working on was obviously important to her. She would tell him if and when she was ready. As he navigated in and out of the coves of Carters Creek, they talked about wines they liked and hobbies they enjoyed. They shared similar interests in politics, and because of the time she'd spent in Richmond in college, they discovered they had many mutual acquaintances.

They waited until the sun dipped below the horizon before tying up at the dock in front of the Tides Inn. The lobby and restaurant were crowded, as expected on a Saturday night of a holiday weekend. The hostess took his name and told them to check back in fifteen minutes.

"I forgot about Monday being Columbus Day," Alistair said. "This probably wasn't the best night for us to come here. My friend Roy is the bartender in the Chesapeake Restaurant. He's off tonight—his cousin is getting married—otherwise he could help us out with a table."

"It's a spectacular night. I don't mind waiting."

"Let's walk around," Alistair suggested.

They wandered to the edge of the property and sat down on a metal bench overlooking the water. Lights gleamed from the boats at the dock, and the air hinted of autumn without being chilly. Was he actually considering trading this peaceful setting for the chaos of the city?

When they checked back with the hostess, they were shown to their table. Alistair ordered a bottle of pinot noir from SIMI winery and several items from the light fare menu, including a dozen oysters on the half shell, bourbon-glazed fish bites, and a platter of assorted cheeses.

The prospect of moving to New York continued to weigh heavily on his mind during dinner, and as they were finishing the last of the wine, he told Olivia about Henry's job offer. Much to his relief, she didn't think him crazy for considering it.

"It sounds like you had a challenging career you enjoyed," she said. "I don't blame you for wanting it back. I can't imagine how hard it was to give it all up when your wife got sick."

"I never thought twice about it, honestly. And it turned out to be the right decision. My wife loved the outdoors. We had some wonderful days together."

She leaned closer to him, her gaze meeting his. "May I ask you a personal question?"

"Of course," he said, bracing himself.

"When you made the decision to leave your job, did you ever consider what you would do after . . ." She stopped herself.

He shook his head. "I truly believed she'd beat the cancer. I'd made enough money to last our lifetimes. The plan was for us to live out our days in this tranquil place we both loved so much."

Olivia placed a hand on his. "You made a great sacrifice for your wife for all the right reasons. I don't know many men who would've done such a thing. Your wife was a lucky woman to have you by her side. But she's gone now. You need to live life for yourself. Resume your career in New York if that's what you want."

The sensation of Olivia's hand on his made him uncomfortable for all the right reasons, and he gave hers a little squeeze before pulling his away. "That's the problem. I'm not sure that's truly what I want. New York and the Northern Neck are very different places, and I love them equally as much."

As Olivia sipped her wine, he observed her luscious lips and replayed the kiss from Sunday night in his mind. While he wasn't sure he was ready for a full-blown relationship, he thought maybe a sexual fling was exactly what he needed.

"Why can't you have the best of both worlds?" Olivia asked. "If you reclaim your life in New York, wouldn't you spend long weekends down here, maybe a week in the summer? Isn't that what you did before Mary Anne got sick?"

"Actually, no. My parents owned the house back then. I didn't inherit it until my father died of a sudden heart attack three months before Mary Anne was diagnosed with cancer. There is way too much involved in maintaining the property for it to be a second home."

A breeze rustled her hair. "I can see that."

"Besides, this is my home now."

She smiled. "Home is where the heart is."

But his heart still belonged to Mary Anne, and she was no longer here.

CHAPTER NINETEEN
OLIVIA

Olivia sat close to Alistair on the way home from the Tides Inn. The spark of chemistry between them had ignited during dinner. She could no longer ignore—no longer wanted to ignore—the connection they shared. Her body ached for him, and it was all she could do not to run her hands through his dark hair where it curled at the nape of his neck. While she'd been attracted to Robert, she'd never experienced such unabashed lust for him. The romance novels she'd been reading had fueled her fire, and she was prepared to throw caution to the wind if it meant satisfying her deep sexual yearning.

After securing the boat, Alistair and Olivia walked up the dock together. His arm brushed against hers, sending a bolt of electricity through her body.

"Thank you for a lovely evening," she said when they neared his house.

He turned to her, the moonlight casting a warm glow on his brown eyes. "It's still early. Would you like to come in for a nightcap?"

"That's probably not a good idea. I can't promise I won't try to kiss you again," she said with a nervous laugh.

"Then let me be the first to kiss you." He took her face in his hands and brought her lips to his, kissing them lightly at first and then with increasing urgency as their lips parted and tongues met.

She drew away from him. "Are you sure this is what you want?" she asked, her voice deep with lust.

He ran his thumb across her lips. "I'm sure about my attraction to you, which is as sure as I can be about anything right now."

Right answer. She was leaving at the end of the month. She wasn't looking for a permanent relationship. She was looking to satisfy the sensual side of her she'd kept locked up for far too long.

Not wanting to appear overeager, she said in a reluctant tone, "All right. But I don't need any more alcohol."

"How about a cup of tea?"

She nodded. "Tea would be nice."

He placed a hand at the small of her back as they continued on to the patio. "Make yourself at home." With a flick of his grill lighter, he set the firepit ablaze. "I'll only be a minute." He disappeared through the sliding doors into the kitchen.

While he was gone, Olivia rested her head against the back of the chair and closed her eyes. Ten minutes later, he emerged from the kitchen carrying a small tray with two cups of tea and a bottle of Blanton's bourbon. He set the tray down on a nearby table and handed her a mug of tea. Popping the cork off the bourbon, he held the bottle out and said, "Fancy a splash?"

"None for me," she said, placing her hand over her cup. "I can't believe you drink bourbon in your tea."

"This isn't just any bourbon. I consider the vanilla and caramel flavors in the bourbon my sweeteners."

She laughed. "Your substitute for honey."

"Or liquid courage, depending on how you look at it."

Olivia smiled, relieved to know she wasn't the only one who was nervous.

He dragged one of the other chairs close to her and sat down. "I wanna be honest with you, Olivia. I'm attracted to you. What man wouldn't be? You're beautiful and smart and fun to be with. But I'm afraid of disappointing you. I married my high school sweetheart. I've only been with one woman in my life."

This admission took her totally by surprise. Whatever she'd been expecting from him, that surely wasn't it. *What a dear man,* she thought.

She set her teacup down on the tray and shifted her body toward him. "I hardly see that as a negative, Alistair. But if it makes you feel any better, we're not so different in that regard."

A quizzical expression crossed his face. "How so?"

"I told you I divorced my husband, but I never told you why our marriage ended. When our friends in Charleston ask, even though I suspect they already know the truth, I tell them my marriage to Robert simply ran its course." She breathed deeply before continuing. "After twenty-eight years of marriage, my husband experienced an epiphany. He discovered he was gay."

Instead of the repulsion she'd expected, Alistair's face filled with compassion. "That must've been difficult for you."

She shrugged. "In some ways, it was a huge relief. For years, I'd blamed myself for the problems in our sex life. But it wasn't me who turned him off. It was women in general."

He brushed a strand of hair off her forehead. "For your sake, I'm glad your husband finally came out of the closet. You deserve better."

She placed her hand on his cheek. "Thank you for saying that, Alistair. I needed to hear it. I've been afraid to hope for better. Being alone is safe. And I'm happy being alone. I'm not looking for anything long term. But companionship with someone who treats me like I deserve to be treated would be nice."

He appeared disappointed at first, and she thought she'd blown it, but then he said, "Let's just see where it takes us."

"I'm not unlike you in one regard. Aside from a few dalliances in high school and college, and my marriage to a homosexual man, my experience with men has been very limited. That's why when I kissed you the other night . . . well, it surprised me as much as it surprised you."

He chuckled. "While your kiss caught me off guard, it provided the jolt I needed to rejoin the real world. And I thank you for that."

Alistair stood up and pulled her to her feet. Taking her by the hand, he led her through the family room and down a short hallway to the master bedroom. The room was decorated in white and shades of gray with a tufted headboard adorning the king-size bed. A large armoire occupied one wall, and an upholstered bench the space at the foot of the bed.

They faced each other, and she lifted her arms while he tugged her black silk top over her head. They fumbled with buttons as they peeled off clothes. Naked, they fell onto the bed together and made love with frenzied desire. They climaxed at the same time and lay panting in each other's arms.

"That was incredible," Alistair said. "I don't think either of us has anything to be ashamed about in the lovemaking department."

She rested her head on his chest. "I have to admit I'm relieved."

A naughty smile appeared on his lips. "I think we should try it again, just to make certain it was as good as we thought."

She laughed, thinking there was no way it could be as good. But the second time was better and the third even better than that. Alistair was a tender lover who knew exactly which buttons to push, and her orgasms nearly blew her mind.

"I'm pretty sure I just saw fireworks," she whispered to him before falling asleep in his arms.

~

When Olivia woke the following morning, daylight was already streaming through the window. Carefully, so as not to disturb a sleeping Alistair, she lifted back the covers and rolled out of bed. She gathered up her clothes and was headed to the adjoining bathroom when his voice filled the silent room. "Hey! Where're you going?"

She stopped in her tracks but didn't turn around. "To make the walk of shame back across the yard to Lena's cottage."

"But why are you leaving?"

She heard the sheets rustle, and when she turned around, covering her nakedness with her clothes, he was sitting up in bed. "I'm unaware of the proper protocol in these types of situations. I assumed you wouldn't want to see me this morning."

"Not only do I want to see you this morning, I want to spend the whole day with you. And I have it all planned out." He ran his hand across the mattress beside him. "Come back to bed. It's Sunday morning. We'll sleep awhile longer, and then after I make you the best omelet you've ever eaten for breakfast, we'll have a paddleboard race across the creek, which I will win, and then we'll go fishing for our dinner."

Olivia scrunched up her face. "Ugh. Fishing again?"

His head bobbed up and down like a child's. "You know it. The rockfish are biting. We'll catch a mess of 'em, and I'll cook 'em up for our dinner."

"That's an offer I can't turn down." She dropped her clothes on the floor and climbed back into bed. "But just so you know, you don't stand a chance against me on the paddleboard."

"Ha. We'll see about that," he said, wrapping his arm around her and drawing her close.

Olivia snuggled up against him. Alistair had returned from New York a happier person—energized and willing to take chances. Maybe the job offer had renewed his confidence in himself. Maybe the hustle and bustle of the city served as a reminder that life was going on without him. Or maybe getting away from the house where he'd nursed his dying wife had enabled him to finally put that part of his life behind him. Whatever it was, Olivia approved.

~

They spent the day as he'd suggested. He cooked her the best omelet she'd ever eaten. He beat her in the paddleboard race across the creek, although she came in a very close second. And they caught a mess of rockfish for dinner. Actually, he caught all the fish. She sat on the bow of the boat, sunning and reading.

When they returned to the dock midafternoon, he went to the grocery store in Kilmarnock while Olivia, determined to accomplish the daily word goal she'd set for herself, retreated to her study to work on her manuscript. She wasn't sure why, she just knew she wasn't ready to tell Alistair about her project. Was she afraid he would laugh at her as he'd done when she'd told him about the Kate Scapades? Or was she worried he would think less of her for writing something frivolous like a romance novel as opposed to a literary work of fiction? They'd never discussed their preferences for literature. She'd never seen him reading a novel, and the few books on the shelves in their family room offered little insight. Maybe he wasn't the literary snob she'd once been. Regardless, she couldn't risk getting shot down this early in the process.

At five thirty, Olivia showered and dressed in long khaki shorts and a white cotton blouse with a sweater tied around her neck. She dried her hair and put on makeup, checking her reflection in the mirror one last time before turning off the bathroom light. Grabbing the bottle of sauvignon blanc chilling in the refrigerator, she walked next door and found Alistair in the kitchen preparing the fish for the oven.

She yearned to press her lips against the back of his tanned neck but asked if he'd like a glass of wine instead.

"I've got a beer." He gestured at the Heineken on the counter and reached for the bottle of wine. "Here, let me open that for you."

"I can do it," she said, making a big show of unscrewing the wine cap.

"I like a woman with muscles," he said, pinching her bicep.

She filled a glass with wine and set about making a cheese grits casserole. Once the casserole was in the oven, she tossed arugula with slices of ripened pear, goat cheese, and sugared pecan pieces. They worked alongside each other in the kitchen as though they'd done it for years, with jazz music playing softly in the background and cool air flowing through the open sliding glass doors. All seemed right in her world for a change. She would focus on the here and now and not think about the future.

When they'd finished eating and the dishes were done, they sat close together by the firepit in companionable silence, sipping snifters of brandy.

He reached for her hand, bringing it to his lips. "Would you like to have a sleepover?"

"A sleepover?" She giggled. "How old are you, ten?"

He laughed. "After last night, I feel like a kid again. I'm serious. I want you to spend the night with me. Go to Lena's and get your pajamas or gown or whatever you sleep in, and slippers, and some clothes for in the morning."

"Aren't you worried what the neighbors might think?"

"What neighbors? The closest ones live too far away to see what goes on at my house." He tilted her chin toward him. "We don't know what the future holds for either of us outside of the next three weeks. Why not spend every moment we can together? Unless you have someplace you'd rather be."

Leaning into him, she bit his lower lip. "There's no place I'd rather be than here with you."

And she meant it. As much as she loved Charleston, she was beginning to feel a strong attraction to the Northern Neck—one that had more to do with Alistair Hoffman than the scenery.

CHAPTER TWENTY

LENA

Lena wanted to present an image of a fashionable middle-aged woman when she introduced herself to the followers of the *High Living in the Lowcountry* website. She purchased several new outfits from the plethora of women's boutiques on King Street and booked an appointment at an upscale hair salon that offered professional headshots as part of their services.

"I feel like a washed-out hag," she told Angie, the stylist, a striking woman in her midthirties with spiked hair and a nose ring. "I want you to color it blonde. I'm thinking a warm shade like honey."

Angie gasped. "Are you kidding me? Most women your age would kill to have your hair."

"But I'm tired of being gray-headed," Lena argued. "I'm fifty-four. I want to look my age."

"Your hair is not gray, honey. Your hair is silver. Believe me, there's a difference." She ran her fingers through Lena's locks. "It's thick and healthy. If you want a change, I suggest taking off some of the length and adding layers to frame your face."

Lena acquiesced, but she was pleased with the result and accepted Angie's offer to do her makeup. When Angie took her photograph with their professional camera in front of their white screen, Lena appeared ten years younger.

She used the photograph in her introductory post, which she published on Monday of her second week in Charleston. In the short write-up, Lena introduced herself as Olivia's longtime friend and explained that she would be contributing regularly to the blog during her month-long stay in the area. She spoke of escaping her life in Virginia for a much-needed break and praised the hospitable citizens of Charleston for offering her a warm welcome when she needed it the most. She included one of her favorite images—a silhouette of a man and woman drinking martinis at the rooftop bar of the Market Pavilion Hotel with the pink skyline of the city at sunset in the background.

The post received a sizable number of hits and comments from readers encouraging Lena to share more of her wonderful photographs. On Tuesday, she published an article featuring some of the most popular varieties of oysters grown in the state's marshes and creeks. The accompanying photographs made mouths water. The post received nearly a thousand hits with hundreds of comments from readers complimenting her informative article.

Thrilled with the response, Lena was ready to devote all her time to taking photographs and researching topics for the blog. If only she could find a way to graciously back out of her internship with Jade. Their relationship had continued to deteriorate as Jade had grown increasingly more demanding and critical. Lena's opportunity came on Wednesday morning, when she accidentally broke one of Jade's polarizing filters during a shoot at Magnolia Gardens.

"You're an idiot!" Jade screamed. "I don't know why I even bother with you. You lack any talent whatsoever for photography."

Lena desperately wanted to tell Jade to shove her camera up her rear end, but the words got stuck in her throat. She blinked back tears during their long drive home from Magnolia Gardens and scurried off as soon as Jade had parked in the driveway and turned off the engine.

She walked straight to Poogan's Porch and asked for a table on the second-floor porch. When the waitress arrived, she ordered the mac and cheese and a glass of chardonnay. She needed comfort food to calm her nerves and booze to give her the courage to terminate her relationship with Jade.

She'd devoured the mac and cheese and was on her second glass of wine when her phone rang with a call from Jade. She sucked in a deep breath, steeling herself for the lashing to come when she told Jade she would no longer be her assistant. But Jade didn't give her a chance to speak before blurting, "I have an emergency, and I need your help. I've received an offer on my business. I have to fly to Nashville right away to meet with the potential buyer. Can I count on you to stay with Mom?"

"But what about the storm?" asked Lena, thinking of Hurricane Michael preparing to make landfall in the Florida Panhandle. Forecasters were predicting Charleston could experience high winds and heavy rainfall as the remnants of the storm cut through the southern states before heading out to sea.

"That's why I need to leave immediately, to get out ahead of the storm."

"But the storm's headed toward us. Aren't you worried about leaving your mother in a hurricane?"

"By the time it reaches South Carolina, it'll be downgraded to a tropical storm. You and Mom will be fine without me. I'm booked on a flight through Charlotte departing in two hours. I need to leave for the airport soon. Mom is taking her nap. The sheets on the guest bed are clean. Get here as soon as you can."

Lena pulled the phone away from her ear, staring at it in disbelief. Jade wasn't asking Lena; she was ordering her to stay with her mother. If she wasn't so fond of Phyllis, she would've told her to go straight to hell. But she *was* fond of Phyllis. And she'd been paying close attention to the elderly woman's physical condition since discovering the bruises a week ago. Phyllis's hair was often greasy and her clothes soiled. While

Lena had seen no further signs of physical abuse, she wouldn't put it past Jade to leave her mother home alone.

"How long will you be gone?" Lena asked as her mind raced. She would miss her afternoon photo expedition, but she'd taken more than three hundred images the past few days that needed editing. And she could use the downtime to write more content for the blog.

"I'll be back tomorrow afternoon at the latest," Jade said in an impatient tone.

"Are you okay with me using your computer? I have a lot of editing to do."

"I prefer that you don't. You should have your own laptop." Jade ended the call before Lena could argue.

She gaped at the phone in her hand. *Did I just imagine that call, or is this woman for real?* From over the balcony railing, she noticed thick, dark clouds building in the west. The situation smelled like week-old fish to Lena. Jade was leaving her mother in the path of a hurricane, to fly into a hurricane, to meet with a potential buyer for her business. With today's modern technology, why not Skype?

Lena signaled the waitress for the check. She handed her the credit card, guzzling the remainder of her wine as she waited for the receipt. She racewalked down Queen Street to Olivia's condo, where she packed a canvas tote with items she needed for her overnight stay and then grabbed her camera bag before leaving the building and walking toward Church Street. As she replayed the phone conversation in her mind, she realized Jade had been right about one thing—Lena totally needed her own laptop. She would purchase one with her credit card. She'd been charging a lot to Charles recently—her trip to the salon, her new wardrobe, and several meals in the more expensive restaurants. She felt he owed it to her—past wages for years of servitude.

Phyllis was coming down the stairs, calling out for Jade, when Lena let herself in the back door. She rushed to her side. "Phyllis, it's me,

Lena. Jade had to go out of town suddenly on business. She'll only be gone one night. I hope you don't mind if I stay with you."

"Mind? I'm thrilled." Phyllis reached her hands out and cupped Lena's cheeks. "You're a breath of fresh air around here."

Lena smiled at the compliment. "How do you feel about running an errand with me?"

"Are you kidding me? I don't know how long it's been since I last left this house. Where're we going?"

"I need to make a trip to the Apple computer store on King Street. I didn't think to drive my friend's car. We'll have to ride in an Uber. Is that okay with you?"

"It's better than okay. It's an adventure. I've never been in an Uber, but I've heard plenty about them on the news." As Phyllis felt her way to the front door, Lena trailed closely behind, accessing the Uber app on her phone and requesting a ride.

"Do they sell ear-ma-bobs at the computer store?" Phyllis asked.

"I'm sure they do. What happened to the ones I gave you?"

"Jade took them back. She was mad as a hornet that we went snooping in her desk."

Lena was glad Phyllis couldn't see the disgusted look on her face. What kind of woman deprived her visually impaired mother of the chance to listen to audiobooks?

Phyllis waved her arm in the direction of the stairs. "Will you be a dear and fetch my handbag from my room?"

"Sure thing." Lena pocketed the phone and dashed up the stairs.

"And grab my iPad while you're up there," Phyllis called after her. "It's on the nightstand. I'm hoping the people at the store can fix it. I can't seem to get it to work properly."

Even though the iPad was an older version, Lena suspected whatever trouble Phyllis was having was due to user error. "We'll have the computer geniuses take a look at it."

Lena found Phyllis's room once again in a complete state of disarray—even worse than the last time she'd visited. She would give it a thorough cleaning while Jade was gone. Grabbing the handbag and iPad, she hurried back down the stairs, opening the front door as the Uber was arriving.

"Hold on to my arm, Phyllis. I don't want anything happening to you on my watch."

"I'm ninety years old, Lena," Phyllis said, shuffling alongside her on the sidewalk. "I want to enjoy what time I have left instead of wasting my days sitting in front of that blasted television. Worst-case scenario, I break my hip and die during replacement surgery. At least then I'll get to see my beloved husband and all my friends."

She gave Phyllis's hand a squeeze. "My friend, how I admire your positive attitude."

When they reached the low-slung sedan, she opened the door, holding Phyllis firmly by the arm as she climbed into the back seat. She ran around to the other side and slid in next to Phyllis.

The driver, a man named Elijah with a shaved head and dark beard, asked, "Which store are you going to on King Street?"

"The Apple computer store," Phyllis said.

Elijah chuckled. "The Apple computer store it is."

As he sped north toward the shopping district on King Street, Phyllis chatted with Elijah about the problems she was having with her iPad while Lena scrutinized the dark clouds as they billowed over the tops of buildings, praying she got Phyllis home safely before the rain set in.

When Elijah pulled up to the curb in front of the Apple Store, Lena thanked him and hurried around to the passenger side, gripping Phyllis's arm as she hauled her out of the back seat.

"Is this it? Is this the Apple Store?" Phyllis asked, her body shivering with excitement. "I've always wanted to come here."

Techno Granny, Lena thought, smiling to herself.

The store was empty aside from a handful of customers. "We got lucky," Lena said. "I've walked by this store many times. It's almost always crowded no matter what time of day. I guess the rest of the city is making preparations for the storm."

"Humph. I've seen a lot of hurricanes come and go in my lifetime. But I've been listening to the weather station. This storm won't amount to a hill of beans by the time it gets to Charleston."

"I hope you're right." While Phyllis and Jade seemed convinced the storm would amount to nothing, Lena couldn't ignore the forecast—a potential for forty-mile-an-hour winds, heavy rainfall, and the possibility of tornados. Although she'd loaded up on groceries that morning, she hadn't thought to bring any food with her to the Dowdys' house. Surely Jade had made a trip to the Harris Teeter before departing for Tennessee.

A young man wearing the official cobalt-blue employee shirt approached them, introducing himself as Christopher. "How can I help you, ladies? Are you shopping for anything specific today?"

"I'd like a thirteen-inch MacBook Pro with Touch Bar, Touch ID, and Retina display," Lena said.

Christopher's baby face registered surprise, as though he'd been expecting a difficult sale to an electronically challenged woman. "That was easy. Are you sure you don't want to explore other options? We're anticipating an announcement of a new release for the MacBook Air any day now."

"I've done my research, and the MacBook Pro I described is the one I want." She smiled back at him. "But thanks anyway."

Christopher spoke into his headset, summoning one of his coworkers to fetch the computer. "Your MacBook will be out in a minute. Can I help you with anything else while we wait?"

"Not for me," Lena said. "But my friend is interested in some earphones."

Christopher turned his attention to Phyllis. "What sort of earphones are you looking for?" He regarded her with a quizzical expression as he realized that something was not right with her sight.

Phyllis cupped her hands over her ears. "I want headphones, the kind that fit over my ears and block out everything else around me." She removed her iPad from her handbag. "And something's wrong with this thing. It keeps stopping in the middle of my audiobooks."

He took the iPad from her. "Wow! How old is this iPad? Did you purchase it back in the dinosaur age?" He flashed a wide smile, revealing two adorable dimples.

Phyllis brought a hand to her hip. In contrast to the stern look on her face, she said in a teasing tone, "Don't get fresh with me, young man. I may be old, but I'm not *that* old."

He laughed. "Yes, ma'am." He fiddled with the iPad for a minute. "I see you have a lot of contacts. Do you have an iPhone?"

"Yes, but I couldn't put my hands on it if I had to. I don't have any use for it anymore. My daughter, the one who lives up in Boston, is the only person who calls me. And she always calls me on my house phone."

He handed her back the iPad. "You can talk to one of our Geniuses, but honestly, I don't think you'll get the performance you're looking for out of this iPad. If you're interested, I can show you the iPad mini 4, which is smaller and lighter with more up-to-date technology."

Phyllis pounded the table beside her. "Hook me up, as you young people say."

"Done. Now let's go check out the headphones." Christopher took hold of Phyllis's elbow and guided her across the showroom to a table display of Beats headphones. She tried on several before deciding on a pair of red ones.

As Lena watched the exchange, she found herself feeling sorry for Jade for missing out on this fun side of her mother.

"Are you sure you can afford both the headphones and the iPad?" Lena whispered to Phyllis while they waited for Christopher to transfer Phyllis's contacts to her new iPad.

"I have plenty of money, my dear. And I certainly won't be taking it with me where I'm going."

Lena laughed. "No, I guess you won't." She admired the old woman's outlook on life and wished she could be more like her.

Christopher processed their credit card charges and handed each of them a white plastic bag with the Apple logo. "You may not be aware of this, but there are a lot of apps for the visually impaired," he said to Phyllis. "You can even have a live video call with a trained person who can help you find something you may have lost or match the colors of your clothes, those kinds of things."

"Really?" Phyllis and Lena said in unison.

"What's it called?" Phyllis asked.

"I'm not exactly sure," he said. "But I'm sure you can google it."

~

Back at the house, the women spent the remainder of the afternoon at the kitchen table setting up their new electronic devices. Lena helped Phyllis discover several apps designed for the visually impaired that would unquestionably make her life easier.

It was past six o'clock when Lena got up and went to the refrigerator. "We should think about dinner." Opening the door, she was shocked to find the shelves empty. "How do you feel about takeout?"

Phyllis pressed a hand against her chest. "I can hardly stand the excitement. A visit to the Apple Store and take-out dinner all in one day."

Lena removed an unopened bottle of chardonnay from the refrigerator door. "If you're a really good girl, I'll let you have a sip of wine, as long as you promise not to tell Jade."

Pinching her fingers together, Phyllis zipped them across her lips. "Mum's the word."

Phyllis insisted they order from McCrady's Tavern. While they sipped their wine, they used Lena's new laptop to study the menu and locate a food delivery service. Phyllis ordered the scallops, Lena the swordfish, and they both got the salad with baby gem lettuces.

After dinner, Lena walked Phyllis upstairs to her room. Her bath would have to wait until the morning. It had been a big day for the old woman, and she was eager to get into bed with her new iPad and headphones and listen to the hot new bestseller they'd downloaded together—*Where the Crawdads Sing* by Delia Owens.

Lena straightened the room, clearing a path on the floor from the bed to the hallway.

"Believe it or not, there's a method to my madness," Phyllis said about the mess. "I know where everything is in this room."

"That may be so, but there's no point in risking a fall if you have to get up to use the bathroom during the night."

"You're right, of course." Phyllis slipped her arms out of the sleeves of her blouse. "Thank you for today. I don't know when I've had so much fun."

"I should be thanking you, Phyllis. You're delightful company." Lena's eyes traveled to the purple marks on Phyllis's arms. "I hope I didn't give you those bruises when I was helping you in and out of the Uber."

"Even if you did, it was worth it."

When Phyllis struggled to unclasp her bra, Lena said, "Here, let me get that for you."

Standing behind Phyllis, unclasping the bra, Lena was shocked to see bruises in varying shades of green, purple, and yellow up and down her back. Some of them had been there awhile. A week ago, when she'd first noticed bruises on her arms, she hadn't thought to look at her back. "Your back is black and blue, Phyllis. Did you fall?"

"No, I didn't fall," Phyllis snapped. She quickly slipped her gown over her head. "She doesn't mean to be so rough. She's just impatient. She forgets that I bruise easily."

"Who is *she*, Phyllis?" Although Lena already knew who, she dreaded hearing it just the same. Once Phyllis accused Jade of physically abusing her, Lena would have to do something about it. And she had no idea what that something would be.

Phyllis whispered her daughter's name. "But please don't tell her I told you."

CHAPTER TWENTY-ONE

OLIVIA

Alistair insisted on showing Olivia as much of the Northern Neck as he could possibly fit in during her limited stay in Virginia. They took a day trip to Tangier Island in his boat, hiked the trails of Belle Isle State Park, visited nearby wineries, and shopped the neighboring towns for antiques. They cooked dinner together every evening, and after hours of tender lovemaking, they fell asleep in each other's arms.

On Tuesday, they traveled across the river in his boat to Merroir, the original of Rappahannock Oyster Company's six restaurants situated at the edge of the water in Topping, Virginia. Seated at a picnic table under an orange umbrella, they spent much of the afternoon sampling oysters and a variety of craft beers and wines. With a bright blue cloudless sky, the day was warm enough for shorts and T-shirts. She'd drunk way more than Alistair, who appeared to be sober, and on the way home, sitting on the leaning post beside Alistair, Olivia rested her head on his shoulder. She'd nearly dozed off when he said, "On our first day together in Urbanna, you said something that really stuck with me."

She opened her eyes, looking up at him without lifting her head. "What'd I say?"

"That you know what it's like to lose your spouse when it's not your choice. Your husband didn't die, Olivia, but like me, you're mourning the loss of that relationship. I miss my wife something crazy. She was a beautiful person, and I loved her dearly. But as much as I miss the person herself, I also miss the comfort of having a soul mate, someone who knows me better than myself, at my side day in and day out." He paused for a minute before continuing. "I'm not sure I'm even making any sense. What I'm trying to say is I'm beginning to think it's possible to have that kind of close relationship with another person. I think that's one of the reasons you and I are so attracted to each other. We can identify with each other's pain. I think maybe the fate gods brought us together." He snickered. "It's no surprise that Lena had something to do with it, whether intentionally or not. She's always been my guardian angel."

Olivia, as had become her habit, listened to Alistair talk without commenting. He seemed to have a lot to get off his chest. But it worried her that he might be getting too serious about their relationship. They'd agreed, often even joked, that their affair was only about sex. She thought he understood she wasn't looking for commitment. She was looking for companionship.

Despite their numerous outings, Olivia managed to carve out time to work on her manuscript. For most of her adult life, she'd experienced insomnia in phases. Some nights were better than others. She rarely had trouble falling asleep at bedtime, but when she woke during the night to pee, she'd often be awake for hours, unable to flip the switch to turn her brain off. Since beginning work on *Marriage of Lies*, the insomnia had gotten worse. The moment she opened her eyes, her characters nudged their way into her thoughts. It hadn't been a problem at Lena's. She'd simply prop herself up in bed, grab her computer off the nightstand, and type away for several hours. At Alistair's, so as not to disturb him, she tiptoed down the hall to the kitchen. He never even missed her until the fourth official night of their sleepovers.

It was around four o'clock on Thursday morning, and she was typing so fast on the keyboard, she didn't hear him enter the room. When she sensed him standing behind her, she fell back in her chair, hand pressed against her pounding heart. "Jeez, Alistair! Don't sneak up on me like that. You scared me."

He bent at the waist, peering over her shoulder at her computer. "What're you working on? Is that your project?"

"Yes!" she said, and slammed her laptop shut.

He straightened, hands in the air. "I get it! You don't want me to read it."

"It's not just you, Alistair. I'm not ready for anyone to read it."

"Whatever, Olivia," he said, and went back to bed.

Olivia felt guilty for hurting Alistair's feelings and for lying to him. She *was* ready for someone to read her manuscript. Just not him. When she'd told him about her involvement with the Kates, he'd laughed at her. He'd called the Kates absurd and frivolous, which they were, but Olivia had facilitated the Scapades, which made her equally as absurd and frivolous. How could she trust him to give constructive criticism on her romance novel? Her fragile ego required nurturing. As a novice novel writer, she needed someone she could rely on for honest feedback. Someone who understood the romance genre. Someone like Lena.

Sitting straight up in her chair, Olivia opened her laptop, placing her hands on the keyboard as she navigated to the *Hi-Low* website. She hadn't hesitated when Lena had asked to take control of the blog for the remainder of her stay. And Olivia was pleasantly surprised at the *Outsider's Look at Charleston* campaign. Lena's images were breathtaking, particularly the candids capturing stolen moments between locals and tourists. And the articles were informative, well written, and engaging, especially the introductory piece where she spoke of the warm welcome the people of Charleston had extended to her when she needed it the most. Based on the comments, her followers loved Lena and were cheering her on.

She thumbed off a text to Lena. Kudos on a job well done on the blog. Much impressed. Have a huge favor to ask. If you have time, would you be willing to read a few chapters of a novel I'm working on? Know I can count on you for an honest opinion. She hit send before she could change her mind, then held her breath. She didn't expect Lena to respond at four in the morning, but she set the phone, screen up, on the table beside her computer just in case.

Inspired by the notion that someone might actually read her words, Olivia refocused her attention on her manuscript and worked straight through until after sunrise. Alistair returned to the kitchen for coffee around seven thirty.

"Would you like pancakes for breakfast?" he asked with little enthusiasm.

She stood and gathered her things. "No thanks. I'm gonna go. I have a full day of writing ahead of me. But I wanna get out on the water for a bit first. Can I interest you in a paddleboard race?"

"Not today. I need to check in at the Jumpstart." Normally he kissed her goodbye, but he didn't so much as cast a glance in her direction as she left the room.

After an hour of vigorous paddling on the water, Olivia showered, dressed, and settled in at the desk in the study. She was thrilled to see Lena's response to her text. Send it on. Have plenty of time. I'm staying with a friend's elderly mother while she's out of town on business. Can't wait to read it.

Olivia saved her first ten chapters in a new document and fired it off to Lena in an email with a quick note: *Excuse the grammar errors. Be honest with your feedback. If you hate it, I can take it. I have thick skin.* After all, she'd survived her husband leaving her for another man.

With gentle wind wafting through the open window, Olivia worked straight through the rest of the morning and the afternoon with no interruptions. She'd entered the zone. She'd given her characters the lead, and they were showing her the way. She wrote like a madwoman, the words seeming to fall out of the sky onto her computer document.

She ate a container of yogurt for lunch and several slices of apple slathered with almond butter for a midafternoon snack. At six o'clock that evening, she went to the kitchen for a well-earned glass of wine. From the window, she could see Alistair moving about in his kitchen. She had not heard from him all day. Not a single text or a shout-out from across the yard. He was obviously still irritated at her for slamming her computer shut on him that morning. He was pushing too hard—wanting more from her than she was ready to give. She was only now coming to terms with the emotional fallout from her divorce.

While sadness weighted her chest, she knew it was for the best. She couldn't afford the distraction of a serious relationship. Requests for ads on her blog and income from affiliate marketing had crept back up, thanks to Lena, but that income was peanuts compared to the salary she needed to continue her lifestyle in her waterfront condo in Charleston. Since no other options for a sustainable career had presented themselves, all of her eggs had landed in the *Marriage of Lies* basket.

She turned her back to the window and leaned against the kitchen sink. She'd been a fool to think they could have companionship without commitment. Even if she wanted more from their relationship, which she wasn't sure she did, logistics complicated their situation. She lived in Charleston, he in the Northern Neck. Or maybe New York City if he accepted the job offer.

She took her wine outside to the deck. The sky was heavy with clouds, and the wind had picked up as the remnants of Hurricane Michael pushed through the area. The gloomy weather did little to improve her mood. She felt restless and lonely after spending the day at her computer. Was she even cut out for the reclusive life of a writer? Being alone in Charleston, where sidewalks and restaurants were always teeming with tourists and locals, had never felt lonely. But here, with the waves lapping the shore and a formation of geese flying overhead, she found being alone depressing.

Suddenly, she wanted to be anywhere but in the empty cottage. She grabbed her purse and the keys to Lena's van and headed out. With windshield wipers on full speed, she made the ten-minute drive to Kilmarnock, where she circled the downtown area until a parking space opened up in front of the Dub Shack.

She parked the van and pulled the hood of her coat up over her head, making a dash for the door. The restaurant was casual and crowded, every booth on the upper level occupied. She nudged her way between two middle-aged men at the bar who appeared to be alone. The one on her right, handsome and fit with sandy hair and blue eyes, was working his way through a plate of baby back ribs, while the one to her left, red-faced with a large belly, was nursing a beer.

Red Face thrust his sweaty hand at her. "I'm Steve. What's a pretty little thing like you doing dining alone?"

She gave his hand the Ice Queen stare. She was in no mood to be hit on. "A girl's gotta eat."

She flagged the bartender down, a nice-looking young man she guessed to be about thirty. "I'll have a glass of your house red. And I'd like to see the menu when you get a chance."

The bartender placed a menu in front of her. "We're all out of the specials tonight. It's the craziest thing. Everyone decided to come out in the storm instead of staying at home."

When the bartender left to fetch her wine, Steve scooted his upholstered bar chair closer to her. "I know everyone around these parts, and I never forget a face, especially one as pretty as yours. That means you're either new to the area or a tourist."

"I'm neither. I'm here for work."

As she glanced at the menu, she felt Steve's creepy gaze on her, lingering on her breasts. The bartender brought her wine, and she ordered the Hawaiian chicken sandwich. "To go," she added with emphasis.

The bartender jotted her order on a notepad and turned away, his attention already on another customer.

"What is it that you do for a living?" Steve asked.

"I'm a romance writer." As the words escaped her lips, she realized her mistake.

Steve broke into a wide grin, revealing nicotine-stained teeth. "You don't say. I'd be happy to assist you in your research."

"Bartender! Cancel my order," she called to the bartender, who was flirting with a pretty blonde at the other end of the bar. "I'll just pay you for the wine." She slapped a twenty-dollar bill on the counter, pushed her stool back, and left the restaurant in a hurry.

She drove Lena's van at top speed, anxious to get back to the safety of the cottage. She heated a can of chicken noodle soup and topped off the glass of wine she'd abandoned earlier. While she ate, she researched topics relating to self-publishing romance novels. Maybe she was adapting more easily than she thought to the life of a reclusive writer. As an authorpreneur—marketer, editor, graphic designer, formatter—she would wear many hats. The versatility appealed to her, and she refused to let reports of the saturated romance market get her down. She had more than two weeks left in her house exchange with Lena. She would stay holed up in the cottage until she finished her first draft.

If she worked hard enough, maybe she wouldn't miss Alistair so much.

CHAPTER TWENTY-TWO

ALISTAIR

Alistair felt like a schoolboy with his first crush. He knew he was being overly sensitive. He didn't need the emotional drama. Not today of all days, on the second anniversary of Mary Anne's death.

Why had Olivia slammed her computer on him? She was either hiding something or she didn't have enough faith in him to share her work. And he didn't want to be with someone who didn't trust him.

Mary Anne had been the ideal woman for him—honest and trustworthy until the day she died. They'd always agreed about most things. They'd finished each other's sentences, instinctively known what the other was thinking. He knew it wasn't fair to compare his current lover with his dead wife. They were different in so many ways. Olivia possessed an independence Mary Anne had lacked. And Olivia was so damn sexy, a sophisticated woman who carried herself with such poise in the stylish clothes she wore. And their lovemaking was tender and exhilarating. One minute he yearned to caress her fit body until she climaxed, and the next he wanted to drive deep into her, ravishing her.

Sure, he was sex-starved. The last year of her life, Mary Anne had been too sick to even think about sex, making a grand total of three years he'd gone without it. But his attraction to Olivia was about more than sex. He felt alive with her. His heart beat faster, pumping blood through his veins and awakening nerve endings. She invigorated him. He wanted to try new things with her, take her on trips to places he'd never been. He was even considering asking her to spend Christmas in New York with him.

He debated how to spend his day. He'd caught up on all his chores. He needed to make an appearance at the café, but that could wait until later. Hurricane Michael had been downgraded to a tropical storm, but the potential for thunderstorms was too high to risk going out in the boat. *Back to feeling useless and insignificant.* He'd felt so needed when taking care of Mary Anne during her illness. But he'd done nothing of importance since her death, nothing that impacted the lives of others. Being in New York, where the crème de la crème in all the major industries made decisions that affected the world, made him long to be a part of the rat race again.

Alistair sat down at the kitchen table with a fresh cup of coffee and his laptop. With thoughts of moving to New York at the forefront of his mind, he spent an hour searching for available apartments in desirable areas. He made a list of the ones that met his criteria, but further investigation would require a real estate agent.

He called his sons—first Josh, who was out of the office at a meeting, and then Mike.

"How's the shoulder, bud?" he asked his youngest when Mike picked up on the second ring.

"Much better, Dad. Thanks. I'm glad you called. I've been thinking about you today. Are you okay?"

"I'm hanging in there. Today is hard on all of us. How are *you?*"

Mike let out a sigh. "It helps to stay busy."

Keep your mind occupied so your heart doesn't have time to feel.

"Staying busy usually worked for me," Alistair said. "Which is one reason I'm calling. I'm hoping you can recommend a good Realtor who represents properties in Manhattan."

"Does that mean you're seriously considering Henry's offer?" Mike asked with excitement in his voice.

"*Considering* is the operative word, son. And researching available apartments is part of that consideration."

"I understand. I know several Realtors who deal in high-end residential properties in Manhattan, but I think you should work with Holly Bennett. You'll like her. Not only is she smart, she's a top seller in the market. And she lists all the best properties. I'll text you her contact info when we hang up."

"Thank you. I'll give her a call right away." Alistair paused, not wanting their conversation to end. "So what else is new with you? Everything going okay with work?"

"Work's busy but good." Several long seconds of silence elapsed before Mike continued. "I took Emily out on a date. Remember that nurse I met the night of the accident? You know, the doctor's daughter I told you about."

Alistair could hear the smile in his son's voice. "I remember. Does that mean you broke up with Stacy?"

"Yep. Your advice hit home. You never know when the right girl might come along. You should take your own advice, you know."

"Meaning?" Alistair said, although he knew full well what his son meant.

"Meaning you, too, should keep an open mind about women. You never know when a nice one might come along."

Propping his elbow on the table, Alistair buried his face in his free hand. "I don't need another lecture about your mom not wanting me to be alone."

"I promise not to lecture you anymore if you'll agree to let Josh set you up with his friend over Christmas."

Olivia popped into mind. "We'll see." Alistair lifted his head. "I should let you go, son. I know you're busy. We'll talk soon."

After ending the call, Alistair checked the time on his phone. Almost noon. His eyes traveled to the window. The worst of the storm wasn't expected until later in the day. Gray clouds and chilly temperatures provided perfect weather to drive over to Shirley Plantation for a wine tasting and cozy lunch by the fire at the Upper Shirley Vineyards. Not something he wanted to do alone. A dim light gleamed from Lena's upstairs window, and he imagined Olivia typing away at her computer, working on her secret project. He considered sending her a text, suggesting the outing, but to spend the day with another woman felt like a betrayal to Mary Anne's memory.

The café it is! He grabbed his keys and left the house. He'd have to take his chances that Johnny, the chef at the café, had chosen a hearty soup for one of the day's specials.

The Jumpstart was packed with locals, and a line three deep stood at the counter waiting to place their orders with Jasmine and Jess. Alistair slipped behind the counter and passed through the workspace to the kitchen. Johnny stood at the griddle, looking harried as he prepared sandwiches and ladled soup into bowls. "It's really busy today. Where's Sherry?" Alistair asked.

"She has the flu," Johnny said without looking up from the griddle. "At least that's what she claims."

Alistair furrowed his brow. "Do you have reason to doubt her?"

"I don't want to throw anyone under the bus, boss, but let's just say our manager's been sick a lot lately. We're swamped, as you can see. We could really use her help."

"I'm happy to pitch in." Alistair went to the supply room and returned with a black apron bearing the café's logo—a steaming mug of coffee with "Jumpstart Café" in block font beneath it. Slipping on the apron, he said, "Tell me what to do."

"You can take this food out to the customers." Johnny motioned at the plates lined up on the stainless-steel table beside him. "The table numbers are written on the tickets."

For the next two hours, Alistair delivered orders and cleared dirty dishes from empty tables. Once all the customers had been served, he helped Jasmine and Jess refill beverage dispensers and tidy up the seating area.

"We've missed seeing you, boss," Jasmine said as she rearranged Danish to make the tray look fuller. "We heard your son was in an accident. Is he okay?"

"He's doing great," Alistair said. "I talked to him on the phone a little while ago. Thanks for asking."

Jasmine smiled. "I know you're relieved."

Alistair nodded. "You have no idea."

"We're sure glad you showed up when you did," Jess said. "If business keeps up like this, we'll have to hire another waitress. Sherry's been . . ." She cast a nervous glance at Jasmine, who nodded for her to continue. "She hasn't been around much lately."

Alistair pressed his lips thin. "Johnny mentioned something about that. I'll look into it. In the meantime, if you need help, call me. Both my cell and home numbers are on an index card by the phone in the office."

Jess finished replenishing the self-serve bar with plastic lids and packets of sweeteners and came to stand beside Alistair. "So, boss," she said with a playful grin that hinted at trouble. "There's this woman. She was in here a lot last week, although we haven't seen her in a few days. She's beau-ti-ful."

"I bet she is," Alistair said with an eye roll. This wasn't the first *beau-ti-ful* woman his two young friends had tried to hook him up with.

"She's smart too," Jess added. "She's a writer, staying at a friend's house on Carters Creek while she researches a novel she's working on."

Alistair's ears perked up. "Did you happen to catch her name?"

"Olivia something or other," Jess said.

Trying not to sound too interested, he said, "And you say she's working on a novel."

Jess nudged Alistair with her elbow. "A romance novel. Maybe you can help her with her research. You know, the sexy scenes where the man sweeps the woman off her feet."

Alistair forced a smile. "The two of you are incorrigible. Did your mothers ever tell you that?"

"All the time," they said in unison.

He turned his back on them, busying himself with wiping down the counters. No wonder Olivia had slammed her computer on him. She was writing a *novel* about the intimacy they'd shared. *Damn!* She'd never cared about him. She was simply using him for sex. He felt hurt that she'd exploited him and angry at himself for allowing it to happen.

Alistair worked through the afternoon in a broody silence, with patrons arriving in a steady stream for late lunches and specialty coffee drinks. While Jasmine and Jess took care of the customers, Alistair tackled the list of repairs that needed to be made around the café—a leaky sink in the women's restroom and a cabinet that had come off its hinges in the supply room, among others.

He left the café around five thirty and drove straight to the Tides Inn, where he parked himself on a stool at the bar in the Chesapeake Restaurant. Roy placed a Stella in front of him. "Alistair. Dude. How're you holding up? I know this is a tough day for you."

Alistair guzzled half the beer and wiped his mouth with his napkin. "I promised myself I wouldn't burden you with my problems."

"I'm a bartender. Listening to people's problems is part of my job." Roy planted his beefy elbows on the bar. "You look particularly down in the dumps this evening. Not that the anniversary of your wife's death isn't enough."

"You know me too well." He downed the rest of his beer. "I need something stronger. Maker's Mark and water on the rocks, please."

Roy put ice in a glass and then added a healthy shot of bourbon and a splash of water.

Alistair drained the glass in one gulp. "Hit me again."

Roy did as he asked, handing him the glass along with a dinner menu. "Do yourself a favor. Order some food to soak up that booze. You'll thank me in the morning." He moved to the other end of the bar to assist a rowdy group of golfers who, judging by their behavior, had spent their day drinking in the bar rather than playing golf.

As he perused the menu, he thought back to Saturday night, when he and Olivia had dined on the terrace. She'd looked so lovely in her black silk top and skinny jeans that hugged her shapely hips. They'd made love for the first time that night. Did she sneak out of bed after he'd fallen asleep to make notes about the sex? While that didn't sound like something Olivia would do, he was hard-pressed to come up with another explanation as to why she'd kept her novel a secret from him.

Mary Anne had been an avid reader. She'd preferred mysteries, but on occasion, she'd read one of Lena's romances. When she'd become too ill to leave the house, he'd bought books for her at Walmart. Once, he'd made the mistake of bringing home what he thought was a romance but turned out to be erotica. Alistair smiled, thinking about how incensed she'd been. "I will not have that smut in my house. Take it back to the store next time you go."

Was it possible that Olivia was writing erotica?

"What's it gonna be?" Roy asked when he returned. "You've had plenty of time to look at the menu, not that you don't already know it by heart."

"A half pound of steamed shrimp and another Maker's and water," Alistair said, sliding his empty glass to Roy.

Roy looked at the glass and back at Alistair. "Do you really think you need another drink?"

"If you don't give it to me, I'll find a bartender who will."

"Okay, man," Roy said, pouring him another bourbon and water. "But this is the last one, so savor it." He took the menu and disappeared into the kitchen.

When he returned ten minutes later with Alistair's shrimp, Roy said, "So are you ready to tell me why the urgent need to get drunk?"

Alistair peeled a shrimp, dipped it in cocktail sauce, and popped it in his mouth. "Not really, but I know you'll pester me until I do."

He told Roy all about Olivia—how they'd met, the slamming of the computer that morning, and what he'd learned from Jess and Jasmine about the romance novel she was writing.

"You shouldn't just assume she's writing about you," Roy said. "I can think of a hundred reasons why she'd want to hide her computer screen from you."

"But she said she was working on her project."

"You've forgotten how sneaky women can be. She could've been ordering you a present. Or she could've been shopping for sexy lingerie to surprise you. Hell, for all we know, she could've been looking at porn."

Alistair scoffed. "Looking at porn? Your mind's in the gutter, Roy. Olivia's not the type to watch porn."

Roy wadded up a cocktail napkin and tossed it at Alistair. "For her novel, dude. She might've been researching porn for her novel."

Alistair hung his head. "I get your point. I should probably give her a chance to explain. I'll go see her in the morning."

But with his curiosity growing, he didn't want to wait until morning to talk to her. When he left the Tides Inn forty-five minutes later, as his truck swayed in the wind and he had to dodge several downed tree branches in the road, he came up with the perfect excuse to visit the cottage tonight.

He parked his truck in his driveway, and ducking his head against the wind, he dashed across the yard to Lena's. Olivia answered the door in her flannel pajamas. Only she could make flannel pajamas sexy.

"I just wanted to check on you, to make sure you're weathering the storm all right."

"I'm fine," Olivia said in a curt tone.

"Do you mind if I come in for a minute? Lena sometimes gets water in her basement when it rains this hard." No need to tell her it had only flooded one time, back when Hurricane Isabel hit in 2003.

"By all means," Olivia said, stepping out of his way. "I didn't realize the cottage had a basement."

"Other than the furnace, there's not much down there."

She followed him into the kitchen, surprise crossing her face when he opened an out-of-the-way door in the corner. "And all this time I thought that was a broom closet."

He was down the stairs and back up in less than thirty seconds. "All dry."

"That's a relief," she said, closing the door behind him.

He spotted a glass of red wine beside her open laptop on the coffee table in the living room. "I didn't mean to interrupt your work."

She followed his gaze to her computer. "About this morning . . . I owe you an apology, Alistair. I don't know why I didn't tell you from the start, but this project I'm working on is a romance novel. I thought maybe you'd think it was silly. I'd never even read a romance novel until I picked up one of Lena's out of boredom. Anyway, I got this idea for a plot, and the words just came to me out of the blue. I figured, why not see where it takes me."

"I never would've thought you silly, Olivia. I think you're wonderful."

When he moved to take her in his arms, her hand shot out. "I'm sorry, Alistair. I can't afford the distraction right now. I really need to finish this first draft."

His mouth fell open. *She can't afford the distraction?* She was working on a romance novel, not a merger involving two Fortune 500 companies. He thought about what she'd told him. That she'd never read a romance novel until now. That the idea for the plot came to her out of the blue. Not once, during all the time they'd spent together, had she mentioned her pressing deadline. It didn't make sense that her project was suddenly more important than him. She was totally hiding something. "Are you writing about us?" he asked.

When she hesitated, he knew he'd been right all along. "If you even think about publishing it, I'll sue you for slander."

He stormed back across the yard to his house, where he later passed out at the kitchen table, one hand gripping a framed photograph of Mary Anne on their wedding day and the other his bottle of Blanton's bourbon.

CHAPTER TWENTY-THREE

LENA

Jade texted Lena on Thursday morning: The deal is taking longer than expected. I'll be home sometime tomorrow afternoon. She didn't inquire about her mother's well-being or express any consideration as to whether staying an extra day with Phyllis suited Lena. While she was angry at Jade for her callous attitude, she was relieved to postpone the inevitable conversation regarding her mother.

Even in light of the bruises, Lena was having a hard time wrapping her mind around the idea of Jade physically abusing her mother on purpose. *She doesn't mean to be so rough. She's just impatient. She forgets that I bruise easily.* And Lena could see how that could be true. As she herself had witnessed, Jade was too self-absorbed to have much patience with others around her. Nevertheless, Jade needed to be reminded that her mother was fragile and should be treated with tender loving care.

In any event, Lena enjoyed the older woman's company and was more than happy to stay a little longer. Phyllis seemed to be thriving with the change of pace.

After helping her bathe and dress in clean clothes, Lena made Phyllis promise to stay in her recliner while she went to the condo for Olivia's car. Phyllis was as delighted as a child at an amusement park when they ventured off to the Harris Teeter in the Volkswagen Beetle with the convertible top down.

"Whee! This is fun," Phyllis said, waving her hands over her head. "I can't see where I'm going, but I feel like I'm riding in a dune buggy."

As Lena loaded up the cart with food, Phyllis touched and smelled everything in the produce department as though she'd never been to the grocery store before. She was exhausted by the time they got home, and after a cup of tomato basil soup and a grilled cheese sandwich for lunch, she retired to her room for a long nap.

The rain from the tropical storm held off, but because of the wind, they spent a quiet afternoon inside with Lena editing her images and Phyllis listening to her audiobook. Lena prepared Phyllis's favorite chicken parmesan recipe for dinner, the best Lena had ever eaten, and then tucked Phyllis into bed early with her iPad and headphones. Fighting off sleep, she stayed up past midnight reading the first chapters of the romance novel Olivia had sent for her feedback.

~

On Friday morning, as Jade's return from Nashville drew near, Lena and Phyllis sipped coffee together in the garden. Thinking she might never be invited back to the Dowdys' house, Lena said, "I want you to be able to get in touch with me if you ever need me."

She recited her cell number and made Phyllis repeat it, over and over, until she'd memorized it. "In case you forget, I'm going to write my name and number on several slips of paper and leave them where you can easily find them—in your wallet, the drawers of both your nightstand and the table beside your recliner, in the pockets of your favorite cardigans, and one on the bulletin board beside the wall phone in the kitchen."

Phyllis's face darkened. "You sound as if you're going away. Will I ever see you again?"

"We never know what tomorrow will bring," she said in a solemn tone. "But you can always call me if you need me."

When Jade finally arrived home around three that afternoon, Lena said, "I need to speak with you in private." With a quick glance at Phyllis, who was in her recliner listening to Dr. Phil on the television, she added, "Outside."

Jade dropped her suitcase at the foot of the stairs and followed Lena out the front door. "Look, if you're mad because I was late getting back from Tennessee—"

Slinging her overnight bag on her shoulder, Lena turned to face her. "Your mother warrants better treatment than you're giving her. Her clothes are filthy. She doesn't bathe regularly. And you plant her in front of the television for hours on end. You took her earbuds away from her, so she couldn't listen to her audiobooks. What kind of person does such a thing?"

"I needed my earbuds for a conference call."

"And what? You forgot to give them back to her after you were finished? Your mother is a wonderful woman, a delight to be around. She's not going to live forever, you know. And you'll be sorry you missed out on this time you could've spent together."

Jade stiffened. "You've been a thorn in my side since the day we met. Mind your own business, Lena. My mother and I are doing just fine."

Lena took a step closer to her, staring her down. "Oh really? You didn't think I was such a thorn in your side when you asked me to drop what I was doing to stay with Phyllis while you flew off to Nashville."

Jade rolled her eyes. "As if you were doing anything important."

"Whether I was or wasn't is beside the point. You took advantage of me. You said you'd only be gone for twenty-four hours. You knew all along you weren't coming back until today, didn't you?"

A smirk appeared on Jade's lips. "Think what you want."

"I'll tell you what I think," Lena said, nostrils flaring. "I think you're responsible for the bruises on your mother's back and arms."

Jade snorted. "I don't know what you're talking about," she said in a dismissive tone that left little doubt in Lena's mind.

"Oh yes you do." Lena pointed her finger at Jade's nose. "If you don't stop hurting her, I'm going to report you to the authorities."

"As if they'd believe you over me." Drawing herself to her full height, Jade spun on her heel and strode up the sidewalk.

"Needless to say, I quit as your assistant," Lena called after her. "I'll drop your equipment off tomorrow."

She ran to the end of the sidewalk where Olivia's car was parked on the curb. Flinging the canvas bag in the passenger seat, she started the engine and sped off down the street. But the more distance she put between herself and Jade, the heavier her actions weighed on her. She'd permanently severed all ties with Jade, which meant she would no longer be aware of what was going on with Phyllis. Why hadn't she thought to get contact information for Phyllis's other daughter, Marie? Lena needed to seek professional help about the situation. But she decided it best to wait until she'd calmed down before calling the authorities.

Her cell phone rang as she was parking the Beetle in the garage at the condo. She rummaged through her purse for her phone, glad to see Kayla's number on the screen and not Jade's.

"Hi, Mom! Guess what? I'm in Charleston. I came down to visit a friend. We'd like to take you out to dinner tonight if you're free."

Suddenly weary, her head fell back against the headrest. "Back up a minute, Kayla. What're you doing in Charleston? And who is this friend?"

"It's a long story, actually. I'd rather explain everything in person."

While having dinner with a stranger didn't appeal to her, the thought of seeing her daughter brought a smile to Lena's face. For the past week, she and Kayla had been carrying on a continuous texting conversation without a single argument. It was time to test out this new relationship in person.

"Can we make it a late dinner? I've been staying with an elderly friend for a couple of days and need a little time to unwind."

"Sure. Let's say eight o'clock at the Peninsula Grill. I know things haven't been great between us lately, Mom. I've been confused about where I want to live and stressed out about finding a job. But you'll be happy to know, I'm putting my life in order. Good things are happening for me. And I can't wait to share them with you."

Her daughter sounded more upbeat than she had in years. "And I can't wait to hear about them. I'll look forward to seeing you at eight," Lena said and ended the call.

Her legs ached to pound the sidewalks, and her fingers itched to press a shutter button. But not with Jade's camera. She couldn't risk something happening to it. She would have to use her own.

She took her bag up to the condo, changed from her sandals into comfortable walking shoes, and grabbed her camera. The downtown streets hummed with locals and tourists enjoying a leisurely Friday evening. Lena walked for nearly two hours, snapping dozens of candids. If they turned out, considering her outdated equipment, the shots would be perfect for the blog. Next time she spoke with Olivia, she planned to suggest changing the name of the blog from *High Living in the Lowcountry* to *Quality Living in the Lowcountry*. Not only would the new name provide a fresh start after the fiasco with the Kates, but she thought *Quality Living* sounded more inclusive of the types of people she wanted to attract.

She showered and dressed in a simple black dress with a high collar, three-quarter-length sleeves, and a swing skirt she'd purchased from J. McLaughlin. With time to spare, she made a detour by the Dowdys' to return the camera equipment on her way to the restaurant.

The driveway was empty, and the house seemed eerily quiet as she walked around to the back. She hated to leave the expensive camera equipment on the porch and was relieved to find the door to the study unlocked. Dropping the camera bag in Jade's desk chair, she hurried out of the house and back down the driveway before anyone could see her.

Lena, relieved of the burden of her toxic relationship with Jade, walked with a spring in her step as she cut over to Meeting Street and headed north toward the Peninsula Grill. Her thoughts shifted to her daughter. Who was this friend Kayla had mentioned? One of her sorority sisters from Chapel Hill? Or maybe it was a girlfriend from high school who had moved to Charleston after college. Lena was in no way prepared to see the man who was standing beside her daughter, both sipping from flutes inside the Champagne Bar at the Peninsula Grill.

When he noticed Lena in the doorway, Golden Casanova moved through the crowd to greet her. "Mrs. Browder, I'm Zack Phelps," he said with hand extended. "I owe you a sincere apology for the circumstances surrounding our first meeting. That night . . . well, it should never have happened that way. I promise you, my mama taught me much better manners."

Lena was pleased to see that he'd shaved off his beard and cut his hair so that it curled at the nape of his neck. He was a handsome man with strong facial features and twinkling blue eyes. But good looks didn't let him off the hook for the torment he'd put her through.

"Young man, I can assure you, Kayla's mama taught her better manners as well."

Kayla appeared at their side, two flutes of champagne in hand. "Mom! Jeez. Give Zack a break. He apologized."

Zack chuckled. "It's fine if she wants to give me a hard time. I earned it. I only hope that by the end of dinner tonight you will have forgiven me."

Kayla handed Lena a flute. "Don't ruin the mood, Mom. We're celebrating."

"By all means, don't let me be the party pooper." She took the glass from Kayla, who had never looked more gorgeous in over-the-knee brown suede boots, a color-block button-up skirt in shades of autumn leaves, and a short orange sweater that revealed three inches of her bare firm midriff. "What're we celebrating?"

Kayla lifted her flute. "Life. Love. Charleston. This city is fabulous. Don't you just love it here, Mom?"

Lena nodded. "I do love it here." They clinked glasses, and Lena took a sip of the dry champagne.

Kayla gave Lena the once-over. "You look amazing. What're you wearing?" She spun her around. "Very Audrey Hepburn. And you cut your hair. I have to say Charleston agrees with you."

Lena beamed. "That it does."

The room was packed with patrons, with every seat at the bar occupied, and the cozy atmosphere had a good vibe. She would come back another time to do a feature write-up for the blog.

"How did the two of you meet?" Lena asked, her eyes on her daughter. "Are you in a relationship? Is he the friend you're staying with?"

Kayla tilted her head back, her blonde mane trailing down her spine, and laughed out loud. "That's a lot of questions at once, Mom."

"I didn't even ask the most important one," she said, her expression all business. "How's Biscuit? It terrifies me to think of her being left alone with your father. My poor dog will starve."

"No worries. I brought Biscuit to Charleston with me. We can go visit her after dinner if you'd like. And yes, Zack and I are in a relationship. I'm staying with him in his uncle's carriage house."

Lena wondered if Kayla and Zack were sharing a bed in his uncle's carriage house. *Of course they are. Isn't that where you first met him, in your daughter's bed?*

She shifted her gaze to Zack. "How does your uncle feel about having a golden retriever shedding all over his carriage house?"

"He doesn't mind. He has two Boykin spaniels of his own."

The hostess approached them. "Your table is ready now, sir."

"I hope you don't mind eating outside," Zack said to Lena as they left the crowded bar. "Kayla thought you might appreciate the courtyard."

"I don't mind a bit. I love the outdoors, and the courtyard sounds lovely."

The hostess led them down a path of old bricks through a garden of lush greenery and landscape lighting to a table draped in a white cloth, set for three. After a serious discussion with the waiter about the wine list, Zack took the liberty of ordering a bottle of Albariño wine from Spain and a dozen oysters on the half shell for the table. He was growing on her by the moment.

The night breeze rustled the palmetto fronds, and jazz music played softly from hidden speakers. It was a night for romance, and the young couple sitting opposite Lena was obviously in love.

She placed her folded hands on the table. "So about your relationship. Where'd you meet, and how long have you been seeing each other?"

Kayla blushed. "Mom! What's with the Spanish inquisition?"

"*You* invited *me* to dinner," Lena said. "Which I take as a sign that you want me to know about your relationship."

Zack placed his hand over Kayla's. "She's right, you know. We've got nothing to hide, Mrs. Browder. It's just that our relationship, because of logistics, has been off and on since we met in Richmond last December."

Lena did her best to hide her surprise. "You've known each other since December?"

"Yes, ma'am. We met at a bar in Shockoe. Kayla had already come home for winter break, and I was still finishing my exams at VCU. Although we talked all the time on the phone, we only managed to see each other a couple of times during the spring semester. After graduation in May, I went to Europe for the summer. I'd only just returned and had driven to Richmond to get my belongings out of storage when we had our embarrassing encounter two weeks ago."

Has it only been two weeks? Lena thought. *So much has happened, it seems like a lifetime ago.*

The waiter arrived with their wine, presenting the bottle to Zack for inspection before pouring a sample to taste. Once Zack approved the wine, the waiter filled a glass for each of them and quietly left the table.

"Anyway, Mrs. Browder, I'm crazy about your daughter. We have no idea where our relationship will lead. For now, we're happy spending as much time together as possible."

To be young and in love again, Lena thought with an expression of reminiscence on her face. *Will I ever find that kind of happiness with a man again?* She bit down on her lower lip to keep from laughing out loud. She didn't know what to do with the man she had, let alone how to get a new one.

"I appreciate your honesty," Lena said, and took a sip of her wine. "You mentioned an uncle. I assume you're from Charleston."

"Born and bred. My father left my mother when I was ten. I haven't seen him since. Mom's brother, Uncle Owen, has been more of a father to me than my own ever was. His two sons, my cousins, were like my brothers growing up, but they've both moved out west, and I hardly ever see them anymore."

The waiter brought the platter of oysters and took orders for their main courses—pan-roasted scallops for the ladies and a New York strip for Zack.

"Do you have a job, Zack?" Lena tried to appear nonchalant as she forked an oyster from its shell.

Zack nodded as he slurped down an oyster. "I'm a graphic designer for a marketing firm here in Charleston."

"Zack's a talented illustrator," Kayla said, holding her chin high.

He shrugged off the compliment. "It's really just a hobby."

"Guess what, Mom? I met with someone in the admissions department at the College of Charleston today. I've decided to go back to school."

Lena nearly choked on her oyster. "You what? When I asked you last week about graduate school, you said you'd had enough school."

"I also said I wanted to work in a hotel. If I take classes next spring and fall, I can earn a second degree in hospitality and tourism management with a concentration in hotel management." Kayla set down her fork and wiped her mouth with her linen napkin. "I know what you're thinking, and I don't expect you to support me. I plan to get a job, waitressing or something, while I'm in school."

She'd wanted her daughter to find some direction in her life. She never imagined that would include a move to Charleston. "Where will you live?"

Kayla blushed. "With Zack."

Lena was mortified. They'd only been in a relationship since December. And not a very serious one from the sound of it. But she had to give Kayla the freedom to make her own choices, even if those choices turned out to be mistakes. "How does your uncle feel about having another tenant?" *And how does your father feel, Kayla, about you living with a man? My guess is he knows nothing of it.*

"My uncle is fine with it," Zack said. "He loves Kayla."

"And the rent's free," Kayla added.

"No way, Kayla. You can't live there and not pay rent. I did not raise a freeloader."

"Uncle Owen is a semiretired criminal attorney," Zack explained. "He travels a lot. I take care of things while he's gone, including his dogs, in exchange for free rent. Believe me, his dogs are a handful. I could use Kayla's help."

"And what if things don't work out between the two of you?"

"I'll find a new roommate. Or I'll move in with you," Kayla said with a mischievous glint in her eye.

Zack placed his napkin on the table. "On that note, I'll excuse myself for the restroom."

Lena watched him go. "Who said I was moving here permanently?"

"You're totally making the move. You just haven't gotten that far along in your thinking yet." Kayla reached across the table for Lena's hand. "You're like this whole new person. You seem so happy. Being away from Dad has been good for you. And I'm so proud of you for finally standing up to him. I shouldn't say this about my own father, but I feel like I have a right to since you're my mother. Dad is not a nice person, Mom. He doesn't deserve you. And you deserve better."

Kayla's words were music to Lena's ears. She hadn't realized it until that very moment. She'd needed her daughter's approval before she could seriously consider divorcing her husband.

CHAPTER TWENTY-FOUR

ALISTAIR

Alistair arrived at the café before opening on Saturday morning to meet with an employee candidate. While he waited, he wandered around the empty restaurant, jotting down notes of changes he wanted to make.

He'd worked at the café all day on Friday and was enjoying his interaction with customers as he served them delicious treats from his kitchen. Jess had shown him how to take orders and process credit card payments, and Jasmine was teaching him how to make the specialty coffee drinks and smoothies. In the afternoon, when the lunch crowd had died down, he'd spent over an hour in the kitchen with Johnny, discussing his suggestions for new menu ideas.

"In addition to our tried and true," Johnny had said, "I'd like to switch up the menu from time to time to incorporate seasonal offerings. We should be taking advantage of locally grown fresh fruits and vegetables in the summer and featuring items with pecans, pears, and pumpkins in the fall."

Alistair had considered the idea. "I love it. Why are we not doing this already?"

Johnny had hunched his shoulders, his long arms and big hands out by his sides. "I've mentioned it to Sherry a number of times. She never seemed interested."

Alistair had given Johnny a slap on the back. "Well, I own this place, and as of this minute, you have full creative control of the menu. I'm always available for taste tests if you need feedback."

Johnny had let out a belly laugh. "I'll remember that."

Now, as he stood looking up at the chalkboard menu, Alistair saw that Johnny had wasted no time in implementing changes. The board itself was a masterpiece, with a cornucopia of small pumpkins and fruits and autumn leaves drawn in colored chalk in the bottom left-hand corner. The menu items, including several hearty soups, made Alistair's stomach rumble. He could hardly wait until lunchtime to try the roasted turkey panini with brie, cranberry, and spinach.

His interviewee, a friend of Jess's, had recently lost her waitressing job in a neighboring town when the restaurant where she worked had closed. She arrived precisely at six fifteen. An attractive young woman in her late twenties, Janice wore her silky black hair pulled tight in a perky ponytail. Alistair brewed them both a coffee and motioned her to a table by the window, sitting down opposite her. "Thanks for meeting me so early. Things get hectic in a hurry when we open at seven."

"No problem at all. I'm used to early hours. I appreciate the opportunity, Mr. Hoffman. I'll be honest with you. I really need this job. I'm a super hard worker, and I have plenty of waitressing experience."

When she listed the upscale restaurants where she'd worked, he thought Janice overqualified for the job at the Jumpstart, but who was he to look a gift horse in the mouth? As they talked on, Jess and Johnny came in through the back door and busied themselves in preparation for the morning rush.

"The job's yours, if you want it," Alistair said finally. "You were destined to work here anyway."

Her dark eyes grew wide. "Oh really. Why's that?"

"Because your name begins with J. We have Jess, Jasmine, and Johnny, and now we have Janice."

She laughed. "You're right. It is destiny." She held her hand out to shake. "Thank you, Mr. Hoffman. I promise you won't be sorry. When can I start?"

He glanced at the clock above the chalkboard menu. "How's now?"

Janice beamed. "Now works for me."

As they stood, he said, "And Janice, please call me Alistair."

After turning his new employee over to Jess for training, Alistair went to the café's small office at the back of the building behind the kitchen. He dove into the mountain of bills that had amassed in Sherry's absence. In the past two days, he'd left several messages for his manager but had heard nothing in return. His anger mounted when she appeared in the doorway of the office, wearing a tight-fitting wool dress and high-heeled boots—dress more appropriate for lunch at a country club than work in a café.

"You don't need to worry yourself with the bills, Alistair. That's my job," she said with a smug smile.

As he peered at her over the top of his reading glasses, he realized he'd never cared for her. "It's apparent to me that you haven't been doing your job," he said, gesturing at the envelopes and invoices scattered about the desk.

She dropped her smile, and her body grew rigid. "I've been sick."

"A lot lately, so I've heard." He pointed at the door. "Close the door and have a seat. I'd like to hear about your illnesses."

She slid onto the metal folding chair beside the desk. "My health is really none of your business. I'm entitled to my sick days. If I don't use them, I lose them. That's your policy."

"Which I plan to change immediately."

"Why are you so angry at me? Did I do something else wrong?"

He propped his elbows on the desk and steepled his fingers. "The truth is, Sherry, I'm having a hard time finding anything you've done right around here lately. You've been neglecting your responsibilities, which is unacceptable. I'm sorry to say our business relationship has run its course."

Her hand flew to her chest, fingering the string of pearls around her neck. "Are you firing me? I've been the manager here for ten years."

"And that's part of the problem. The café needs a fresh perspective. You'll receive two weeks' severance pay." He held his hand out to her. "Can I have your keys, please?"

She gawked at his hand incredulously. "But who's going to manage the café?"

"You're looking at him."

"I'll sue you for wrongful termination," she said in a threatening tone.

"You'll never make it to court. I have plenty of reasons to fire you. All documented." He wiggled his fingers. "Keys, please. I have work to do."

She stood abruptly, digging her keys out of her purse and dropping them into his hand. "Fine. I never liked working here anyway."

"That much is obvious." He got up from his chair and followed her to the back door, bolting it behind her before returning to his office.

As the morning wore on, when he discovered errors in the accounting system and room for improvement in their budgeting and cost management, he felt even better about his decision to fire Sherry. He possessed enough business sense to set their affairs right again. But then what? Did he hire someone to replace Sherry? He couldn't very well manage the café himself from New York. He'd had no luck in finding a buyer for the café, not that he'd tried very hard.

Around eleven o'clock, during the lull between the breakfast and lunch crowds, he called Jess into his office.

"What's up, boss?" she asked, plopping down in the metal chair.

Removing his reading glasses, he massaged the bridge of his nose. "I fired Sherry a little while ago."

"Yes!" Jess mouthed, giving the air a fist punch.

"I agree!" Alistair said with a chuckle. "We're definitely better off without her. For the time being, I plan to handle the big-picture responsibilities myself. Payroll and bank deposits, those kinds of things. But I need someone to manage the front end. Which, as you know, I'm still learning. I'd like for you to be my line manager."

"Me?" Jess said, jabbing her thumb at her chest. "What about Jasmine? We do the same job."

"You and Jasmine are both hard workers. I won't argue that. But you're older and you've been here longer. Therefore, I think you've earned this opportunity."

"I'm only a year older, and I've only been here six months longer. We've been splitting the duties, picking up Sherry's slack, for a while now. Why don't you make me opening manager and Jasmine closing manager? Things will be much easier now that we have Janice. Thank you for hiring her, by the way."

"And thank you for recommending her. She's a welcome addition to the staff." He sat back in his chair as he considered her suggestion. "Having co-managers could work. Although, if I have to go out of town, I'm placing you in charge."

Jess moved to the edge of her chair. "That's fine."

"All right, then," he said, tossing his hands in the air. "We'll give it a try."

Jess jumped to her feet. "Can I tell Jasmine?"

He smiled at her enthusiasm. "By all means. You can also tell her I'm giving both of you a small raise."

"Thank you, boss," she said, offering him a high five.

Jess had no sooner left his office when Henry Warner called. "Henry, my man, I didn't expect to hear from you so soon."

"Alistair, I'm glad I caught you." He sounded frantic, as was expected of a managing director of a New York investment firm. "I know I gave you until the end of the year to make a decision about rejoining the firm, but something's come up, and I really need you now."

Alistair suddenly felt sick to his stomach. The timing couldn't be worse. No way could he move to New York anytime soon. "Can you elaborate? What exactly do you need from me now?"

Henry told him about the deal they were working on. "You've worked with these gentlemen before, Alistair. They specifically asked for you. We're talking about a substantial commission if this deal goes through. We're meeting with the clients on Wednesday. I'd need you in Manhattan no later than Tuesday at noon. We'll put you up in the corporate apartment."

With a heavy heart, Alistair said, "I have obligations here. I can't just up and leave."

"It'll only be for a week, ten days max. After that, you can take the rest of the year to decide if you want to come back full-time."

Alistair let out a sigh. "I don't know, Henry."

"Take the weekend to think about it. We'll wing it on our own if necessary, but we stand a better chance of closing the deal with you on board."

Alistair promised he'd get back to him by Sunday night before ending the call. He thought about all the events that had happened since his return from New York. His affair with Olivia. The anniversary of his wife's death. The turmoil at the café. And now this invitation from Henry.

He leaned his head back against the chair, lifting his face heavenward. "Why'd you have to leave me, Mary Anne? I don't know how to make big decisions without you. If you're looking down on me from up there, please give me a sign."

CHAPTER TWENTY-FIVE

LENA

Lena was shopping online for camera equipment when Kayla called on Saturday morning to invite her on a mother-daughter outing. "I was hoping we could go for brunch and then do some shopping. Zack recommended Five Loaves Café. Wanna meet there at eleven thirty?"

"That sounds lovely," Lena said. "I'll see you then."

She scrolled through the photographs she'd taken of Kayla posing in front of the iron garden gates of the Peninsula Grill the previous evening. Her daughter made for a striking figure with her long blonde hair and toned body. If the blog progressed as Lena hoped, she would have Kayla model some of the clothes from the boutiques and vendors she planned to showcase.

Lena had enjoyed the night out with Kayla and Zack. They'd lingered for a long while after dinner. She told them about her photography and the blog. She'd even told them about the Dowdys, including her concerns that Jade was physically abusing Phyllis and her confrontation with Jade upon her return from Nashville.

When they'd finally left the restaurant around eleven, they'd gone for the promised visit with Biscuit. Zack's uncle's compound consisted of an imposing Federal-style main home and adjacent carriage house situated amid manicured grounds with grand porches and bluestone terraces. They'd sat together in the courtyard for over an hour, sipping glasses of cabernet while Biscuit frolicked in the grass at their feet. Kayla was a happier person, and as a result, she was kinder to and more considerate of her mother. Or perhaps the change in their relationship had nothing to do with Zack. Maybe Lena and Kayla were simply able to relax and be themselves with Charles out of the picture. Regardless, instead of questioning Kayla's transformation—her sudden maturity—Lena vowed to embrace it.

She remembered Kayla's words from the night before. *You're like this whole new person. You seem so happy . . . Dad is not a nice person, Mom. He doesn't deserve you. And you deserve better.*

Being near Kayla was yet another reason for Lena to make a permanent move to Charleston.

She was leaving the condo to meet Kayla when the elevator doors opened and two police officers emerged—a young man and an older woman, both tall and physically fit. The policewoman's gaze shifted from her notepad to Lena to the brass number four on the wall beside Olivia's door. "Are you Lena Browder?"

"I am." Lena's first thought was of Kayla, that she'd been in an accident. "Is my daughter okay?"

The officers remained silent, staring at her with deadpan expressions.

Panic rose in her chest. "Please, God. Tell me nothing has happened to my daughter."

The officers exchanged a glance. "We don't know anything about your daughter, ma'am," the policewoman said. "I'm Officer Wise, and my partner is Officer Cole. We need you to come with us to police headquarters. You're wanted for questioning in a case we're working on."

Relief that Kayla wasn't involved morphed into fear that she herself was in some kind of trouble. "What's the nature of this case?"

"It involves an assault and battery on an elderly woman," Officer Wise said.

Lena smelled a rat. The only elderly person she knew in Charleston was Phyllis. And yesterday, she'd accused Jade of abusing Phyllis. Was Jade blaming her for the bruises on Phyllis's back, or had something else happened to her elderly friend? "Am I under arrest?"

"Not yet," Officer Cole said. "For now, we just need to ask you a few questions."

She had no choice but to go with them to tell her side of the story and straighten out this mess. Lena slipped her hand in her purse for her cell phone.

"What're you doing?" Wise said, yanking the bag away. "Are you carrying a concealed weapon in there?"

Lena felt light-headed. "I was looking for my phone to call my daughter. She's expecting me to meet her in ten minutes for lunch. She'll be worried when I don't show up at the restaurant."

Wise dumped the contents of Lena's purse on a nearby console table. Her wallet, cell phone, a memory card for her camera, and a handful of coins spilled out. Satisfied there was no weapon, Wise scraped the contents back into her purse.

Cole jabbed at the elevator button. "You can either ride with us or drive your own car."

"I'll drive my own car to save you from having to bring me back after the inquiry."

"You mean, if you're not further detained," Cole said as the elevator doors opened.

Lena gulped and followed them into the elevator.

They parted on the ground floor. Lena went to the garage for Olivia's Volkswagen while Cole and Wise waited for her in the patrol car parked on the curb outside of the building. She tailed the patrol car closely as they raced down Broad Street to Lockwood Drive to an area of Charleston she'd never been before.

Lena called Kayla on the way, explaining that something important had come up and she wouldn't be able to meet her for brunch.

"I hope nothing's wrong," Kayla said in a concerned tone.

Lena debated how much to tell her daughter. "I'm not sure, honestly. Something has come up with Phyllis, my elderly friend I told you about last night. I'll call you back when I know more." She hung up before Kayla could press her for more information.

When they arrived at the police station, Wise and Cole escorted Lena to a windowless interrogation room where Detective Lauren Malone was waiting to question her. The detective was young and pretty with a thick mane of auburn hair and a steely glare that sent chills down Lena's spine. She motioned Lena to an empty chair opposite her. "Have a seat."

Lena did as instructed. "Look, Detective, I'm from Virginia. Phyllis Dowdy is the only elderly person I know in Charleston, so I have to assume this is about her. I consider her a friend. Please tell me she hasn't been hurt in any way."

Malone's expression softened a bit. "Your *friend* has accused you of pushing her down a short flight of stairs. Her daughter claims she came home from a business trip to Nashville and found her mother lying on the kitchen floor. Phyllis underwent surgery this morning for a partial hip replacement."

Lena gasped. "Oh no! Poor Phyllis."

"We've interviewed Phyllis and Jade separately. The details of their reports match. These are very serious crimes, Mrs. Browder. Assault and battery and elder abuse are felonies. Both carry up to a twenty-year sentence. I'd like to hear your side of the story. Where were you between three and five yesterday afternoon?"

Perspiration broke out on Lena's forehead and trickled down her back. After taking a moment to compose herself, beginning with the day she first met Jade, she recounted the events leading up to the discovery of the bruises and her confrontation with Jade upon her return from Nashville.

When she'd finished talking, Malone said, "That's all well and good, Mrs. Browder. But you still haven't answered my question. Where were you yesterday between three and five p.m.?"

"Well, let's see," Lena said, staring up at the ceiling as she thought about the events of the previous afternoon. "Jade got home from her trip around three. After our brief exchange on the sidewalk in front of their house, I returned to my friend's condo where I'm staying. I went out for a walk with my camera. I was gone for a couple of hours."

After grilling her extensively about street names and times and the images she'd captured, Malone stood abruptly and left the room. "I'll be right back," she said, but she was gone for more than two hours.

Lena was frantic by the time she returned. "Without an alibi to confirm your whereabouts during the time of Mrs. Dowdy's accident, I have no choice but to arrest you for the crime. You'll be held in custody until your arraignment on Monday morning." She gestured to a phone on a nearby table. "You may use the phone. I suggest you call your attorney."

Lena removed her phone from her purse. "May I use my own phone?"

Malone held her hand out as if to say, *Be my guest.*

Lena's hands shook as she entered the numbers on the screen, and she willed her voice to remain calm when she heard Kayla's voice. "Listen carefully, Kayla. I'm at the police station. There's been a terrible misunderstanding. Phyllis fell and broke her hip. She's accusing me of pushing her down the stairs. I'm being charged with assault and battery and elder abuse."

Lena heard a sharp intake of breath on the other end of the line. "That's horrible, Mom! You of all people. You'd never hurt a fly. How can I help? Should I call Daddy?"

"No! Whatever you do, don't call your father." There was only one person she trusted implicitly. She hated to bother him, especially when he had so many problems of his own. "Call Alistair. I'll text you his number."

"You don't have to spend the night in jail, do you? They're only questioning you, right?"

"No, sweetheart. They've arrested me. I'll have to stay in jail until my arraignment on Monday morning. I need to find an attorney."

"Do you want me to call Zack's uncle? From what I understand, he's one of the best criminal attorneys in Charleston."

"Maybe. I don't know what to do. See what Alistair says." Lena brought a trembling hand to her face. "Oh, honey. I'm so sorry to put you in this position. I've ruined your weekend."

"Please! This isn't your fault, Mom. You would never do something like this. Hang in there. Help is on the way."

A torrent of tears threatened as she ended the call and stared down at her lap. She'd read dozens of news stories about innocent people being accused of crimes they didn't commit that had landed them in prison for decades. Surely that wouldn't happen to her.

She'd never felt so alone in her life. Alone and terrified out of her mind. But despite her fear and loneliness, she found it very telling that her husband was the last person she wanted to turn to during the worst crisis of her life.

CHAPTER TWENTY-SIX

OLIVIA

Olivia stalked Alistair like a lovesick teenager, rushing to the nearest window every time she heard his truck start up or the crush of gravel in the driveway. If only he didn't live so close.

You're just stir-crazy, Liv. You're not used to being cooped up with virtually no human interaction.

The remnants of the tropical storm had ushered in the first significant cold weather of the season, and after a brisk walk on Friday morning, she'd settled herself on the sofa in front of the gas fire and commenced a writing spree that had lasted for more than twenty-four hours. Between periodic visits to the window to spy on Alistair and frequently checking her email for Lena's response to the chapters she'd sent, she managed to write nearly ten thousand words. She ate salads and drank hot tea. She commended herself for saving money by not dining out. If she were in Charleston, she wouldn't have been able to resist the temptation to visit one of her favorite restaurants.

Alistair had left the house midmorning on Friday and returned late afternoon. He stayed home on Friday night, turning the light out in his master bedroom by eleven. On Saturday morning, she'd been awake, working by the fire, when she'd heard his engine start up before six.

She'd hurried to the kitchen window in time to see his truck turning around and driving slowly down the driveway. She'd gone upstairs to her room and crawled into bed, curling up beneath the warm covers. Not only did she miss the feel of his warm body next to hers, but she missed everything about him. His smile. His dry humor and sharp wit. His omelets. She'd had her chance on Thursday night, but she'd sent him away. *I can't afford the distraction right now. I really need to finish this first draft.* And finish it she would, if she wanted to keep her condo and pay her bills.

She'd dozed off and slept dreamlessly for three hours. When she'd awakened around nine, her characters were once again at the forefront of her mind. After a short writing sprint of six hundred words, she'd taken a long walk. Showered and dressed in jeans and a sweater, she was in the kitchen slathering deli mustard on a slice of grainy bread around one o'clock that afternoon when Alistair returned home. Her body ached for him as she watched him get out of his truck and hurry inside. How she longed to feel his arms around her. She was still standing there ten minutes later, daydreaming of making love to him with a half of her uneaten ham sandwich in hand, when he emerged from the house carrying a duffel bag. She flew out the front door and across the lawn, stopping when her bare feet encountered the gravel in the driveway.

"Yoo-hoo, Alistair! Are you going somewhere?" She felt the heat rising in her face. "Not that it's any of my business. I was just so worried the last time you left town when Mike had his accident. I hope the boys are okay. Do you need me to get the mail or take out the trash for you while you're gone?"

Tossing his duffel in the back seat of his truck, he slammed the door and walked toward her. "I appreciate your concern, and thanks for the offer, but I shouldn't be gone long. I'm on my way to Charleston. Lena's daughter, Kayla, called me a little while ago. Lena's been arrested. The situation is serious. She wants me to come."

Lena? Arrested? The house swap had been Olivia's idea. If Lena had gotten herself into trouble in Charleston, Olivia's town, she needed to be there. "I'm going with you. Give me a minute to pack." Before he could object, she turned away from him and hopped on cold feet back across the yard.

Alistair followed her into the house. "Seriously, Olivia. You don't need to do this. I know you're busy with your book. I can handle the situation alone."

"I'm coming," Olivia said, already halfway up the stairs. "End of discussion."

"We need to get on the road," he called after her. "What can I do to help you get ready?"

"Turn off the fire and lock everything up," she hollered back.

Between packing an assortment of clothes and gathering her toiletries, she paused for a brief moment at the window. She would miss the view. The cottage. Her sanctuary. While she complained about being isolated, the truth was, she'd fallen in love with the Northern Neck and hated to leave. But she knew Charleston. Not only could she show Alistair around, but she could help Lena find whatever assistance she needed.

She lugged her suitcase back downstairs, handing it to Alistair to take to the car while she straightened up the living room and the kitchen. Slipping her laptop into her tote bag, she took one more look around the downstairs before locking the front door.

Alistair was waiting for her in the truck with the engine running, and he took off down the driveway before she could buckle her seat belt. When they reached the main road, he turned left toward Irvington.

"Exactly what kind of trouble is Lena in?" she asked.

"Kayla didn't know much, only that it had something to do with one of Lena's friend's elderly mother."

"Right. I remember Lena mentioning her."

He jerked his head toward her. "You've been in touch with Lena?"

"Of course. Why does that surprise you?"

"Because until you showed up two weeks ago, I'd never heard Lena mention you."

Ouch! "Lena and I were never that close in college, but we were friends nonetheless. When we reconnected that day in the Atlanta airport, we both realized how desperately we needed a friend." *Take that, Mr. Wise Guy. Why didn't Lena reach out to you, her supposed best friend, instead of running away?*

Alistair came to a rolling stop at the main intersection in Irvington before speeding off toward White Stone. "What exactly did Lena tell you about this friend's elderly mother?"

"Only that she was staying with the mother while the friend was out of town on business."

"And when did she tell you this?" Alistair asked.

"On Thursday, when I texted her asking if she'd be willing to read my first chapters." Olivia realized her mistake right away.

He tightened his grip on the steering wheel as they ascended the Rappahannock River bridge. "So you let her read your novel but not me?"

"Yes, Alistair, I did. After I was so rude to you about it, I realized that I needed someone to read it, to see if it had any potential. Lena seemed to be the right person for the job considering her fondness for romance novels."

He pursed his lips as he thought about it. "I guess that makes sense."

Olivia stared out the window at the boats cruising at fast speeds on the river below them. "For the record, Alistair, I'm not writing about us." She paused. "Okay, so maybe that's not entirely true. I'm not writing about you and me. My protagonist is a woman attempting to move on with her life after discovering her husband is gay."

Some of the tension drained from his body. "I can see how that would be therapeutic for you."

"And cheaper than seeing a shrink," she said with an awkward laugh. "Truth is, I've learned quite a lot about myself. So many things about my marriage make sense to me now."

"Good. As long as I'm not a part of your story."

Hostile. This is going to be a long ride. "What else did Kayla tell you about Lena's arrest?"

"Lena's friend's mother claims that Lena pushed her down the stairs. The mother suffered a broken hip as a result of the fall."

Olivia's jaw dropped. "That's absurd. Lena would never do something like that."

"Right? Kayla's trying to find out more. She promised to call me when she does."

"How did Kayla get involved? Last I heard, when I saw Lena in Atlanta, her daughter was one of the reasons she was running away from home."

"Their relationship has been troubled since Kayla went away to college. But it sounds like they're trying to make amends. Kayla is down there visiting her boyfriend, who coincidentally is from Charleston and has an uncle who's a criminal attorney. The uncle is out of town for the weekend, but Zack, the boyfriend, is trying to track him down."

Olivia knitted her eyebrows. "I'm curious who the uncle is."

"Kayla didn't mention any names."

"My ex-husband is a corporate lawyer. If the uncle is unavailable, I know of several other criminal attorneys."

"I'll keep that in mind." When they came to a T intersection, Alistair made a right-hand turn onto Highway 33 and reclined his seat slightly. "We have a seven-hour drive ahead of us. You might as well get some work done." He eyed her laptop in her bag at her feet. "I need to make one quick phone call, and then I'll be quiet so as not to disturb you." He lifted his phone from the console to his ear.

While he talked, Olivia listened to his side of the conversation. "I'm glad I caught you, Jess. The timing's horrible, I know, but I have to go out of town on an emergency. Are you and Jasmine okay to hold down the fort for a few days?"

He paused while Jess talked.

"No, it's not the boys this time. I'm helping out a friend. How's business? Do our customers like the new menu?"

Another pause.

"Glad to hear it. The turkey panini is my favorite as well. Listen, Jess, I don't want you to hesitate to call me if you need me. Otherwise, I'll be in touch in a couple of days."

"Is everything okay at the café?" Olivia asked after he'd ended the call.

"It will be in time. I had to fire Sherry this morning, but Jess and Jasmine are very capable."

No wonder he's been spending so much time at the café. "Who's going to take Sherry's place?"

"I am. At least for now."

She wanted to ask him how that affected his pending job offer in New York, but she decided it best not to pry. She removed her computer from her bag and opened it on her lap. "You don't have to be quiet on my account. Just pretend I'm not here. Listen to the radio or whatever you'd normally do."

"If you're sure," he said, already reaching for the volume knob.

Olivia actually *did* mind, but it was his truck, and he was driving. She preferred working in silence, and it took her at least thirty minutes, until they were merging onto the interstate toward Richmond, to focus. Once she got into her zone, however, she was able to work solid until the ringing of Alistair's phone startled her several hours later.

Looking up from her computer, she saw a sign welcoming them to Fayetteville, North Carolina. Eavesdropping, she surmised that the call was from Kayla.

"You're kidding."

"She does? Hmm, that's not good. Poor Lena."

"All right then, that's what we'll do."

"I'm not sure yet. I'll text you when I get in."

He dropped the phone back into the cup holder. "That was Kayla."

"I gathered," Olivia said. "What'd she say?"

"Zack was able to get in touch with his uncle. His name is Owen Dixon, and he's agreed to take the case," said Alistair.

"Owen would be my first choice for the job. He and my ex went to law school together at the University of South Carolina. His wife, Diane, was a friend of mine. Poor thing, she passed away a few years ago from a stroke."

That seemed to resonate with Alistair, and a sympathetic look crossed his face. "Apparently, he's already spoken to the police about Lena's case. He confirmed that the woman, the friend's mother whose name is Phyllis, is accusing Lena of pushing her down the stairs. They are charging Lena with assault and battery and elder abuse. She'll have to stay in jail until the arraignment hearing on Monday morning."

Olivia lifted her phone from her bag and conducted a Google search. "Both charges are felonies. If convicted, she could go to prison for a very long time."

Alistair nodded, his expression grim. "It's very serious. There's one bit of good news. The police are allowing Kayla and me to visit her tomorrow."

"I know Lena will be glad to see you."

"We'll need a place to stay," Alistair said. "Can you recommend a good hotel?"

Olivia had assumed she'd stay at her condo. She didn't think Lena would mind, and she couldn't afford a hotel room in downtown Charleston. "You're welcome to stay at my condo with me, if you don't mind sleeping on the couch."

With his eyes on the road, Alistair said, "I don't feel right about that, Olivia. You and Lena exchanged homes for the month. Technically, she's renting the condo from you. It seems like an invasion of privacy."

"You're right," Olivia said with a sigh. "I wouldn't be happy, either, if Lena suddenly showed up at the cottage. There's a boutique hotel across the street from my condo. I'll see if they have any availability, but I'm warning you, the rates will be high on a weekend night during peak season."

"It doesn't matter. Book two rooms and charge them to my American Express." He tugged his wallet out of his back pocket and set it down on the console.

She located the website and requested two nights' accommodations at the HarbourView Inn. "There's only one suite left. It's six hundred and fifty dollars a night, but it has a bedroom with a king and a sitting room with a sleeper sofa."

"Book it."

She completed the reservation and returned his credit card to his wallet.

"We're going to need gas soon," Alistair said, glancing down at his dashboard. "We might as well get dinner when we stop."

"That's fine," she said, returning her attention to her computer.

They drove another thirty minutes before exiting the interstate in Lumberton. After filling up with gas, they continued on to a Chick-fil-A, where they went inside to use the restroom and ordered their food to go.

She offered to drive as they were walking back to the car. "If you need a break."

"I'm fine. I'm used to driving long distances."

Olivia didn't argue. Dusk had fallen, and she hated driving in the dark. After she'd eaten her sandwich, she tried working some more on her manuscript, but the bright computer screen in the darkened truck strained her eyes. She attempted to make idle conversation with Alistair—about the damage from the recent hurricane to the Florida Panhandle and his plans to spend the upcoming holidays with his sons. She even tried talking to him about fishing, but his mood was sullen, his responses curt. He was undoubtedly concerned about Lena, but Olivia sensed something else was bothering him as well—the situation at the Jumpstart Café or his pending job offer in New York.

The dark highway loomed ahead of them. Small cars zipped in and out around them, but Alistair drove in the right-hand lane at a steady speed just above the speed limit. The songs on his country music station sounded the same to her, but she didn't dare suggest changing it. She'd brought headphones with her, and she yearned to listen to one of her audiobooks on her iPhone, but she feared she'd come across as rude.

Coming with him to Charleston had been a mistake. Did she have an ulterior motive, or had it simply been a split-second decision?

It was almost ten o'clock and her nerves were frayed by the time they arrived at the hotel. When he turned his truck over to the valet attendant, she retrieved her suitcase from the back seat and headed across the street.

"Where're you going?" Alistair called after her.

"I'm staying at my condo," she said over her shoulder.

She heard him say, "Suit yourself," but she kept walking without looking back.

CHAPTER TWENTY-SEVEN

LENA

The memory of Kayla's encouraging words helped Lena make it through her first desolate night in jail. *This isn't your fault, Mom. You would never do something like this. Hang in there. Help is on the way.*

She certainly hoped help was on the way. She didn't know how much more she could take. She'd shed a steady stream of tears since she'd ended her phone call with Kayla the previous afternoon. She'd bawled throughout the booking process, especially when they'd strip-searched her, forced her to shower, and given her this god-awful orange jumpsuit to wear.

Lena had a clear view of the clock on the wall in the hallway outside her cell. Every second that ticked off the clock of the seemingly endless hours wore her down more, like a hammer pounding a nail. Her cellmate, Juana, whose expression was set in a permanent scowl, said they were fortunate to be able to see the clock. But Lena thought maybe it was better not to know the time. She cowered in the corner of her bed at the sounds from the neighboring cells, the crying and screaming of obscenities and calling out for the guard. The thin mattress was lumpy, her pillow hard as a brick, and the smells from the commode assaulted her nose. The food was inedible, and her stomach ached from hunger.

Juana claimed it could be worse. "This ain't nothing compared to prison. Trust me, I been there a time or two myself."

With nothing to do but wait, Lena passed the time by reflecting on the events of her life that had led her to this juncture. She was a pushover, letting people take advantage of her at every turn. Charles. Kayla. Jade. She asked herself why she'd even agreed to stay with Phyllis. But she knew the answer. She'd been afraid to tell Jade no. Sure, she felt sorry for the old woman. Phyllis's own daughter neglected and abused her. But she'd genuinely enjoyed Phyllis's company and considered her a friend. Why had Phyllis turned on her? She'd introduced her to audiobooks, taken her on outings to the computer and grocery stores, cleaned her room, and cooked her favorite recipe for chicken parmesan. *And this is the thanks I get.*

In the blink of an eye, she'd lost control of her life based on an accusation against her. She'd refuted the accusation with her version of the story. Why did the police believe Phyllis and Jade over Lena? Was it simply a matter of two against one? What proof did they have, aside from Lena's inability to verify her whereabouts at the time of the accident? What happened to innocent until proven guilty?

When a guard escorted her to a cubicle in the visitation room late Sunday morning, Lena broke into a hysterical fit of crying when she saw Kayla perched on the stool with Alistair standing behind her. Despite their brave smiles, she could tell they were shocked to see her being treated like a common criminal.

When Lena lifted the phone receiver to her ear, Alistair spoke to her in the familiar voice that had comforted her throughout much of her lifetime. "We're gonna get you out of this mess, Lena. We've been through a lot together. I'm here for you now, and I won't leave you until the charges have been dropped."

Kayla snatched the phone away from him. "Hang in there a little while longer, Mom. Zack's uncle has agreed to take your case. He doesn't get back from his trip until late tonight, but he'll be here in the morning for the arraignment."

"But what if he can't get me out?" she sobbed. "What if I have to go to prison for the rest of my life? I'm so scared. I don't understand why they're taking Phyllis and Jade's word over mine."

Kayla cocked her head to the side, looking up at Alistair with a bewildered expression. He nudged her off the stool and sat down. "I need you to stop crying, Lena, and tell me about these so-called friends of yours."

The fear in Kayla's beautiful blue eyes weighed heavily on Lena. Who wouldn't be terrified seeing their mother in a convict's jumpsuit? Lena sat up straighter in her chair. She needed to prove her strength to Kayla. She would fight these charges. She would not be the victim of Jade's appalling charade.

"Okay." She swiped her tears away and sucked in a deep, unsteady breath. "I can do that."

"Why don't you start by telling us how you came to know the Dowdys?"

Lena's grip on the phone tightened. "I met Jade my second day in Charleston. We were both on the dock at Waterfront Park photographing the bridge, and we got to talking. We went for coffee afterward, and Jade told me about her wedding photography business. She asked if I wanted to be her assistant, and I jumped at the chance to work with a professional. She seemed friendly enough at first, but it didn't take long for me to realize she's not a nice person."

"Why'd you continue working with her?" he asked.

Lena shrugged. "Because I was learning a lot. Putting up with her foul moods seemed a small price to pay for the experience. Jade's a genius. I'll give her credit for that."

"When did you first meet the mother?"

"The same day I met Jade, but later. She offered to lend me some of her equipment. She suggested I come to their house for dinner and to have a look in her supply closet."

Lena suddenly remembered returning the equipment before meeting Kayla and Zack for dinner on Friday night. The accident must have already happened, which explains why the Dowdys' house had seemed so quiet at the time.

"Anyway," Lena continued, "Phyllis has age-related macular degeneration. She sees very little, but she still has a lot of spunk and gets around very well considering her limitations. When I met her that first night, it was obvious that Jade was neglecting Phyllis. I felt sorry for her, so I spent some time with her, and we became friends."

Alistair's lips parted in a gentle smile. "I'd expect nothing less from my kindhearted best friend. You're always looking out for those less fortunate than you."

Am I? Lena wasn't sure that was true.

"Explain to me why you were staying with Phyllis," Alistair said. "Where was Jade?"

"Jade's home and business is in Nashville. But she's been living in Charleston for the past six months, taking care of her mother. She got an offer on her business and flew up there last week to discuss the terms with the potential buyer. It happened last minute. She was only supposed to be gone for one night. Whether or not she'd planned it, she was gone for two. I've seen the bruises. On two separate occasions when I was staying with her. Jade is the one abusing Phyllis. Not me."

"Where are these bruises?" Alistair asked.

"On her back and arms. I confronted Jade about them when she returned from her trip to Nashville."

Alistair moved to the edge of the stool. "Wait a minute. Are you saying you accused Jade of abusing her mother?"

She gave him a solemn nod. "I was worried about Phyllis. I told Jade if I found out she was responsible for the bruises, I would report her to the authorities."

Comprehension crossed Alistair's face. "So she was running scared, and she turned you in to the police before you could beat her to it."

"That's the only thing that makes sense," Lena said. "I can't figure out why Phyllis went along with her, though. I thought we were friends."

With elbows propped on the table, phone tucked under his chin, he said, "Because Jade threatened her. And Phyllis is terrified of Jade."

A faraway look settled on his face, and Lena could see the wheels in motion in his brilliant mind. "What're you thinking, Alistair?"

"I have an idea. I'm not sure it'll work, but it's worth a try." He got to his feet, holding the phone up so he and Kayla could both hear Lena. "Do either of you know anything about the hospitals around here?"

Kayla shook her head. "No, but I can ask Zack. He's waiting in the car for me."

"You're not planning to visit Phyllis, are you?" Lena asked.

"I am, actually. Unless you think her daughter might be permanently stationed at her bedside."

Lena let out a sarcastic laugh. "*Devoted* is not a word I'd use to describe Jade. But I'm warning you, Alistair. Jade is a formidable woman. I'd hate for you to make the situation worse."

"I'll be careful. I promise." He winked at Lena. "What about other family members? Does Jade have any siblings?"

"Yes! She has a sister, Marie, who lives in Boston. Phyllis speaks of her younger daughter fondly, but I get the impression she doesn't visit often."

"What do you know about Marie?" he asked. "Is she married? Does she have children? A career?"

"She's a doctor, an orthopedic surgeon," Lena said. "And she has a family. That's all I know."

The guard entered the room, signaling that their time was up.

"I'm so sorry to have dragged the two of you into this mess." Lena locked eyes with her daughter through the window. "Zack mentioned at dinner that his uncle is semiretired. Are you sure he doesn't mind taking my case?"

"Not at all," Kayla said. "He's happy to help."

Alistair added, "Olivia says Owen's the best in town."

Lena's face brightened. "I forgot to ask you about Olivia. How is she? Is she enjoying the cottage?"

"Seems to be. She came with me, actually. She's staying at her condo. I hope you don't mind. There was only one hotel room available."

"Why would I mind? It's her condo. Tell her to push my stuff aside." In the midst of the chaos of the past few days, she'd forgotten about the sample chapters Olivia had sent her. "Oh! And tell Olivia I haven't had a chance to email her back, but I loved her chapters. She has a gift, and she absolutely must keep writing."

Alistair smiled, and there was a warmth in his brown eyes that Lena hadn't seen since Mary Anne died. "I'll be sure to tell her. I know that'll make her happy."

Kayla took the phone from Alistair. "Mom, are you sure you don't want me to call Dad? I think he should know about this situation. We're gonna need money for bail."

"Please don't call him, Kayla. I left home for a number of reasons, one of which was to prove to myself that I can stand on my own two feet. I can't admit defeat at the first sign of trouble. Alistair can post bail, and I'll pay him back."

Alistair took the phone one last time. "Stay strong, sweet Lena. We're gonna get you outta here first thing in the morning."

Lena gulped back yet another sob as the guard led her from the room, separating her from the two people she loved most in the world.

CHAPTER TWENTY-EIGHT

ALISTAIR

Alistair and Kayla left the police station and walked together to the parking lot. The crisp autumn air felt refreshing after being locked up in a windowless room for an hour. He couldn't help but wonder how Lena must feel being behind bars.

Kayla's young man was waiting for her, leaning against the hood of a gray Ford Explorer. He was handsome in an artsy way with hair a tad long for Alistair's taste, but the way Zack looked at Kayla left little doubt that his feelings for her were genuine.

Kayla made the introductions, and the men shook hands. "I've known Kayla her entire life," Alistair said. "She's like a daughter to me. If you hurt her, you'll have to answer to me."

"Alistair!" Kayla's face beamed red as she nudged him with her elbow.

"I'm just looking out for you." He placed an arm around Kayla's waist in a half hug.

"How'd it go with your mom?" Zack asked with concern in his blue eyes.

Kayla looked down at the ground. "She's trying to be brave, but I can tell she's scared."

"I appreciate your uncle's willingness to help," Alistair said.

"Of course. I only wish he were here now, although I doubt there's much he could do on the weekend."

Kayla moved over beside her boyfriend. "What can you tell us about the hospitals in the area? Where would the ambulance have taken an old lady with a broken hip?"

He stared up at the sky as he thought about it. "Probably Roper, which is not far from here. Or if her condition was more serious, MUSC, the Medical University of South Carolina. It's right next door to Roper. Why? Are you planning a visit?"

Alistair nodded. "I'm not sure what good it'll do, but it's worth a try. I'm fresh out of better ideas."

"I hope you know what you're doing," Kayla said. "What if someone figures out who you are? You won't be of any use to Mom if you're in jail with her."

"Trust me, I have no intention of going to jail. Just being in the visitation room gave me the willies."

Kayla smiled. "I know what you mean."

Zack opened the passenger door of his Explorer. "Can we give you a lift?"

"No, but thanks. I have my truck."

Zack pointed in the direction of a bridge off to his left. "You'll wanna go back toward downtown past the Ashley River Bridge. Take a left onto Calhoun, and Roper will be immediately on your left."

Alistair got in his truck and drove out of the parking lot. At the bare minimum, he aimed to have a word in private with Phyllis in the hope that he'd gain some insight into the accusation she'd made against Lena. Ideally, he'd have a chance to speak with Marie. She was an orthopedic surgeon. Surely she'd flown to her mother's bedside when learning of her broken hip.

He had no trouble finding the hospital or an empty space in the parking deck. He stopped at the gift shop in the lobby and bought a bud vase with three yellow roses and a sprig of baby's breath before proceeding to the information desk.

"Can you tell me what room my aunt is in, please? Her name is Phyllis Dowdy."

The elderly volunteer typed on her computer's keyboard and then smiled up at him. "She's in room number 435." She pointed him to a nearby bank of elevators.

Alistair, having spent a lot of time in hospitals when his wife was sick, knew how things worked. Nurses were usually too busy to pay much attention to visitors, and they rarely spent more than a few minutes with a patient at any given time. He was relieved to find Phyllis alone in her room. She was sitting up in bed—her gray hair matted to her head as though it hadn't seen a brush in days—jabbing her finger at an iPad in her lap.

Alistair knocked lightly on the door. "Excuse me, Mrs. Dowdy?"

She looked straight at him, but he knew she couldn't see him. "Yes. Who's there?"

"I'm Al Hoffman, a volunteer here at the hospital. I wanted to stop by to see if I can help you with anything or get you something."

She lifted the iPad, holding it out to him. "Please! My vision's impaired. Can you help me find an audiobook on my iPad? I'm looking for a Mary Higgins Clark novel. I've forgotten the title, but it was released earlier in the year. Last spring, I think. I know it's on here somewhere. My friend downloaded it for me a few days ago."

Alistair wondered if that friend was Lena. "Of course." He entered the room, placing the bud vase on the windowsill, and then removed the iPad from her hands. The Audible app was open on the screen, and the Mary Higgins Clark title was at the top of her list of books. "It's in your library. We just need to download it." He clicked the download arrow. "It'll only take a minute. Do you mind if I sit down while we wait? I want to make sure it's working for you before I leave."

"Of course not. I could use the company."

He pulled the desk chair up close to the bed. Bags of clear fluid hung from a pole, dripping through plastic tubing to the IV in her right arm, while monitors on the wall behind her indicated a strong heart rate, her blood pressure, and her oxygen saturation levels.

"How're you feeling today?" he asked.

Her blue eyes were alert, despite the disease. "Pretty good for an old lady with a broken hip."

Alistair feigned surprise. "A broken hip? That sounds painful. How did it happen? Did you have a fall?"

She gripped the blanket with her gnarled fingers. "My daughter claims I fell down the short flight of stairs between my dining room and kitchen."

"Your daughter *claims* you fell down the stairs? Do you not remember how it happened?"

Phyllis scrunched her face up, as though confused. "Not really, no. I've lived in that house going on forty years. I may be blind, but I know my way around."

"Were you alone at the time?" Alistair asked. "Is it possible that you tripped over something?"

"My daughter was with me. She says . . . well, never mind what she says. I don't think she's right."

Her daughter says what? That Lena pushed her. And Phyllis doesn't think she's right?

Alistair decided not to press her about the fall. "Does your daughter live in Charleston?"

"One of them does. At least temporarily. Jade's my caretaker. My other daughter, Marie, lives in Boston."

Bingo, Alistair thought. "And what does Marie do?"

"She and her husband are both doctors."

"You must be very proud," Alistair said. "What kind of doctors are they?"

"She's an orthopedic surgeon, and he's a cardiologist. I have two granddaughters, Lizzie and Kelly, ages ten and eight."

Alistair accessed the contacts app on Phyllis's iPad and searched for Marie. There was only one Marie, a Marie Murphy with an address listed in Boston. Removing his phone from his pocket, he snapped a photograph of the contact information.

"Does your daughter in Boston know about your accident? Being an orthopedic surgeon, I imagine she's concerned about your recovery."

"I'm not sure if Jade even called her. She says she did, but she and Marie don't get along so well."

Whether they got along or not was beside the point. Wouldn't Jade have called her sister about something as serious as their mother's accident? Unless she was hiding something.

"Here." He gently placed the iPad in Phyllis's hands. "I believe this is the novel you're looking for." He spotted a set of red headphones on the bed table. "Would you like me to put your headphones on?"

"That would be lovely, dear man. Thank you. You've spared an old blind woman hours of boredom. I was waiting for Jade to show up, but no telling when that'll be."

He secured the headphones over her ears and tapped the play button. "Can you hear it?" he asked in a loud voice.

She gave him a thumbs-up, rested her head back against the pillows, and closed her eyes.

She was a lovely woman. He could see how Lena would befriend her. Phyllis said her *daughter* was with her when the accident happened. She didn't mention anything about a friend being there at the time.

Alistair slipped out of the room and rode down in the elevator, exiting the hospital through the same doors he'd entered. He walked to a nearby picnic area and sat down at a round metal table. Locating the image of Marie's contact information on his phone, he tapped her number into his keypad and placed the call. The line rang three times before a woman answered.

"May I speak with Marie Murphy, please?"

"Who's calling?" the woman said in a curt but friendly voice.

"My name is Alistair Hoffman, and I'm calling from Charleston. I'm a friend of a friend of your mother's. Are you aware that Phyllis had a bad fall and underwent partial hip replacement surgery yesterday?"

There was a gasp followed by silence. Just as he'd suspected. Jade had not told her sister about their mother's accident.

"I'm sorry. What did you say your name was? And who is this mutual friend you and my mother share?"

"My name is Alistair Hoffman. Lena Browder is our mutual friend."

"Oh Lena, of course. Mom talks about her all the time. Do you know if my mother's okay?"

"I've just left her hospital room at Roper. She seems fine. More than fine, actually. I admire her spunk."

"Mom is one of a kind. My sister and I aren't on the best of terms, but I can't believe she wouldn't call me about something this important."

"I'm fairly certain I know the reason for that." In delicate terms, Alistair explained everything he knew about the situation—Lena suspecting Jade of physically abusing Phyllis, and Phyllis blaming Lena for the fall.

"I can't believe this," Marie said in an incredulous tone. "I wouldn't put it past Jade to do something so underhanded, but this is totally out of character for Mom."

"I could be wrong, but I have a feeling Phyllis isn't aware that charges have been brought against Lena." Alistair watched as a middle-aged woman supporting an elderly woman's arm walked past him, making him think of Lena and Phyllis. "Lena and I have been best friends since childhood. I can say with absolute certainty that she would never do something like this. She really cares about your mother, Marie. She thinks of her as a friend."

"From what I've heard from Mom, the feeling is mutual. Thank you for calling me, Alistair. I'll be on the next available flight to Charleston. One way or another, I *will* get to the bottom of it."

As he ended the call, Alistair felt more optimistic than he had since learning of Lena's arrest. The first pangs of hunger struck, and he rose from the table in search of food. He crossed through the main section of the MUSC campus and over Ashley Avenue to a quaint-looking sandwich shop. He ordered a turkey and swiss on rye and went upstairs to the outdoor porch to wait for his order. Over the railing, as he observed a young couple walking hand in hand on the sidewalk below, the reality of his circumstances hit hard. He was having lunch alone in a strange restaurant in one of the most romantic cities in the world. With the remainder of the afternoon stretching ahead of him, he wished he could call Olivia, but she couldn't even stand to be in the same hotel room with him, let alone show him her town. She'd been so moody during the trip. Why had she even bothered to come?

Out of the blue, the dream he'd had the night before came back to him. He'd been out on his boat with Mary Anne, toasting the life they'd shared with champagne.

"Don't be afraid to love again or feel guilty about loving another," she'd said to him. "Follow your heart, Alistair. You're a wonderful man who deserves to be happy."

He'd asked Mary Anne for a sign, to help him decide about accepting Henry's offer. She'd pointed him in the direction of love instead. He was tired of being sad and alone. The time he'd spent with Olivia had given him a glimpse of the fulfilled life they could have together. If she would consider giving him another chance, he would take it. And this time, he wouldn't mess it up.

CHAPTER TWENTY-NINE

OLIVIA

Olivia had been staring at a blank document on her computer screen since returning from a sunrise yoga class in the park. Not only was she distracted thinking about Alistair and Lena, but she worried that her condo was sending off bad writing vibes. She felt like a fish out of water in her own home. She missed the Northern Neck, the view of Carters Creek, the country roads and small-town living.

She showered, dressed, and slipped on her most comfortable walking shoes. She craved she-crab soup. There was nothing better for lunch on a chilly day, and she knew just where to find the best in town.

The Mills House Hotel bustled with activity. Guests moseyed about the lobby, and a crowd of locals—many of whom she recognized—mingled around the tiered fountain in the outdoor courtyard at a post-wedding brunch. A chef made omelets at a buffet table that stretched the length of the far side of the gardened terrace, while servers wearing white shirts and black vests offered drinks from behind a bar opposite. Olivia made her way to the restaurant and was waiting at the hostess stand outside the Barbadoes Room for a table when she heard someone calling her name. Turning in the direction of the voice, she spotted a hand waving at her above the sea of people. The sea parted, and Kate

Baker emerged with Kate Bradford at her side. Hair teased and makeup applied to perfection, both women wore slinky dresses and over-the-knee black boots with spike heels.

Ugh! Just my luck to run into the Kates when I've only been back in town for less than twenty-four hours.

"Liv, darling," Kate Baker said, pressing her cheek against Olivia's. "Where in the world have you been? We've been trying to reach you."

Olivia's eyebrows shot up. "Since when are the two of you a *we?*"

"We're friends now, believe it or not," Kate Bradford said.

Kate Baker brought her finger to her lips. "But don't tell anyone. If you blow our cover, it'll ruin our gig."

"What gig?" *Careful, Liv. The last thing you need is to get caught back up in their drama.*

"You're not gonna believe it," Kate Bradford said, and then lowered her voice. "We've been asked to do a reality TV show."

Olivia blinked hard, not sure she'd heard her correctly. "A reality TV show? You're kidding me."

"This is no joke, Olivia," Kate Baker said, pursing her Botox-injected lips. "As a matter of fact, that's why we're here. We're meeting with the producers in a few minutes."

She'd assumed the Kates were at the hotel for the wedding brunch. "Good for you. Enjoy your meeting."

When she turned back toward the hostess stand, Kate Bradford grabbed her by the arm, spinning her back around. "Wait! There's a part in this for you too."

"We've been trying to get in touch with you," Kate Baker said. "Did you block our numbers from your phone, you naughty woman?"

Olivia blushed. Not only had she blocked their numbers, but she'd deleted their numerous emails without reading them. "I've been out of town."

"That explains why you were never home when we stopped by," Kate Bradford said.

They actually came to my condo? How do they even know where I live?
"Well I'm here now," Olivia said. "What's so urgent?"

Kate Baker steepled her fingers under her chin as though praying.
"The producers want to talk to you about buying your blog posts, the
Kate Scapades. Isn't that fab?"

Buy my blog posts? Now the Kates had her full attention.

Kate Bradford consulted her Apple Watch. "It's almost time for
our meeting. But now that we've found you, we can't let you get away.
Please say you'll hang around to meet with the producers. The show
won't happen without the blog posts."

Olivia tried to sound calm, even though her heart was pounding
in her chest with excitement. "I'm not going anywhere. At least not for
a while." She gestured at the Barbadoes Room. "I'll be in the dining
room, getting a bite of lunch."

"Awesome!" Kate Bradford said. "Don't leave the restaurant until
one of us comes for you."

Kate Baker added, "If you need to find us, we'll be right around the
corner in the Best Friend Lounge."

They wiggled their fingers at her as they teetered off in their boots.
Olivia stood in shocked silence, watching them go. When the hostess
alerted her to an open seat at the bar, she crossed through the restaurant
in a daze. Settling onto the barstool, she ordered a bowl of she-crab soup
and a glass of sauvignon blanc from the bartender, Jackson, whom she
was well acquainted with from previous visits. She rarely drank during
the day and never when eating lunch alone. Not only was she rattled
by her conversation with the Kates, but she was nervous about meeting
the producers.

*Put your big-girl pants on, Liv. This could be your big chance. If noth-
ing else, you could earn enough from the sale of the blog posts to pay off your
credit card bill. Question is, can you stand working with the Kates again?*

She sipped her wine, her appetite for the creamy crab soup suddenly vanished. The television above the bar was tuned to CNN, the

box in the bottom right of the screen showing the time. Her concern mounted when an hour passed with no sign of either Kate. Maybe the producers had opted not to move ahead with plans for the show. Or maybe they'd decided not to use her blog posts after all.

By the time Kate Bradford finally appeared, she'd convinced herself that no amount of money was worth being involved with the Kates again. She'd already paid her tab and was preparing to leave.

"Sorry that took so long," Kate said. "The producers are ready to take a break from our meeting to talk to you now."

Olivia slid off the barstool to her feet, slinging her tote bag over her shoulder. "I've given it some thought, and I don't think it's a good idea for me to be involved with your reality show. But thanks for thinking of me." She crossed through the dining room toward the main lobby.

Kate, in her high heels, struggled to keep up with her. "I don't understand, Liv. It'll be fun. We work so well together."

Fun? Work so well together? Is she delusional?

"I'm working on a new project that requires my undivided attention."

Kate's heels clicked on the marble floor as they passed the reservations desk and rounded the corner to the front entrance. "Please, Olivia. Just hear them out. This venture will require zero effort on your part. The blog posts are already written. All you have to do is sell them to the producers and deposit your big fat check in the bank."

Olivia stopped in her tracks as she considered how big and fat the check might be. "All right," she said with a reluctant sigh. "I guess it can't hurt to meet with them."

Kate took her by the arm and dragged her over to where Kate Baker was waiting by the fireplace in one of the lobby's many lounging areas. She flung open the door to the corner bar, gave Olivia a gentle shove inside, and closed the door behind her.

Big-girl pants, Liv, she reminded herself as she stood inside the door.

A young man and woman in their early thirties rose from a round table in the corner to greet her. With dark hair and striking features, they looked enough alike to be twin siblings. They wore loafers and skinny jeans, and their intense brown eyes scrutinized her from behind retro eyeglass frames. They introduced themselves as Stephanie and Ryan. No last names.

Ryan motioned her to the leather banquette. "Please have a seat."

Olivia slid onto the leather banquette across from Stephanie and Ryan. "I love this cozy space. I've been here several times for drinks with friends."

Memorabilia from the acclaimed Best Friend of Charleston steam locomotive—from which the lounge was named—adorned the wood-paneled walls and shelves behind the bar.

"The owner was nice enough to let us meet in here," Stephanie said. "The Mills House is one of my favorite hotels in Charleston. We're considering filming a scene from one of our episodes in the lobby or courtyard."

Ryan shuffled several files on the table in front of him. "What a stroke of luck having the Kates run into you today. We've been trying to set up a meeting with you."

Olivia placed her hands in her lap to stop them from shaking. "I've been away on a writing retreat. I'm working on a novel."

A look Olivia identified as intrigue passed between Stephanie and Ryan. "We're quite fond of your writing," Stephanie said. "We'd love to hear more about this novel in a minute."

Ryan smiled. "Your Kate Scapades blog posts are fresh and funny and packed with vibrant details that bring the events to life. How much did the Kates tell you about our plans for a reality show?"

"Very little, except that you'd like to base the show on the blog posts."

"That's correct," Ryan said, and spoke for a few minutes about their vision for the show. "Your blog posts are a strong foundation from which to start. If you're interested, we'd like to make an offer to purchase the copyrights from you."

"Logistically, what would that entail?" Olivia asked.

"You would simply delete the blog posts from your website and hand the content over to us," Stephanie said.

"We're prepared to offer you a fair price." Ryan scrawled a number on a scratch piece of paper and slid it facedown across the table to Olivia.

Olivia lifted the paper and read the number. Other than a slight narrowing of the eyes, she managed to keep a straight face. Fifty thousand dollars was five times what she'd anticipated. *This is where an agent would come in handy. You were married to an attorney. Play hardball.* "Make it seventy-five, and we've got a deal."

Ryan didn't hesitate. "Sixty-five, and we keep all the media—videos and images."

Olivia held his gaze. "Sixty-five, you keep the media, and give me exclusive behind-the-scenes coverage during filming."

Ryan nodded. "Done. That's a win-win for both of us. We'll tap into your audience to start, and as popularity for the show grows, so will your following." He extended his hand to Olivia. "Do we have a deal?"

"We have a deal." She shook his hand first and then Stephanie's.

"We'll need your contact information." Stephanie's fingers flew across the keyboard of her laptop as Olivia called out her cell number as well as her addresses, both snail mail and email. "Our legal department will contact you early next week to get the ball rolling."

Olivia wanted to pinch herself that this was really happening.

Stephanie closed her laptop. "Coincidentally, we noticed your visiting contributor is taking your blog in a new direction."

Olivia debated how much to say, but then she decided it best to be honest. "Not a new direction. The direction I originally intended for *High Living in the Lowcountry* before I got waylaid by the Kate Scapades. Lena, my contributor, has been helping me by publishing fresh content while I've been focusing on my novel. Going forward, my goal is for us to work together to keep the younger audience entertained and, at the same time, attract an older following."

"I look forward to seeing how you manage that," Stephanie said.

Me too! If such a broad objective is even obtainable. If Lena is willing to work with me. If Lena isn't in prison.

Ryan sat back in his chair, crossing his long legs. "Tell us more about this novel you're working on."

They nodded their heads in approval as she told them the basic premise of *Marriage of Lies*.

"When do you expect to be finished with the novel?" Ryan asked.

"In early spring." Now that her immediate money problems had been solved, she could afford to take her time with the manuscript.

"As I said earlier, we're big fans of your work. Pass it along when you've polished it to perfection. I can't make any promises, but I can definitely get it in front of our movie producers."

Movie producers? "That would be great. Thanks." Sensing their meeting was coming to a close, Olivia stood to leave.

Stephanie and Ryan walked her to the door. "One more thing," Ryan said. "Are you willing to work with us to expand on your blog posts to make full episodes?"

And get sucked back into the lives of Kate Bradford and Kate Baker? No thanks. "I have too much on my plate at the moment. However, I'd be willing to consult whenever needed." Which would enable her to keep one foot in the door with the production company.

"That would be wonderful." Opening the door, Stephanie gestured for Olivia to go ahead of her to the lobby.

The Kates rushed over to them. "How'd it go?" Kate Baker asked.

"Looks like we have ourselves a show," Ryan said, draping an arm around each of the Kates' shoulders.

"Let's call for a bottle of champagne," Stephanie suggested. "Olivia, I hope you'll join us in the celebration."

"I wish I could," she lied, eager to get away from the Kates. "I need to get back to my novel."

Bidding them farewell, she hurried out of the main lobby entrance onto the crowded sidewalk. She walked on air as she crossed the street and made her way toward home. She'd been more anxious about her financial circumstances than she'd realized.

She wanted to share her news with someone. And that someone was Alistair. But it wouldn't be right to brag about her good fortune when Lena was in so much trouble. She removed her phone from her bag, disappointed to see there were no missed calls or texts from him. She yearned to reach out to him, to ask about his meeting with Lena and see if she could help in any way. But texting seemed so impersonal, and she was afraid he'd ignore her call. She needed to set her eyes on him, to talk to him face-to-face. Lucky for her, she knew exactly where to find him.

CHAPTER THIRTY
ALISTAIR

Alistair's heart fluttered at the sight of Olivia sitting by the fireplace in his hotel's lobby, thumbing through a magazine. Her black jeans were snug on her shapely thighs, and the pale pink color of her cashmere sweater softened her complexion. She was so damn hot. He warned himself to proceed with caution—she was a worldly woman, and he was a simple man.

When she noticed him standing near the check-in desk, she dropped the magazine on the coffee table and crossed the lobby to greet him. "There you are! I've been waiting for over two hours. I thought maybe you'd call after your visit with Lena. How is she? I've been so worried."

Alistair experienced a stab of guilt. "I'm sorry. I should've called." His eyes darted around the small lobby. "I'd prefer to have this conversation in private."

"Let's go for a walk," Olivia said, heading for the door before he could protest.

He had no choice but to take off after her. Never mind that he'd been strolling around downtown for hours. His leather loafers had rubbed blisters on the backs of his heels, and keeping up with Olivia took some effort.

They walked two blocks before either of them spoke. "So how is she?" Olivia asked.

"She's hanging in there. Lena is stronger than she thinks she is."

"I feel so helpless. Is there anything I can do for her?"

He shook his head. "Not at the moment. After talking to Lena, I'm convinced more than ever that Jade is the one abusing her mother, not Lena."

"Then we'll have to figure out a way to prove it," Olivia said with a determined set of her jaw.

They walked down East Bay Street to the seawall. As he stared out across the harbor, he considered whether to tell Olivia about his visit with Phyllis. "I did something earlier today that seemed like a good idea at the time, but now I'm not so sure."

Olivia turned her back to the water, leaning against the railing. "What'd you do?"

"I learned from Lena that Phyllis has another daughter, Marie, who is an orthopedic surgeon in Boston. It dawned on me that Marie may have flown to Charleston to be with her mother after the fall. And I thought maybe she could shed some light on the charges her mother had brought against Lena. So I went to Roper Hospital to visit Phyllis, thinking I might run into Marie."

He told her what Phyllis had said about the fall, how he'd found Marie's phone number on her iPad, and then about his call to her when he left the hospital.

Olivia covered her mouth with her hand. "There's probably a law against that, Alistair. If you're not careful, you'll find yourself in jail with Lena. What'd you learn from Marie?"

"Apparently, Jade and Marie don't get along. While she'd heard plenty about Lena from her mother, Marie had heard nothing of Phyllis's accident from her sister. When I told her about the accusations against Lena, she said she was jumping on the next plane to Charleston."

"That's great news! Is she going to call you when she learns something?"

"I assume she will. She has my number."

Olivia turned back around to face the water. A gentle breeze rustled her honey-colored hair, and Alistair yearned to take her in his arms, to bury his face in her neck and inhale her sweet scent. He couldn't help himself. She'd gotten under his skin, and there was nothing he could do to shake his feelings for her.

Olivia touched his arm lightly, sending a tingle down his spine. "You did the right thing, Alistair. You may very well have saved Lena from going to prison."

"Let's not get ahead of ourselves. Lena is still in a lot of trouble."

They watched a pelican dive headfirst into the water, emerging seconds later with a fish in its mouth.

"I can't believe any woman would beat her own mother," Olivia said.

"I'm terrified of what Jade might try to do to Lena next."

"At least she can't get to her while she's in jail."

"Thank heavens for small favors."

They left the railing and headed back toward the hotel. They'd gone several blocks when Olivia veered off to the right, down a cobblestone side street. She motioned to him. "Come this way. Let's walk through the park."

As they strolled along the path bordering the marsh, flocks of seagulls flew overhead and people walking dogs on leashes passed by.

"Seems like everyone in Charleston has a dog," Alistair said. "Is having one a prerequisite to living here?"

She snickered. "That's true. A lot of people have dogs, but not me. Although there are times when I've wished I had one."

As they got closer to his hotel, Olivia seemed hesitant to part. "Something truly remarkable happened to me today. I'd like to tell you about it, but it feels wrong to be happy when Lena's in jail."

He palmed his forehead. "I'm so sorry. I completely forgot. Lena specifically asked me to tell you that she loved your chapters. She'd been preoccupied and hadn't had a chance to email you yet. She thinks you have a gift and encourages you to keep writing."

"She said that?" Olivia's smile was broad, and her green eyes sparkled. He'd underestimated how much her writing meant to her.

"Her exact words," Alistair said. "Lena is a very supportive person. She would want you to brag about this truly remarkable thing that happened to you today."

This brought a smile to her face. "In that case, can I buy you a drink? The rooftop bar at The Vendue hotel offers the best sunset views in town."

With a sweep of his hand at the sidewalk in front of them, Alistair said, "Lead the way."

They walked up the street to The Vendue and through the lobby to the elevators. The rooftop lounge was surprisingly crowded for a Sunday evening, and they had to fight their way to the nearest bar. Once they got the bartender's attention, Olivia ordered an Absolut Citron and Alistair a Palmetto Pale Ale.

Olivia patted her sides, as if looking for her ever-present tote bag. "Stupid me. I offered to buy you a drink, and I've forgotten my wallet."

He tugged his wallet out of his back pocket. "No worries. I've got mine." He removed his credit card and handed it to the bartender. "Keep the tab open."

They took their drinks to the far corner of the roof and stood at the railing. The sun had begun its descent below the horizon, casting a pink glow over downtown. Alistair followed Olivia's finger as she pointed out the various church steeples. "Saint Philip's is there, and Saint Michael's over here."

"The view is spectacular." Alistair wasn't prone to snapping photographs on his iPhone, but this was one shot he couldn't resist. "Pose for me."

"Cheers." She held her glass up, offering a sweet smile.

He admired the image, an attractive woman with the city of Charleston at sunset in the background.

A table for two opened up nearby, and they quickly staked their claim.

"Now tell me what remarkable thing happened to you today," Alistair said once they were seated.

"It's the craziest thing, Alistair. I still can't believe it." She folded her arms on the table. "So . . . I went to The Mills House Hotel for lunch today. They have the best she-crab soup in town. You'll never guess who I ran into."

"I have no clue." Other than Olivia, Alistair knew three people in Charleston. One was in jail, and he doubted Zack and Kayla had gone to The Mills House for lunch.

"Kate Baker and Kate Bradford."

He racked his brain. She spoke as though she expected him to know who these women were.

"You know," Olivia said. "The Kate Scapades, the women who took my blog hostage."

Recognition crossed his face. "I thought you were avoiding them."

"I was. And still am. Sort of." She sipped her drink. "The Kates have been offered a reality TV show. They were at The Mills House meeting with producers. I've been ignoring their emails, otherwise I would've known about it. The producers have been trying to get in touch with me about buying the copyrights for my blog posts."

With his head cocked to the side, Alistair regarded her with a curious expression. "A reality TV show? And this is a good thing? No offense, but I'm not a big fan of reality TV."

Her face fell. "It's a good thing because they're paying me a very handsome price for the copyrights."

"Does this mean you'll have to work with the Kates again?"

"They offered me a job on their production team, but I turned them down. Well, not completely. I agreed to consult as needed. And there's even more exciting news. I negotiated a deal that gives my blog exclusive behind-the-scenes coverage during filming."

Olivia was absolutely thrilled about this new development. Who was Alistair to put a damper on her excitement? "This calls for a celebration. I'll get us some champagne."

His spirits plummeted as he returned to the bar and waited for the bartender to pour two glasses of champagne. The news of the TV show served as a reminder that Olivia would be returning to Charleston at the end of the month. He'd known all along that was the plan, of course. Had he subconsciously been hoping for a different outcome?

Back at the table, he handed her a glass of champagne and toasted her good fortune.

"I can't wait for these charges against Lena to clear," Olivia said. "I'm dying to talk to her about a new vision for my website. If she'll continue working with me, it'll be *our* website. Do you think she'll stay in Charleston?"

"Getting out of jail is the only thing on Lena's mind at the moment. I guess there's a chance she'll move here permanently, especially if Kayla is planning to stay." Alistair hoped a divorce was in Lena's future. It was high time she rid herself of her deadbeat husband.

"I owe you an apology, Alistair. I lied to you." She shook her head. "Let me rephrase that. I didn't exactly lie to you. I just haven't been completely honest. The truth is, I'm only a few thousand dollars shy of being flat broke. I still have my condo, but the rest of my divorce settlement is nearly gone. This windfall from the sale of the blog posts couldn't have come at a better time."

It took a minute for this news flash to sink in. He'd never been in a financial crisis. He came from a wealthy family, and he'd made his own millions in New York. He couldn't imagine what she'd been going through or why she'd felt the need to hide her money problems from him. He considered making a joke about her forgetting her wallet so he'd have to pay for the drinks but thought better of it. "Why didn't you tell me?"

She sighed. "Pride, mostly. The only real job I've ever had was writing copy for an advertising agency right out of college. I continued to work after Robert and I were married, but when my daughter came along, I chose to stay at home with her. After the divorce, I had to figure out a way to support the lifestyle I'd grown accustomed to. It's scary to suddenly find yourself alone when you're used to someone else making all the important life decisions for you. Robert was very generous in our settlement, but I made the mistake of paying cash for my condo, which drastically reduced the money I have to live on. I saw this novel I'm writing as an opportunity to avoid taking out a mortgage or borrowing against the condo or whatever one does in these situations." A smile spread across her lips. "Did I tell you the producers said they could get my novel in front of their movie producers?"

"I believe you left that part out." He clinked her glass again. "Double congratulations." He studied her, admiring not only her beauty but her determination. He imagined the years since her divorce had been difficult for her, yet she'd somehow managed to persevere.

"I owe you an apology as well," Alistair said. "I overreacted when you closed your laptop on me. I was totally out of sorts that day. Thursday was the second anniversary of Mary Anne's death."

"Oh, Alistair. I'm so sorry." She placed her hand on his. "I wish you'd told me."

"You have no idea how sorry I am that I didn't." The warmth of her hand on his made him want to take her in his arms. "I'd like to see this condo of yours, if you're willing to show it to me."

She drained the rest of her champagne and set the empty glass on the table. "What're we waiting for?"

They stopped by the bar to pay their tab before taking the elevator to the lobby. Alistair wondered what was going through her mind when she was quiet on the short walk to her building.

Her condo was small but decorated in Olivia's signature elegant style. She threw open the French doors, and they emerged onto the small balcony. "I wouldn't mind waking up to this view every morning," Alistair said.

She nudged him with her body. "What're you talking about? Your view of Carters Creek is pretty awesome."

"True. I imagine both offer inspiration for a writer."

"One would think," Olivia said. "I tried writing earlier today, but I couldn't get the creative juices flowing."

"You're probably just tired from the long drive yesterday."

"I think it has more to do with what I've discovered at Lena's cottage than what's missing here. These past few weeks, I've been able to settle in, to really concentrate on my work."

He laughed. "Because there's nothing else to do."

"There's plenty to do, if you're motivated to do something."

He turned to face her. "Are you saying the Northern Neck is growing on you?"

"I'm saying the Northern Neck is starting to feel like home. And I've grown quite fond of the handsome man who lives in the house next door." Taking him by the hand, she led him into her bedroom.

CHAPTER THIRTY-ONE

OLIVIA

Olivia fell back against the bed pillows. "That was . . ." Her voice trailed off.

Alistair rolled onto his side, propping himself up on one elbow. "That was what, Olivia? Spectacular? Sensational? You're the writer. How would you describe it?"

Sex between them, up until now, had been frenzied, urgent, even desperate at times, as one might expect from two sexually deprived adults. But this was tender and sweet. Her feelings for him had overwhelmed her, bringing tears to her eyes as she'd climaxed. "Forget the fancy adjectives, Alistair. It was simply lovely."

He dragged the tips of his fingers down her chest and across her bare breasts toward . . .

She brushed his hand away. "No more. Not now. I need food."

He chuckled. "We'll talk about food in a minute. But first we need to settle a housekeeping detail. Lena will need a place to stay when she's released from jail tomorrow. And I have this incredible suite across the road complete with gas-burning logs in the fireplace. Can I convince you to come stay with me?"

She chewed on her lower lip, pretending to ponder his suggestion. "I'd hate for your incredible suite to go to waste. Can I have coffee in bed?"

"You can have anything you want in the bed," he said in a voice deep with lust.

"Then count me in." She threw her feet over the side of the bed. "Since I'm going to share your suite, would you care to share my shower?"

"Oh yeah!" he said, chasing her into the master bathroom.

Their shower was a tantalizing experience that left both of them weak with desire. After dressing, Olivia styled her hair and repacked her small suitcase while he put fresh linens on the bed for Lena.

"Let's talk about food," he said as he wheeled her suitcase through the lobby of his hotel to the elevators. "Where should we eat?"

"Since it's Sunday, our choices are limited. A lot of places are closed. What're you in the mood for?"

The elevator doors closed on them. "Something quick. The sooner we eat, the sooner we can go back to bed." He pinned her against the wall, kissing her.

"I know just the place. Meeting at Market is a sports bar near here with fast service, casual food, and Sunday night football."

"Perfect!" He cast a glance heavenward, saying a silent prayer to Mary Anne for helping him find a girl who loves football.

When the elevator doors opened on the third floor, she gently shoved him away. "If I go with you to your room, we'll never leave. Why don't I hold the elevator for you while you take my suitcase? But hurry before I die of starvation."

When they returned to the front of the hotel, Alistair had the valet summon a rickshaw to take them to the restaurant. The driver, a college student studying marine biology at the College of Charleston, draped a blanket over them and took off toward East Bay Street, his long legs pumping the pedals of his bicycle. For an extra twenty dollars, he took the scenic route—down to Broad, up Church, and through the market.

At Meeting at Market, patrons occupied a handful of tables, and two single men sat at the bar with a lone stool between them. Alistair and Olivia chose seats at the opposite end of the bar and struck up a conversation with the bartender, Sarah, a petite young woman with unruly dark curls piled on top of her head. Based on her recommendation for the best local craft beers, Alistair and Olivia both ordered a Holy City Pluff Mud Porter.

When Sarah handed them menus, Alistair asked, "What's good here?"

"The burger," she said, proceeding to fill two glasses with the dark beer from a tap.

Alistair looked at Olivia, who said, "A burger sounds good to me."

He handed the unopened menus back to Sarah. "You heard the lady. We'll have two burgers, cooked medium rare, and fries." He surveyed the restaurant. "This is my kind of restaurant—a cozy spot to watch Sunday night football."

"I aim to please," Olivia said with a wink.

While they waited for their food, with one eye on the Patriots versus the Chiefs game, they talked about their plans for the following morning. The arraignment hearing would start at nine, and they wanted to be at the courthouse no later than eight thirty.

The bartender delivered their burgers—fat, juicy patties of prime ground beef with melted cheddar cheese. Olivia was taking her second bite when Alistair's cell phone rang. With a quick glance at the screen, he silenced the ring, ignoring the call.

"Who was that?" she asked.

"Nobody." He placed the phone facedown on the bar.

She set her burger down and wiped her mouth with her napkin. "That was clearly somebody, Alistair. Was it Lena's daughter?"

"It has nothing to do with Lena." His tone was snippy. In an instant, the wall had gone up, and Alistair had retreated to that broody place he'd been in during the car ride to South Carolina.

They didn't speak again while they finished their food, and the minute he'd signed the check, she was on her feet and out the door. She walked at a fast pace, half a block ahead of him. She was exasperated by his mood changes. Like the guard of a castle with a moat, he lowered and raised his drawbridge, letting her in and then shutting her out depending on his frame of mind. She'd been honest with him that afternoon about her financial crisis. Didn't she deserve the same courtesy? The crisp night air sobered her, and by the time they arrived at his room, she'd worked out what she wanted to say to him.

When he unlocked the door, she entered his suite ahead of him. Maid service had turned back the bedcovers, leaving a chocolate on each pillow and the logs burning in the fireplace.

"What gives, Alistair? I can either take my suitcase and go back to my condo or you can tell me what's bothering you." She went to stand beside the fireplace, warming her hands. "We need to be honest with each other if we want this relationship to work."

He sank to the end of the bed, raking his hands through his hair.

"Obviously you're worried about Lena," she continued, "but I sense there's something more. I don't understand why you're shutting me out."

He let out an audible breath. "Henry, my friend in New York, called me yesterday morning before we left to come down here. He wants me to work on a deal with him. He gave me until the end of the weekend to decide. That was Henry who called while we were at the restaurant. I didn't answer because I have no idea what to tell him."

So it isn't another woman. Relief washed over Olivia. Not that she'd ever really considered another woman was a possibility. He was still in love with his dead wife. "I don't understand. Why would you keep something like that from me?"

He shrugged. "Guilt, I guess. Why am I worrying about a job while Lena sits in jail?"

"Because, like me, you have faith that Lena will be released on bail tomorrow morning. I'm a good listener if you'd like to talk things through."

He smiled at her. "I'd like that. I've been on my own so long, I've forgotten what it's like to have someone help me make important decisions."

Olivia crossed the room to the hotel phone and dialed the operator.

Alistair furrowed his brow. "What're you doing?"

"Ordering up some chamomile tea. Tea helps me think." After speaking with room service, she sat down by the fire. "Come." She patted the cushion on the chair opposite her. "Tell me everything. I thought Henry gave you until the end of the year to make your decision."

Alistair moved from the bed to the chair. "That was before this deal came up. He only needs me in New York for a short time, about ten days. I can stay in the corporate apartment. He wants me there by noon on Tuesday. I don't even know why I'm considering it. I'm not turning my back on Lena."

"Okay, slow down." She held her palm out to him. "Let's assume for a minute that everything goes well for Lena tomorrow. You could fly directly from here to New York, and I could drive your truck back to Virginia."

"You'd do that for me?" he asked in a disbelieving tone.

She held his gaze. "Why wouldn't I do that for you?"

"It's just a lot to ask, a long way for you to drive alone."

"I'm a big girl, Alistair. I appreciate your concern, but I'll be fine. I'm trying to make it so you can do this deal."

Alistair looked away from her, staring into the fire. "There's also the issue of the café. I told you I fired Sherry. Jess and Jasmine can manage the food service side of the business, but they've never handled the bank deposits or paid bills."

"Those are just logistics, nothing we can't work out. I'm happy to help Jess and Jasmine. If we get stuck, you can FaceTime us and walk us through whatever needs to be done."

There was a knock at the door, and Olivia got up to answer it. The room service waiter placed the tea tray on the table beside the window. She tipped him five dollars on his way out. After pouring honey from a sample-size jar into two cups, she added the tea bags and hot water.

"Is there something else you're not telling me, Alistair? Aside from not wanting to leave Lena? I understand why moving to New York permanently is a huge decision. But what's preventing you from doing this one deal?"

"If I go to New York for ten days, by the time I get back, your month in the Northern Neck will be up."

She spooned the tea bags out of the mugs and placed them on the tray. "I've been thinking about extending my stay. At least until I finish my novel. Lena would have to agree, of course. I would insist on paying her rent."

Alistair looked up at her when she handed him a mug. "That would be awesome." He blew on his tea before taking a tentative sip. "You make a good point. I've been thinking about this all wrong. I can do the deal without making a permanent commitment."

She reclaimed her seat. "Exactly. Treat the deal as a trial run. See how you like it, not only being back in a high-pressure working environment but also living in New York for more than a couple of days."

They sat for a brief spell in silence as they sipped their tea. She could tell by Alistair's pensive expression that he was working out something in his mind. Finally, he said, more to himself than to Olivia, "That's what I'll do, then. I'll call Henry and tell him I need a little more time to work through some issues, but I'll let him know for sure by noon tomorrow. I'll feel better knowing Lena's out of jail. And I want to meet with her attorney. I need to know he'll make her case a priority."

"I've known Owen Dixon for a long time," Olivia said. "I have every confidence in him, and I believe you will as well once you've met him."

Taking her mug and placing it on the carpet beside his chair, he pulled her onto his lap. "I'm sorry I didn't confide in you from the beginning. I shut you out. I did to you what I was angry at you for doing to me. More than anything, I want our relationship to work. Can we make a promise not to keep any more secrets?"

She nibbled on his earlobe and planted a trail of kisses down his neck. "That's a promise I can definitely make."

"We're not exactly spring chickens—"

She play-slapped him on the chest. "Speak for yourself, Alistair. I, for one, have a lot of living left to do."

He pressed his finger to her lips. "Be quiet for a minute and let me talk. What I was trying to say is I want to make the most of the living we have left to do. If I decided to move permanently to New York, would you consider coming with me?"

Is he talking about marriage? Because she wasn't ready for that. At least not now. Maybe never. She was just warming up to the idea of a committed relationship, and if things continued to progress, she would have no scruples about living with him. "I can work from anywhere. Have laptop, will travel. I may need to be in Charleston some during the filming of the show, but I can easily fly back and forth."

"Good." He stroked her cheek. "Knowing you'll come with me will make my decision easier. This trial run will help. I've never felt this torn about anything in my life. I enjoyed working at the café this past week. The simple life of the Northern Neck suits the part of me that loves the outdoors and quiet evenings at home. But when I was in New York, I realized how much I missed the energy of the city. I came home, and you were there, and we spent four of the happiest days I'd known in years."

Her eyes welled up, and when she started to agree with him, he pressed his finger to her lips.

"But then you shut me out, and the loneliness I'd been feeling since Mary Anne's death was even more profound. I know one thing for certain. I do not want to be in the Northern Neck without you. I don't want to be anywhere without you. I want you in my life, Olivia."

She laid her head on his chest. "And I want you in mine. I suggest we put all our misunderstandings and miscommunications behind us and focus on the future."

CHAPTER THIRTY-TWO

LENA

The forty-eight hours she'd spent in jail had been hard on Lena. She was exhausted from lack of sleep and antsy from being confined in a tiny space with cinder block walls and no windows. After breakfast on Monday—if one could call the bowl of runny oatmeal breakfast—a female guard escorted her to the same windowless room where Detective Lauren Malone had interrogated her on Saturday. A man with thinning gray hair and a ruddy complexion rose from his seat and came around the table to greet her.

"Hello, Mrs. Browder. I'm Owen Dixon, your attorney."

She forced a smile as she shook his hand. "Please call me Lena."

"If you'll call me Owen."

She nodded. "Deal."

"How're you holding up?"

"I'm doing okay, considering the circumstances. This has all been a gross misunderstanding. There must be some evidence somewhere that will prove I'm innocent."

"And we'll find it. But first we need to focus on getting you out of jail." Her attorney wasn't necessarily a handsome man, but the twinkle in his blue eyes suggested a sense of humor, and his authoritative manner seemed like a good omen.

He motioned her to the table, and they sat down opposite each other. "Would you like some coffee?"

Yes! She wanted coffee. A pumpkin spice latte from Starbucks, not this bitter brew they called coffee around here. "I'm fine, thanks."

"Coincidentally, I'm very fond of Kayla. She wanted me to tell you she sends her love, and she'll see you after the arraignment."

Lena smiled despite feeling guilty for dragging her daughter into this mess.

"You'll be transferred within the hour to the federal courthouse. The arraignment will go as follows. The judge will read the charges, and you'll enter a plea of not guilty. There'll be a brief discussion about bail. Because your permanent address is in Virginia, the judge may consider you a flight risk. But since you have no prior record, I don't see it being a problem. You'll be asked not to leave the state, to stay out of trouble, and to have no contact with the alleged victim."

Lena gulped back a wave of fear. "What if the judge denies bail?"

"That's not likely to happen. I understand you have a friend willing to post bond?"

"That's correct. Alistair Hoffman. He'll be at the arraignment hearing."

The guard arrived to prepare Lena for her transfer to court. "I'll see you at the courthouse," Owen said. "I just checked my schedule with my secretary. Are you free to meet with me in my office at four o'clock this afternoon?"

"If I'm *free* at four o'clock this afternoon, I'll be there."

He chuckled. "You'll be free. We can decide how to proceed at that time."

The morning played out exactly as her attorney predicted. By eleven o'clock, bail had been posted, Lena had been released from jail, and she stood with her daughter and friends in front of the police station. She hugged each of them in turn—Kayla, Zack, Alistair, and Olivia.

"Can we give you a ride back to the condo?" Kayla asked.

"I drove myself, sweetheart. But thanks." She hugged her daughter once more. "Go! Enjoy your day. I'll call you this afternoon after my meeting with Owen."

Her heart swelled as she watched Kayla and Zack walk hand in hand to his Ford Explorer. He held the passenger door open for her before going around to the driver's side. She had a good feeling about that young man.

Lena turned to Olivia, dangling her car keys in front of her. "This is a little awkward. Perhaps you'd like to drive your own car back to the condo."

She needed a hot shower, clean clothes, and fresh air. She needed her space and time alone. She hated the idea of having to share the condo with Olivia, even if it was Olivia's condo.

"You go ahead. I'm sure you could use some time to yourself," Olivia said, as though reading her mind.

"Can we take you out for a late lunch?" Alistair asked.

Lena salivated at the thought of real food. "As long as we go somewhere nearby. And later is better. I want to decompress for a while first."

"How about Amen Street at two o'clock?" Olivia suggested.

"That sounds perfect." She scanned the parking lot for Olivia's car. She'd been in such a state when she'd driven to police headquarters, she'd paid no attention to where she parked. Spotting the red Volkswagen several rows over, she said to Olivia, "So I'll meet you back at your condo in a few."

Olivia looped her arm through Alistair's. "I'm actually staying at the hotel with him."

Lena let out a little squeal. "That's the best news I've heard in ages. I can't think of two people more suited to each other." She wrapped her arms around them, kissing each of their cheeks in turn. She dropped her arms and prodded them toward Alistair's truck. "You lovebirds go have fun. I'll meet you at the restaurant at two."

She was beyond thrilled for her friends and for herself at the thought of having the condo to herself. Her spirits boosted, she lowered the top on the Beetle for the drive home. When the elevator stopped at Olivia's floor, she was ecstatic to see a large brown box from B&H waiting beside the door. She unlocked the door and toed the package inside. She dropped to her knees and tore open the box, unpacking and examining the camera equipment one piece at a time. The last forty-eight hours had served as a reminder of life's fragility, and she was glad she'd opted to splurge on the higher quality camera body and lens.

She assembled the camera, inserting the battery and SIM card and attaching the lens. Hot shower forgotten, she quickly changed into exercise clothes and running shoes and went out to explore with her new camera. Meandering the neighborhood streets she'd grown to know so well, she rejected window boxes and courtyard gardens as her subjects, choosing instead to photograph the people she encountered—the homeless and elderly, children playing in the park, housewives out walking their dogs.

She walked north to the city market and turned left off East Bay Street, where she found Bessie set up in her usual spot under the brick archway in the second building. The old woman looked up at her from the basket she was weaving in her lap. "Well lookie who's here. I've missed seeing you. Where you been these past coupla days?"

Lena looked down at her feet. "You wouldn't believe me if I told you."

"I'm an old lady, Lena. There ain't much I haven't heard." Bessie squinted her brown eyes as she studied her more closely. "Why the long face?"

Lena hesitated, afraid of what Bessie might think of her.

Setting her basket aside, Bessie slowly got to her feet. "Come now. Tell old Bessie what's wrong."

Lena slumped against the table. "Remember that photographer I've been working with?"

"The one with the blind mama?"

"She's the one," Lena said, and then launched into her tale about the elder abuse charges and her weekend in jail.

Bessie listened intently, and when Lena had finished talking, she said, "Well don't that beat all. This world done gone crazy. What's a mean-spirited person doing accusing a kindhearted woman like you of such a vicious act? I trust you got yourself a good lawyer."

Lena nodded, her head hung low.

"Then you fight hard to prove your innocence. If you need a character witness, you can count on old Bessie. I want you to take my picture and show it to the judge. Tell him old Bessie says you're one of the finest people I know."

Lena's eyebrows hit her hairline. She could hardly believe it. After weeks of begging, Bessie was finally letting her photograph her. "You mean it? I can take your picture?"

"Snap away."

And for the next ten minutes, Lena shot Bessie with her baskets in a variety of poses, including one photograph she insisted Lena share with the judge.

When she finished, Lena gave her a hug. "Thank you for this. I know how much you detest being photographed."

"I don't mind so much if I know the photographer," Bessie said, dropping back down to her chair.

"Would you be willing to let me feature you in a blog post? You've led a fascinating life. I would love to share it with my readers. I'll let you read it first, of course. You can change anything you want."

"I'd be honored. I trust you, Lena. And you need to believe in yourself. Have faith in your innocence."

Too choked up to speak, she kissed the tips of her fingers, pressed them to Bessie's cheek, and hurried off with her head ducked so no one could see the tears in her eyes.

Walking briskly to the park in front of Olivia's condo, she strolled down the pier and paused along the way to snap a few photographs of a blue heron in the marsh. She turned off her camera and continued to the end of the pier where she'd first encountered Jade. If only they hadn't met that day, she wouldn't be in such a mess.

She contemplated the long process ahead of her. She'd have to stay in Charleston indefinitely. Fine, since she had no desire to return to Richmond. But she'd have to find a place to live other than Olivia's condo. Living expenses and attorney's fees would cost a fortune. She'd have to tell Charles about her predicament. He would not hold back. He would lay into her like he always did, treating her like an imbecile.

She fought off that all-too-familiar feeling of loneliness. She'd worn it like a second skin all of her married life. She and Charles had never truly connected, unlike so many husbands and wives she knew.

Lena stomped her foot on the pier. "Then don't tell him about the arrest," she said out loud to herself.

Bessie's powerful words came back to her. *Trust in yourself.*

She could count on Alistair, Olivia, and Kayla for moral support during the trial. As for Charles, she would have to go it alone. If necessary, she would spend every dime of her inheritance proving her innocence. She would be free of the charges and free of Charles. She would divorce him. When she met with Owen that afternoon at four o'clock, she would ask him to refer her to an attorney who could handle it.

Feeling more hopeful about her future, she returned to the condo and luxuriated in a long hot shower. Olivia's scale showed she'd lost two more pounds while in jail, for a grand total of eight since arriving in Charleston. She dressed in a thigh-length gray sweater and slim-fitting black corduroy jeans. She styled her hair and carefully applied makeup. She was not guilty of this monstrous act Phyllis and Jade had accused her of. She would face the charges with confidence and determination. She would not let a misguided old woman and her cruel daughter ruin the new life she was forging for herself in Charleston.

With a few minutes to spare before she needed to leave for lunch, she uploaded the images from her new camera. Better than anything she'd taken before, they needed very little editing. The images were sharp and the lighting soft. But more than that, she'd captured the hidden emotions of her subjects—the despair of the homeless, the joy in the children's smiles, boredom on the faces of the housewives. How ironic that her weekend in jail had afforded her a more heightened awareness of the world around her—people, places, animals. When she came to the images of Bessie, tears once again welled in her eyes. She laughed out loud at the one intended for the judge—Bessie aiming her finger at the camera, a stern expression on her face. But her favorite, the one she would use for her blog post, featured Bessie with her chubby arms laden with baskets and a broad toothy grin on her face.

Lena recognized talent when she saw it, even if that talent was her own. With ideas for future posts flooding her mind, she went online and signed into Olivia's blog. She had much to discuss with Olivia over lunch. She took a few minutes to respond to a few of the many comments that had been posted over the weekend. Warmth radiated through her body as she thought about what she'd accomplished. She'd run away from her meaningless existence in Richmond and was developing a meaningful career of her own.

CHAPTER THIRTY-THREE

ALISTAIR

Alistair and Olivia spent their free time between the arraignment and lunch planning his trip to New York. While Olivia booked his flight, Alistair called Henry to tell him the good news. Henry was delighted to hear Alistair would be joining his team temporarily and filled him in on the important details regarding the pending merger.

They were on their way out the door to meet Lena for lunch when Olivia dragged him back into the room for a quickie. Being with her was never boring. She had looks and brains and an insatiable appetite for sex.

When they finally arrived at the restaurant, they were fifteen minutes late. Lena, sitting in a window booth, was working her way through a bowl of hush puppies. "I know why you're late," she said, barely glancing up from her food. "It's written all over your faces."

Olivia and Alistair slid into the booth across the table from her. "What's written all over our faces?" Alistair asked, feigning innocence.

"It's not so much yours as hers." She waved a hush puppy, dripping with honey, in Olivia's direction. "She's wearing the rosy glow of a sexually satisfied woman."

Alistair, feeling the heat creep up his neck, tugged at his button-down collar. "You're certainly in a good mood for someone who just got out of jail."

"I'm famished is what I am after eating prison food for two days." She popped the hush puppy in her mouth. "Lighten up, Alistair. I'm teasing you. What are best friends for, if not for giving each other a hard time? I'm really happy for the two of you. As I said earlier, y'all are a perfect match."

Olivia smiled over at Alistair. "After a rocky start, we're finally figuring that out."

"I think it's wonderful," Lena said. "You've both been through difficult times and deserve to be happy."

Alistair stared hard at his oldest friend. This was not the dispirited Lena of recent years. The optimistic Lena from their childhood had returned. "What gives, Lena? You haven't been this upbeat in years. Don't get me wrong. I'm glad to see you handling the situation so well."

"Never underestimate the power of retail therapy," Lena joked.

Alistair noticed Olivia staring at Lena with mouth agape. She was definitely acting strange.

"Have you been drinking?" he asked Lena. "I've never known you to enjoy shopping."

Lena pushed the empty hush puppy bowl away. "I ordered some new camera equipment from an online retailer. It was waiting for me at the condo this morning when I got back. I took it out for a test-drive, and I got some remarkable photographs. While I was out, I ran into a friend. She was shocked when I told her I'd been arrested. She told me to believe in myself and have faith in my innocence. I do have faith in my innocence because I didn't do this horrible thing Phyllis and Jade have accused me of. I just spent forty-eight hours in jail, and I'm damn happy to be free. And I'm planning to divorce Charles, so

I'll soon be free of him as well. So yes, I'm in a good mood. I believe I'm entitled."

"Good riddance, Charles." Alistair offered her a fist bump across the table. "I've known you for a very long time, my friend. We've been through thick and thin together. But I've never been prouder of you than I am at this moment."

"Okay. Stop. You're making me cry." Lena dabbed at her eyes with her napkin.

"Don't do that. We can't let tears spoil this happy occasion," Alistair said. "Let's order. I'm starving." After a brief discussion about the food offerings on the menu, he summoned the waitress, a pretty young woman with blonde curls who reminded him of Jasmine.

Olivia ordered the grilled salmon salad, Lena the mussels, and Alistair the fried flounder sandwich. He waited for the waitress to bring their sweet teas before telling Lena about his trip to New York.

"I mean it, Lena. I won't go if you need me here."

"My trial is months away. There's nothing you can do for me now. Besides, you've already done plenty by driving all the way down here and posting my bail."

"Okay then," he said. "But remember, I'm only a phone call away if you need moral support."

Lena's gaze shifted to Olivia. "What I'm going to need is a place to stay after our house swap ends. Do you have any suggestions?"

"As a matter of fact, I do." Olivia gripped the edge of the table as if bracing herself. "How would you feel about extending our swap, maybe even until the end of the year? As you know, I'm working on a novel. Turns out, your cottage has good writing vibes."

"I would like nothing better than to extend our swap," Lena said. "I hope Alistair told you how much I enjoyed the chapters you sent. I'd love to read more when you have them ready."

"I will value your feedback." Olivia extended her hand to Lena. "Then we have a deal on the house swap."

Lena shook her hand. "We have a deal."

The waitress delivered their plates, and they attacked their food.

"You're doing an admirable job with the blog," Olivia said, a forkful of salmon suspended in midair. "I hope you'll consider staying on board."

"Count me in! I have so many ideas for future posts."

"And I have so much to tell you about the Kates. You're—"

Alistair's phone rang, interrupting Olivia. He felt two sets of eyes staring at him as he accepted the call from Marie.

"I'm sorry it's taken me so long to get back to you," Marie said, sounding slightly out of breath. "I've had a lot to sort through. As you suspected, Mom was unaware of the charges against Lena. I'm convinced she was confused at the time she made the statement to the police. My mom is terrified of my sister. It took some doing, but I finally got her to admit that Jade is the one who's been abusing her, the one who pushed her down the stairs."

"That's great news! For Lena, anyway." Alistair locked eyes with Lena and gave her a thumbs-up.

"It's great news for everyone, especially Mom. The police have just arrested Jade. She's going to jail for a very long time. She can no longer hurt my poor mother." Marie paused, and Alistair heard her take in a deep breath. "Mom's distraught over the way Lena's been treated, and she's desperate for the chance to apologize. I'm worried about her. She's extremely agitated, which isn't good for her recovery. I know it's asking a lot, but do you think Lena would be willing to come by the house this afternoon?"

Alistair ran his fingers through his hair. "By law, she can't. Having contact with the alleged victim is in violation of her bond agreement."

"The district attorney's office assured me they are dropping the charges against Lena. She should be hearing from her attorney any minute. Please, Alistair. I know we're not in any position to ask for favors, but it would mean a lot to Mom."

"I'm having lunch with Lena now. Let me talk to her, and I'll get back to you."

Alistair ended the call and put his phone beside his plate. "The charges have been dropped, and Jade's been arrested. Phyllis is asking to see you. But we can't do anything until we hear from your attorney."

As the words left his lips, they heard the muffled sound of Lena's phone, buried deep within her purse. "I don't recognize the number," she said when she finally withdrew the phone three rings later.

"Answer it!" Olivia and Alistair said in unison.

When she accepted the call, Lena mouthed, "It's Owen." A smile spread across her face as she listened. "So it's over, just like that?" She paused. "Phyllis is asking to see me. Is that allowed?" Another pause before she thanked him and hung up.

Lena, a dumbfounded expression on her face, sat staring at the phone in her hand. "Owen says I can see Phyllis as long as we're not alone. I don't believe this." She dropped the phone in her lap and buried her face in her hands.

When they heard sniffling, Olivia said, "Oh, honey. I know this is overwhelming. You've been through so much. I have some tissues." She removed a travel package of tissues from her bag and slid them across the table.

Lena tugged a tissue out and wiped her eyes. "I don't understand how this happened."

"Alistair made this happen. Tell her." She landed an elbow to his ribs.

"Yesterday, after I left you at the police station, I went to see Phyllis at the hospital." He told Lena about their visit and then his subsequent phone conversation with Marie. "As you probably guessed, that was Marie who called a minute ago. Phyllis wasn't aware of the charges. At least she doesn't remember making them. She's upset about the way you've been treated and would like to apologize. It's up to you whether you want to see her. If I were you, honestly, I'm not sure I would."

"I think I should," Lena said without hesitation. "For Phyllis's sake. She's the real victim in all this. I knew deep down she didn't have anything to do with my arrest."

"Fine," Alistair said. "But you're not going alone. I'm going with you."

"Then what're we waiting for?" Lena slid the strap of her purse over her arm. "Let's go."

"Aren't you going to finish your lunch?" Alistair asked.

"How can I eat at a time like this?" She eyed his half-eaten sandwich. "Oh. Sorry. Go ahead and finish."

"I'll take it with me," he said, looking around the restaurant for their waitress. "I just need to pay the bill first."

"Don't worry about the bill," Olivia said. "I'll take care of it. Good luck. Be sure to call me after your visit. I'm dying to hear how it goes."

Sandwich in hand, Alistair slid out of the booth to his feet. "How far is it? Should we get my truck from the hotel?"

"We can walk," Lena said. "You should call Marie to tell her we're on our way."

Pressing his phone to his ear, Alistair lengthened his stride to keep up with Lena as she navigated the streets. After they crossed Broad Street, the business district transitioned into residential, and within minutes they were knocking at the front door of a three-story colonial home.

A petite woman with medium-length dark hair and mesmerizing yellowish-green eyes answered the door. "Lena!" She threw her arms around Lena, hugging her for a minute before extending her hand to Alistair. "And you must be Alistair."

He offered her a smile as he accepted her hand. "Nice to meet you in person, Marie."

"I'm so terribly sorry for the trouble my family has caused you," she said to Lena. "I'm as much to blame as my sister. If only I'd stayed in closer touch with Mom."

Lena squirmed out of Marie's embrace. "I'm not without blame. I suspected Jade was abusing your mother, but instead of going to the police or contacting you, I confronted her, thinking that would make her stop."

"And so she pushed Mom down the stairs and made it look like you did it. She's evil and manipulative, and she's getting what she deserves." Marie opened the door wider and stepped out of the way. "Please come in."

Alistair and Lena entered the house and stood at the bottom of the stairs.

"Jade had already gone to bed when I got in last night," Marie said. "I used her computer to access Mom's online bank accounts. I discovered that Jade has stolen thousands of dollars from Mom over the past few months."

Lena frowned. "Why would she need to steal from Phyllis when her business is so successful?"

"That was my initial response as well," Marie said. "I thought there had to be some mistake, so I contacted a family friend in Nashville, who told me that Jade's photography business has gone bankrupt. One of her assistants left to start her own business, taking two other photographers and all their clients with her."

Lena said, "But she flew to Nashville last week to work out a deal to sell the business."

Marie shook her head. "She lied. She's good at it. Always has been. She went to Nashville to finalize the sale of her house."

Lena cast a nervous glance up the stairs. "How is Phyllis? I've been so worried about her."

"She's doing remarkably well, considering her age," Marie said. "As soon as she's well enough to travel, I'm taking her back to Boston with me. We have a luxury retirement community near my house. She'll make new friends, and I'll get to see her every day."

"But I thought she was opposed to moving to a retirement community?" Lena said.

"Another one of Jade's lies." Marie gestured toward the stairs. "She seems really excited about it. If you're ready, we can go up and see her now."

"I'll wait for you down here," Alistair volunteered.

"Actually, Alistair, Mom asked to see you as well." Marie flashed him a mischievous grin. "She wants to thank the kind volunteer named Al who helped locate her audiobook."

"You mean she knows? And she's not mad at me?"

"Far from it," Marie said. "But I'll let her tell you herself."

The threesome climbed the stairs in single file with Marie leading the way. Phyllis was propped up in bed wearing her red headphones with her eyes closed. Alistair lingered in the doorway so as not to crowd Phyllis.

Sensing their presence, Phyllis pulled her headphones off, letting them dangle around her neck. "Is that you, Lena?"

Lena sat down gently on the edge of the bed. "I'm here, Phyllis. How're you feeling?"

"Better, now that I can hear your voice. I feel just awful about the trouble I've caused you. I don't even remember talking to the police about the accident. I guess I was out of it at the time."

Lena squeezed Phyllis's kneecap through the coverlet. "No need to explain. It was all a big misunderstanding."

"But you went to jail because of me. Was it horrible?"

"I'm relieved I won't be going back," Lena said with a nervous giggle. "But spending the weekend in jail gave me a chance to assess my life and make some important decisions regarding my future."

"Do those decisions involve that dear man, Al? Is he a love interest?"

Alistair moved to the side of the bed. "I'm here, Phyllis. And I'm not a love interest. Lena and I have been best friends most of our lives."

Phyllis smiled up at the sound of his voice. "That's nice. She's lucky to have you."

"I'm the lucky one," he said, giving Lena a wink. "Coincidentally, my real name is Alistair. It was wrong of me to deceive you like I did."

"You were just trying to help your friend. And there's nothing more important in life than true friendship." Phyllis stretched her arm out toward him, and he took her hand, giving it a squeeze.

"Did my daughter tell you I'm moving to Boston? I'll be living in a retirement home, making friends with old people just like me."

Everyone in the room laughed, and they talked on about her move to Boston until Phyllis grew visibly tired. In parting, Alistair kissed her forehead and Lena her cheek, promising to visit again in a day or two.

Marie showed them to the door, thanking them for taking the time to see Phyllis.

"I hope she can rest more comfortably now," Lena said. Her sincere tone made Alistair marvel at how easily she'd forgiven this family who'd caused her so much suffering.

As they'd so often done as children, Alistair and Lena walked hand in hand with arms swinging down the sidewalk, turning left when they reached the street.

"I know what you're thinking, Alistair."

"Oh yeah? What's that?"

"That I'm a pushover. That I got myself into this mess by letting Jade take advantage of me and that I shouldn't be so forgiving of Phyllis."

"Don't go putting thoughts in my head," Alistair said. "That may be what you're thinking about yourself, but that is not at all my opinion of you. Your kindheartedness is the thing I love the most about you."

"When I ran away from home, I made a vow to myself that I would toughen up, stop being everyone's doormat. And my very first morning in Charleston, I fell into the same old trap when I met Jade."

"You don't need to change, Lena. You just need to be more selective about the friends you choose. And, I dare say, your next husband." He risked a glance at her. Her eyes shone with unshed tears, and he knew he'd gone too far. "I'm sorry." He dropped her hand and pulled her in for a half hug. "That was uncalled for."

"It's the truth, and I've always counted on you to tell me the truth." Lena swiped at her eyes with the backs of her hands. "If you feel this way about him, why did you let me marry Charles in the first place?"

"He wasn't so bad in the beginning. I got along with him fine. His success got to his head. He changed. You didn't. Therein lies the problem."

She stopped in the middle of the sidewalk and turned to him. "What do you mean I haven't changed? Everyone changes. People are supposed to grow wiser as they age. Are you saying that's why my marriage failed? Because I'm the same naive young woman he married?"

"Now you're putting words in my mouth, Lena. That is not at all what I'm saying. Growing and changing are two different things. Charles was once a decent guy. He is now an egotistical ass. You, on the other hand, are the same generous, loving soul you've always been." He took her by the shoulders and kissed the top of her head. "You've had an emotional few days. Once things settle down and you've had a chance to think about it, you'll see that I'm right. For now, let's focus on the positive. You're out of jail, and the charges have been dropped."

"And I feel like celebrating." She removed her phone from her purse. "I'll call Husk to see if I can get a table for tonight, and you call Kayla. Tell her what's happened and invite her to dinner."

Alistair remembered hearing Olivia talk about the popular restaurant. "Isn't it hard to get a reservation at Husk?"

"Usually." She held the phone away from her mouth. "But I've been talking to the manager about featuring the restaurant on the blog."

He listened to Lena's side of the conversation, waiting for her to give him the nod before calling Kayla, who was ecstatic to hear the charges had been dropped. "We're having a celebration in your mother's honor tonight at Husk, and we want you and Zack to come." A thought he'd had during the arraignment struck him again. "And if he's available, bring Owen along." He had a sneaking suspicion that Lena and her attorney might have more in common than her court case.

CHAPTER THIRTY-FOUR
LENA

Lena admired her reflection in the mirror. She wore a wrap dress—long sleeved and slinky in shades of purple and gray—with tall black boots. The dress was shorter than dresses she usually wore, and even though she had at least ten pounds to lose before she reached her desired weight, she thought she looked hot, as Kayla would say, not half-bad for a maturing woman.

On the way home from Phyllis's house, she and Alistair had walked up King Street together before parting in front of the Charleston Place Hotel. He'd wanted to buy something special for Olivia, and Lena had gone shopping for a new dress to wear to her celebration dinner. She'd purchased the dress and boots with her own money, the feeling of liberation in being able to do so reinforcing her decision to divorce Charles.

Alistair texted that they were waiting for her in front of their hotel. She stuffed her camera in her purse, locked the door, and rode down in the elevator.

"Wow!" Alistair said when he saw her walking across the street. "You look like the Lena I knew in college."

Lena extended her cheek to accept his kiss. "You're a liar, but thank you for the compliment." She noticed a beige sedan with an Uber decal idling on the curb. "Why aren't we walking? The restaurant is right up the street."

Alistair stared down at Olivia with obvious adoration. "Because my date decided to wear her highest heels," he said of Olivia's brown suede boots with three-inch heels.

"They're the only ones I brought that go with my new bag. Alistair surprised me with it." Olivia let out a squeal as she showed off her new Louis Vuitton tote.

Lena ran her hand across the monogrammed canvas. "That's gorgeous. You've been holding out on me, Alistair. I didn't know you had such good taste."

Alistair said, "I started to get black but decided she needed a change."

Olivia pulled the straps of the bag apart so Lena could see inside. "There's plenty of room for my laptop. It's not exactly a dinner bag, but I couldn't resist showing it off."

"You look very professional." Lena looped her arm through Olivia's. "Our month isn't technically up yet, but since we're extending our swap—and who knows when we'll see each other again—this seems like a good time to take our *after* selfie."

"I agree. We've experienced enough changes in our lives to warrant an *after* shot." Olivia leaned in close while Lena snapped a handful of selfies.

Alistair opened the back door for the ladies. "Let's not keep our driver waiting."

Three blocks later, the Uber deposited them in front of the restaurant. Husk consisted of two renovated historic buildings: the restaurant, a framed two-story Queen Anne–style home with front porches on both levels, and a two-story brick building next door that served as the bar. The threesome found the rest of their party gathered in the corner of the second-floor bar with two bottles of champagne chilling in ice buckets on a table nearby. Kayla, Zack, and Owen each gave Lena a congratulatory hug in turn. A waiter filled six glasses with champagne, and Lena lifted hers in a toast.

"I'd like to thank each of you for your support. I would never have made it through this harrowing ordeal without you. To old friends, new friends, and my precious daughter, Kayla." After clinking glasses, everyone took a sip of champagne. Lena raised her glass again. "And to Phyllis, may she have many more years of good health."

"Hear! Hear!" they all said in unison with their glasses held high.

Kayla elbowed Alistair out of the way to get to Lena. "I'm so relieved, Mom," she said, kissing her cheek. "I can't tell you how worried I've been. Especially after seeing you yesterday in that awful prison uniform. Orange is definitely not your color, but boy do you look hot tonight. Your outfit is glam."

Lena touched her fingertips to her daughter's cheek. "Thank you, sweetheart. You look pretty hot yourself." Kayla looked stunning in black skinny jeans, boots, and a pewter-colored sequined top that showed off a considerable amount of cleavage and bare back.

Kayla drained half her glass of champagne and licked her lips. "After everything that's happened, I don't blame you if you want to go back to Richmond, but I'm hoping you'll stay. At least for a while. I've been such a brat these past few years. I'd like the chance to make it up to you. You'll always be my mom, but I hope that one day we can be friends."

"There's nothing I'd like more," Lena managed to choke out past the lump in her throat. As tempted as she was to tell Kayla of her plans for the future, she felt it only right to tell Charles first that she was divorcing him.

Lena moved around the bar, upstairs and down, taking photographs and asking the bartenders about their signature drinks. And she continued her photo shoot when they entered the restaurant next door. Paige Kelley, the manager she'd been working with to coordinate the interview, greeted them at the hostess stand.

"It's nice to finally meet you," Paige said. "I'm glad we could accommodate you tonight."

"Thank you so much for making it happen on such short notice. My best friend's in town, as is my daughter. It's rare that we're all together." She turned to Olivia standing next to her. "I'd like you to meet my . . ."

"Partner. My name is Olivia Westcoat," she said, holding her hand out to Paige. "Lena and I are co-contributors on our blog. We have an extensive following of readers who will appreciate an inside look at Husk."

"We're grateful for the opportunity." With six menus in hand, Paige ushered them to a large round table in the center of one of two dining rooms on the main floor.

Alistair, trailing closely behind her, whispered, "Don't look now, but every man in the room is watching you. I'm going to have to defend your honor."

"Oh, hush up, Alistair," she said, but she couldn't suppress a grin.

At the table, Olivia seated herself to the left of Lena, and Owen beat Kayla to the chair on her other side.

Owen smiled up at Kayla. "I hope you don't mind, Kayla. I'd like to get to know your mother better."

"Of course." Kayla winked at Lena as she moved to the other side of the table to the empty chair between Alistair and Zack.

Lena said, "I'm so glad you could join us tonight, Owen. I want to thank you again for your representation."

Owen smiled. "Happy to help. I'm glad your need for my services was short-lived."

"If you'll excuse me a minute, I don't mean to be rude, but I need to have a quick talk with Olivia."

"Take all the time you need." Owen opened the wine menu. "In the meantime, if you don't mind, I'll take the liberty of selecting some wines."

"That would be nice." Lena directed her attention to Olivia. "At lunch today, you'd started to tell me something about the Kates when we were interrupted by Marie's phone call."

Olivia gripped Lena's arm. "You're not going to believe this. A TV production company has offered the Kates a reality show. They're purchasing the copyrights to the Kate Scapades blog posts, from which they plan to base the episodes. They've promised *Hi-Low* exclusive interviews with the stars during production."

"That's so exciting," Lena said. She could hardly believe everything was going so well when only a few short hours ago she'd been standing in front of a judge, pleading not guilty to elder abuse charges.

"You've done a great job of attracting more followers," Olivia said. "I can't pay you anything right now, but it won't be long before we start to see an increase in income from advertisements and affiliate marketing."

"I never expected to earn money from the blog. My goal was to attract attention to my images in order to build my reputation. I'm not sure what I'm going to do with my photography. Who knows, I may become a wedding photographer."

Olivia clasped her hands together. "That's perfect for you. As you know, Charleston is a popular wedding destination. Listen to me. I'm being presumptuous, talking like you're moving to Charleston permanently. You just seem so happy here, aside from the Phyllis disaster, of course."

"I have a lot of decisions to make about my future, Olivia, but I'd love nothing more than to stay in Charleston."

"I hope it all works out in your favor, Lena. You're a wonderful woman who has much to offer. And I hope we'll continue to be friends going forward."

Lena smiled. "I'm counting on it."

Olivia refolded her linen napkin and smoothed it out in her lap. "Anyway, I have a lot of ideas for future content for the blog. I was thinking we could have a weekly feature where we interview women with special talents. You can share photography tips, and I can offer advice on writing. We could bring in makeup professionals and fashion consultants, implementing video interviews as much as possible."

"I agree, Olivia! Video is hot right now. I have ideas I'd like to share with you as well. We should schedule a phone chat soon."

"I'm dropping Alistair off at the airport early tomorrow morning, and then I'll be on the highway for the rest of the day. Call me whenever you're free. I'll put you on speaker, and we can talk through our ideas."

"I'll do that." Lena turned her attention back to her other guests, who were in a heated debate about the upcoming midterm election.

"Don't you know it's rude to talk politics at a dinner party?" she said, and they all laughed.

Their waitress, a thirtysomething woman with a heart-shaped face and blonde hair secured at the base of her neck, appeared at the table to take their drink orders. Owen asked for a show of hands for red versus white wines and ordered multiple bottles of each.

Lena glanced at the wine menu in his hands, her eyes growing wide at the prices of the bottles he'd ordered. Once the waitress had gone, Owen leaned in close to Lena. He smelled manly, of woodsmoke and bourbon. "Don't sweat the cost. I've already worked it out with Alistair. He's picking up dinner, and I'm paying for the wine."

"I can't let you do that," Lena said, shaking her head. "It's way too much."

"It's my pleasure, dear lady." His eyes sparkled with the same twinkle she'd seen at the police station.

Lena's gaze shifted across the table to Alistair. "And you are totally not paying for dinner."

"Oh yes I am," he said in a defiant tone. "I've already instructed the waitress to bring me the check."

"But I'm already indebted to you for so much. You posted my bail and rescued me from Jade. If you hadn't gone out on a limb like you did in contacting Marie, I could very well be headed to prison."

"I'll get the bail money back, so that's a nonissue. If you insist, you can reimburse me for the refrigerator I bought for your cottage."

"Oh no!" Lena said, bringing her fingers to her lips. "So that old clunker finally died?"

"They hauled it off to the appliance graveyard," Alistair said. "You can have a tombstone made for it."

"Stop teasing me, Alistair!" Lena fished an ice cube out of her water glass and flicked it at him. She asked Olivia, "Was it a terrible inconvenience?"

"It could've been a lot worse," Olivia said. "When I arrived at the cottage that first day, I was greeted by the stench of a dead refrigerator. But Alistair found a deal on a scratch-and-dent model and had it delivered as soon as they could get it there."

Owen folded his arms on the table. "Well now, Alistair, aren't you the knight in shining armor? You sure know how to make a man look bad."

Everyone, including Owen, laughed.

Paige returned to the table with the waitress when she brought over the wine. "The chef has asked to see you ladies in the kitchen," she said to Olivia and Lena. "He's crazy busy and won't have but a minute to speak, but he thought maybe you'd like to take some photographs."

Lena and Olivia shot to their feet at once. "That would be awesome."

Slinging her camera strap over her shoulder, Lena followed Paige and Olivia through the restaurant to the kitchen, where the staff was hustling about in organized chaos. While Paige explained to Olivia their method for crafting menus, Lena set her camera to video and stood off to the side, out of the way, shooting footage of the food prep process.

The chef, wearing his double-breasted white coat with a mono-grammed *H*, waved to them. "Welcome to Husk," he said, his deep voice booming over the cacophony of noises in the kitchen. Making his way to them, he spoke for a moment about their policy of providing farm-to-table food exclusively from the South. "Please, ladies, proceed with your photo shoot. Don't hesitate to ask if you have questions."

Lena and Olivia returned to the table, talking a mile a minute about different possible angles for their blog post. The waitress had poured the wine in their absence, and Alistair had ordered a number of first courses for the table to share. Olivia told the others about their experience in the kitchen while Lena took a quick peek at the video footage on her camera.

"I'm sure your husband was relieved to hear the charges have been dropped," Owen said in a soft voice meant only for her ears. When she looked up at him, she followed his gaze to her wedding ring.

Lena turned the camera off and placed it in her bag. "Funny you should mention that. My husband doesn't know anything about my ordeal. In fact, I haven't spoken with him since I left home at the end of September. It took me running away to Charleston to face the reality that my marriage is over."

"Your husband is a damn fool."

Lena felt her face grow warm. "Anyway, I have no clue where to begin. I guess I need a divorce attorney. Can you recommend one?"

"You need someone licensed to practice law in Virginia, and it just so happens that an old high school buddy of mine lives in Richmond. He has a solid reputation. At least as far as I know. You might want to check him out with some of your friends."

Because I have so many friends in Richmond to ask. The realization that she didn't know a single soul she could ask about a divorce attorney was yet one more sign pointing her in the direction of a permanent move to Charleston.

He removed his phone from the pocket of his tweed sport coat. "I'll send you his contact info."

"I'd appreciate that."

A server delivered their first courses—fire-roasted oysters, glazed pork belly lettuce wraps, and southern fried chicken skins—and they all sampled a tasting from each platter. Alistair spoke of his upcoming trip to New York, Kayla the job interviews she'd lined up, and Zack the ad accounts he was working on. But it was Owen who kept them entertained with lively tales of his numerous trips to exotic-sounding places Lena would love to visit.

The night came to an end all too soon for Lena, and her spirits plummeted as she bid Zack, Owen, and her daughter goodbye in front of the restaurant.

"We're not going anywhere, Mom," Kayla said. "Zack and I are right here if you need us. In fact, why don't you and I get together tomorrow afternoon for a glass of wine, just the two of us?"

Lena smiled. "I'd like that." She had much she wanted to talk to her daughter about.

Alistair summoned an Uber, and when they arrived back at the hotel, he suggested a walk to the end of the pier. With the lights from the Cooper River bridge glimmering in the distance, they stood in silence side by side at the pier railing.

Wrapping an arm around each of them, Alistair pulled Lena and Olivia close. "I sense a new beginning for the three of us. What say we spend Christmas together in New York?"

Olivia clapped her hands together like a delighted child. "New York? Really! Can we, Alistair?"

"You bet we can. What about you, Lena? Can we count you in?"

Lena thought about how far she'd come in the past few weeks and the challenges she faced in the months ahead as she put her divorce in motion. "You lovebirds go ahead and make your plans without me. Christmas seems like a lifetime away."

Alistair gave her neck a squeeze. "I'll leave the invitation open if you change your mind."

They walked back up the pier and through the park, parting in front of his hotel with hugs and kisses. As she rode in the elevator to the condo, instead of being lonely, Lena felt comforted in being alone. Kayla was with Zack, and Charles was no longer her concern. She had only herself to worry about. *This life is no longer on loan, Lena. This is your new reality. Charleston. Being a photographer. Making your own decisions. You no longer have anyone to answer to but yourself. Maybe one day, when the time is right, you'll find a man as kind and generous as Owen. If that never happens, you'll find the strength to make it on your own. There is absolutely nothing stopping you from going to New York for Christmas. You've put your life on hold for far too long. It's time to live a little.*

CHAPTER THIRTY-FIVE

OLIVIA

Alistair and Olivia arrived in Manhattan late in the day on December 23. Their corner suite at The Ritz was handsomely decorated with antiques and velvet upholstery. White lights glimmered on a Fraser fir by the window, and pine scented the air from bouquets of fresh greens placed on side tables in the living area.

"My girlfriend doesn't understand the concept of traveling light," Alistair said to the bellman as he unloaded Olivia's three large suitcases from the cart. "One of those suitcases is full of shoes. I know because I watched her pack."

"Shoes and handbags," Olivia corrected. "So what? I'm high maintenance. You've known that about me from the beginning. Besides, we're spending the holidays in New York, the most fashionable city in the world. I want to look my best."

Alistair smiled at her. "You always do. And I'm counting on you to look smashing for our appointment in the morning."

He'd been talking for days about a mysterious appointment he'd arranged for them. Olivia couldn't imagine what he had in store for her at nine in the morning on Christmas Eve, but she assumed it had to do with the decision he'd yet to make about moving to New York.

The deal he'd worked on in late October had gone well, and Henry was more insistent than ever about Alistair rejoining the firm. Although they'd discussed the issue ad nauseam, he remained torn between his quiet life in the Northern Neck and the fulfilling career he could have in Manhattan.

Alistair tipped the bellman and closed the door behind him.

Olivia wandered over to the Christmas tree, admiring the jewel-toned ornaments. "Who did all this?"

He came to stand beside her. "Believe it or not, they have an elf for hire on staff here."

"Funny, ha ha," she said, and moved to the window. "The view is incredible. I don't think I realized Central Park is so vast."

"To be exact, there are 20,000 trees, over 200 animal species, all across 843 acres."

She nudged him with her elbow. "Look at you with your Manhattan fun facts. You love it here. Why are you having such a difficult time making the decision to move?"

"You already know the answer to that. I love the Northern Neck equally as much. Henry and his wife have invited us for brunch on New Year's Day. I told him I'd let him know my decision then." He wrapped his arms around her from behind. "You're as tired of talking about it as I am. What say we call the subject off-limits while we're here?"

Olivia cocked her head to the side. "And do what? Make a game-time decision on New Year's Day?"

"Something like that. A gut decision based on how we're feeling after spending a week here."

"Sounds good to me," Olivia said, happy to have a little respite. Although she'd assured Alistair that she would be fine with whatever he decided, she found the uncertainty of not knowing where she'd be living in a month's time unsettling.

"Let's dress for dinner and go have a drink downstairs," he said, planting kisses along the nape of her neck.

"As long as we can get an appetizer. I'm starving." She untangled herself from his hold. If she didn't stop him, they'd end up in bed. And she was starving.

Alistair insisted on being well rested for his mystery appointment. After drinks and several appetizers in the hotel's lounge, they decided to call it an early night instead of going to dinner. At eight the following morning, Olivia answered the door when room service brought up bowls of creamy oatmeal, thick slices of applewood-smoked bacon, and a pot of rich coffee. Alistair was still shaving, and Olivia was already showered and dressed in gray suede leggings, black boots, and a long white cashmere sweater with bell sleeves. She poured a cup of coffee and sat at the table by the window overlooking Central Park. While she would miss her views of Carters Creek in the Northern Neck and the harbor from her condo in Charleston, the view of the park was one she could get used to.

The weather forecast predicted six to eight inches of snow later in the day, and the sky was already heavy with thick gray clouds. Being from Charleston, Olivia was accustomed to milder winters, but she loved the idea of a white Christmas in New York. When they exited the hotel forty minutes later, the air was damp and frigid.

"So this is what people mean when they say it feels like snow," she said, buttoning up her white wool coat.

"We're definitely getting snow today." He took her gloved hand in his and started off toward Fifth Avenue.

"Where're we going?" she asked, struggling to keep up with him. "Don't we need to hail a cab?"

"We're just going around the corner."

When they reached Fifth Avenue, he led her another two blocks to Tiffany's flagship store. A young man wearing a plaid tie and a mischievous grin, as though he was hiding a secret, waited for them at the front door. He let them in and locked the door behind them.

"Welcome to Tiffany's," he said. "I'm Brent Pope, and I will be your salesman today. We don't officially open until ten. You have the store to yourselves until then. Let me know if I can answer questions or show you any of the merchandise."

Olivia's eyes were wide as she looked around the empty store. "So this is your mystery appointment? A private shopping excursion at Tiffany's?"

"A Christmas trip to New York isn't complete without one. Besides, I was having trouble deciding on the right gift for you, so I figured why not let you pick it out yourself."

"That's not fair, Alistair," she said with a playful smack on his arm. "You can't put me on the spot like this. Can you at least give me some suggestions?"

"Actually, I did have one thing in mind." They circled the immense showroom, stopping in front of a showcase of diamond engagement rings.

Is he serious? I'm not ready for a marriage proposal. Or am I?

Turning to face her, as though reading her mind, he said, "You may not be ready for this. You may never be ready for this. But I have absolutely no doubts about my feelings for you. I would love nothing more than to spend the rest of my life making you happy. Will you marry me?"

When she opened her mouth to tell him she wasn't sure she wanted to get married again, the word *yes* rolled off her tongue instead. And as she stood looking up at him, she realized she wanted nothing more than to be his wife.

He blinked hard. "Do you mean it? You'll really marry me?"

She bobbed her head up and down. "I mean it! I love you, Alistair. I want to spend the rest of my life making *you* happy."

His lips met hers, and he kissed her passionately, ignoring Brent, who was watching them from the other side of the showroom. Finally, he ended the kiss and called to Brent. "She said yes! I'm gonna buy this lady the biggest diamond you have."

"That's wonderful news." Brent hurried over to them. "I should warn you, however, that we have some very large diamonds." He walked them to an elevator at the front of the store. "Let's go upstairs to the salon where we keep our most valuable jewels."

When they exited the elevator, Brent motioned them to a lounging area. "Please have a seat. I'll be with you in a moment."

Alistair and Olivia had no sooner settled themselves on a Tiffany-blue velvet sofa when a waiter appeared. "May I offer you a beverage? Champagne perhaps? I understand congratulations are in order."

Alistair cast a questioning glance at Olivia. "Why not?" she said. "We definitely have something to celebrate."

For the next two hours, Olivia tried on rings in all shapes and sizes with a variety of gems. In the end, they decided on a four-carat brilliant-cut diamond in a pavé setting. The ring fit perfectly. To be able to wear it out of the store only added to Olivia's delight.

A light snow was falling when they finally emerged from Tiffany's a few minutes before twelve. "I made a reservation for noon at the Boathouse," Alistair said. "We can taxi most of the way, but we'll have to walk a short distance into the park. Are you up for it?"

Her eyes lit up. "A walk in Central Park in the snow with my fiancé? Are you kidding me? This day is full of dreams come true."

~

Snow continued to fall throughout their celebratory lunch at a table by the window at the Boathouse. Afterward, the restaurant's shuttle driver took pity on them and drove them back to their hotel, where they spent the rest of the afternoon in bed, making love and sleeping off their champagne buzz.

"You'd better get a move on," Alistair said as he dressed for dinner. "It's already six o'clock, and the boys are expecting us at seven. It may take a while to get a taxi in this weather on Christmas Eve."

Olivia was still lounging in bed, too warm and content to move. "I'll get up in a minute." She held her hand out in front her, admiring her sparkling diamond. "I just want to look at my ring a little longer. As much as it kills me to take it off, I'm going to leave it in the safe tonight. Since I was in Seattle with my daughter when your sons visited you at Thanksgiving, I'd really like to get to know them, and them me, before we tell them about our engagement."

Alistair tugged on his gray wool slacks. "Whatever you want, sweetheart. But there's no reason to be nervous. They're going to love you."

"I hope you're right."

And he *was* right. She'd worried for no reason. Josh and Mike greeted her with warm hugs as though she were an old family friend.

Their apartment was festive with a fire burning in the fireplace and a small Christmas tree with blinking colored lights in the corner.

"Something smells delicious," Olivia said, sniffing. "Is that dinner?"

Mike smiled down at his new girlfriend, the nurse he'd met in the emergency room the night of his accident. She was a pretty young woman, petite with thick mahogany hair. "Emily's roasting a beef tenderloin. She's an amazing cook."

Olivia didn't need to know Mike well to tell he was smitten with Emily. "I hope you'll put me to work in the kitchen," she said to Emily.

"No way. I won't be responsible for messing up your killer outfit," Emily said of Olivia's red tartan silk pants and black turtleneck sweater.

Olivia eyed the black apron Emily wore over her gray velvet dress. "Do you have another apron?"

She rolled her hazel eyes. "Sorry. These boys don't own an apron. I had to bring my own."

Emily kept her word, refusing to let Olivia help in the kitchen. While she and Alistair sipped red wine by the fire, Mike, Josh, and

Emily put the finishing touches on a delicious dinner of beef tenderloin, roasted vegetables, and twice-baked potatoes. Having spent the previous three Christmas Eves alone, she particularly enjoyed the company, although being with the young people made her miss her own daughter all the more. She found them engaging, intelligent, and funny. If only Laura could find someone as handsome, successful, and kindhearted as Mike and Josh.

After they'd finished eating, Alistair and Olivia insisted on clearing the table and doing the dishes while Emily sliced the eggnog cheesecake she'd made herself. They took their dessert to the sitting area, where they exchanged their few gifts by the fire. They had a good laugh when the boys gave Olivia the same gift she gave them.

"Cashmere scarves will come in handy if the weather today is any indication of the winter to come," Alistair said with a snicker.

Emily appeared touched that Olivia remembered her with an ocean mist and sea salt scented votive candle.

The boys gave Alistair a handsome burgundy-and-navy Hermès tie. "We want to make certain you're looking your best when you go back to work," Josh said, giving his father's neck a squeeze.

"Work or not, a Hermès tie always makes a statement."

Olivia saw past Alistair's smile to the concern in his eyes. *What's holding him back from making this decision?* she wondered for the umpteenth time during the past two months. She watched as he moved to the window, staring down at Thirty-Ninth Street below. Snow had continued to fall throughout the evening. Based on the boys' best guesses, they were nearing the eight-inch mark.

"I don't see any taxis," Alistair said. "I hate to cut the evening short, but if we don't leave soon, we may find ourselves stranded."

Josh said, "I would offer to drive you, but I've had more than my share to drink."

"I can take you," Emily volunteered. "I only had one glass of wine during dinner."

"And I can ride with her," Mike offered.

"None of you are going out in this mess." Alistair retrieved their coats from the rack beside the door. "I'm sure we can get an Uber."

They hugged the kids and thanked them for a wonderful evening, then wished a Merry Christmas to Emily, who planned to spend the day with her parents.

"We'll see you at The Ritz tomorrow, promptly at noon," Alistair said to his sons.

They waited twenty minutes in the lobby for an Uber—a four-wheel drive with a cheerful driver who'd decorated the Tahoe's interior with flashing multicolored Christmas lights. On the way back to the hotel, Alistair's phone pinged twice with texts from both boys. She's awesome, Dad and Mom would be pleased from Mike and Josh respectively.

The minute they were back in the room, Olivia removed her engagement ring from the closet safe. "I'm not taking it off again."

"We'll tell the boys about our engagement tomorrow at brunch." Alistair produced a sprig of mistletoe he'd plucked from an arrangement of greenery in the lobby and held it over her head while he kissed her.

After a late night of lovemaking, Alistair and Olivia slept in the following morning, making them late for brunch with Mike and Josh.

"Are you two sharing a room here?" Josh asked with a look of fake horror on his face.

Alistair puffed out his chest. "Damn straight. This lovely lady has agreed to marry me."

The boys let out hoots of approval. "Let's order champagne!" Mike suggested.

Olivia laughed. "Don't mind me if I float away on the bubbles from all the champagne I've drunk in the past twenty-four hours."

"When's the wedding?" Josh asked.

Alistair reached for Olivia's hand. "That's up to my fiancée. She may want a long engagement."

"How about Presidents' Day weekend?" Olivia blurted out, surprising them all, including herself. "If we're not already living here, we'll fly back up for the weekend. We can figure out a place to have a small ceremony and luncheon reception for family and a few friends."

The look of approval on Alistair's face told her she'd made the right decision.

After consuming multiple bottles of champagne, the boys returned to their apartment for a nap, and Alistair and Olivia to their room.

Olivia stretched out on the bed and called her daughter to wish her Merry Christmas.

"I'm so happy for you, Mom," Laura said when she told her about the engagement. "I can't wait to meet Alistair."

"I hope you'll come for the wedding on Presidents' Day weekend," Olivia said.

"I wouldn't miss it."

Olivia's heart fluttered. Could her daughter possibly be softening toward her?

When she ended the call with Laura forty minutes later, Olivia noticed Alistair watching her with a contented smile on his face. "What're you thinking about?" she asked.

"How I'm the luckiest man in the world to have found such a beautiful woman."

"I have a surprise for you."

"But you already gave me my present," he said.

She'd given him his main Christmas gift early—an antique barometer too fragile to withstand the trip to New York.

"This is just a little something extra." She got up from the bed and disappeared into the bathroom, emerging ten minutes later in a sexy Santa teddy.

Alistair's eyes popped. "Whoa. You are one hot woman." He rolled off the bed to his feet. He took her in his arms. "Just what I wanted for Christmas. My own personal Santa Baby."

CHAPTER THIRTY-SIX
LENA

Lena was experiencing severe anxiety over her trip to New York. In the past twenty-four hours, she'd picked up the phone a half dozen times to call Owen to cancel. Then, remembering her daughter's excitement over what Kayla referred to as an epic New Year's with Mike and Josh, she'd changed her mind. As thrilled as Kayla was about being in New York for the holiday, she was even more excited about introducing Zack to Mike and Josh, the boys who'd been like brothers to her growing up.

It wasn't the trip itself that was causing Lena angst. It was the thought of staying in the same hotel room with Owen, even if that hotel room was a three-bedroom suite. Lena and Owen weren't exactly strangers. She'd grown quite fond of him since they first met at the police station in October. They'd gone to dinner and parties on many occasions. He was fun to be with, easy to talk to, and always eager to try new things. But her feelings went deeper than fondness. They'd kissed. A lot, actually. She found their make-out sessions pleasurable. He stirred awake feelings inside her that'd been asleep for far too long.

While her attraction to Owen was growing, so were her inhibitions about having sex with him. Aside from Charles, she'd only been with two other men. Boys, really—one in high school and one in college. Her sex life with Charles had lacked passion. She knew little about pleasing a man and was terrified of letting Owen down.

When she'd first broached the subject of the New Year's trip to New York, sensing her discomfort, Owen, ever the gentleman, had booked a suite big enough for Lena and Kayla to share a room and Owen and Zack to have their own. She suspected Zack and Kayla were sharing the same bed in Owen's carriage house, but they respected her by not flaunting their sexual life in front of her.

Despite her reservations about the hotel situation, Lena looked forward to traveling with Owen. With a joie de vivre attitude that was infectious, he could turn a simple trip to the Harris Teeter for a gallon of milk into an adventure.

"Our first trip of many to come." He toasted her with the flute of champagne offered to them by the first-class flight attendant. A driver in a luxury car was waiting at LaGuardia Airport to whisk them off to their hotel.

Lena's unease lessened as soon as she saw the spaciousness of their suite. "This is very nice, Owen. Thank you so much."

When Kayla and Zack scurried off to explore the shops on Fifth Avenue, Lena and Owen joined Alistair and Olivia in the Star Lounge for afternoon tea.

Olivia greeted her with a warm hug. "You look fabulous. How much weight have you lost?"

"I've almost reached my goal." Lena eyed the trays of finger sandwiches and petits fours. "But I'm putting the diet on hold until after this trip."

Olivia laughed. "Good decision."

Alistair brought her in for a half hug, whispering in her ear, "Someone's wearing a rosy glow. Are you and Owen in love?"

"Stop it, Alistair." She pinched the tender skin on the underside of his upper arm, but he held her tight.

"Don't look now, but he's staring at you with pure, unadulterated adoration."

"You're incorrigible. Stop teasing me!" She stomped on his foot and pushed him away.

"Ouch! That hurt, Lena!" He hobbled on his wounded foot to his chair.

Once he'd gotten over his pain and Lena and Owen were seated on the banquette across from them at the table, he said, "Olivia and I have some exciting news to share. We're getting married Presidents' Day weekend. We hope you'll fly back up for the wedding."

"I wouldn't miss it for the world," Lena said. "That's the most exciting news I've heard in a very long time. You both deserve this happiness."

"Forget the tea," Owen said. "Bring on the champagne."

Olivia grimaced. "I've lost count of the bottles of bubbly we've consumed this week. And all the rich food. Ugh. I'm definitely starting my diet tomorrow. Or the next day. Oh, what the heck. Like the man said, 'Bring on the champagne.'"

"To Alistair and Olivia," Lena said once they all had champagne flutes in hand. "I'm thrilled for you, even more so that I had a small hand in introducing you. I wish you a long and happy life together."

Alistair raised his glass to Lena. "And to your divorce. How are the proceedings going, by the way?"

"Charles is being surprisingly amicable. He's as eager for our marriage to end as I am. When I was in Richmond in November to meet with the divorce attorney and move some of my things out of the house, Charles confessed to a long-term affair with one of his business associates."

Alistair shook his head in disgust. "Add *womanizer* to his long list of character flaws."

"Whatever," Lena said. "It alleviates my guilt about divorcing him."

Eager to divert the subject from her divorce, Lena toasted Olivia. "To your bright future as a romance author. I wanted to wait and tell you in person. After reading the first draft of *Marriage of Lies*, I can report that it's one of the best romances I've read. I'll type up some notes and email them to you when I get home."

Olivia fanned herself with her cocktail napkin. "I can't tell you how relieved I am to hear that, even if you are exaggerating."

Lena placed her hand over her heart. "I promise I'm not just saying that. It's really very good."

Alistair gave Olivia a half hug. "Now will you let me read it?"

Olivia cupped his cheek. "You can read it when it's published."

Owen lifted his glass. "I'd like to propose a toast to Lena's new venture."

Lena leaned into Owen on the banquette. "Shh! You'll jinx it."

Alistair sat up straight. "Jinx what? Spill it, Lena. What've you been hiding from me?"

"All right. But keep this to yourselves for now. I've come across an opportunity too good to turn down. A wedding photographer who's moving with her husband to Texas has agreed to sell me her business at a price I can afford. It's a small operation, which is perfect for me."

Alistair and Olivia peppered her with questions about the business until Owen excused himself to go to the restroom.

"Things appear to be going well between you two," Olivia said, her brows dancing across her forehead.

"We're just friends," Lena said, staring into her lap to hide her flushed face.

"Yeah, right," Alistair said with an eye roll.

"Since you'll be making a permanent move to Charleston, you're welcome to live in my condo as long as you like," Olivia said.

"That's very generous of you, but you'll need a place to stay once they start filming the reality show. I found a carriage house for rent. It's tiny but perfect for me. It's time for our house swap to end." Lena poured herself more champagne and shifted in her seat to face Alistair. "I've given it a lot of thought, and as much as I love the Northern Neck, I've decided to sell my cottage. I need the money to buy the business. I know this may come as a shock to you. I will forever worship every memory we made there together."

Disbelief crossed Alistair's face. "Are you sure about this, Lena? I think you're making a rash decision way too soon after your separation from Charles. What's the hurry? Why not give it some time?"

Lena felt flustered. Was she making a hasty decision? "I have——" Owen returned to the table, saving her from having to respond.

There was no more talk of Lena selling her cottage that afternoon, but when they went upstairs to their rooms to change for dinner, Owen asked, "Did something happen while I was in the restroom? I felt like I'd interrupted something important when I returned. Alistair seemed so gloomy when he'd been in such a good mood earlier."

Lena sat down on the sofa in the suite's main sitting room. "He's upset with me for selling my river cottage. He thinks I'm making a rash decision too soon after my separation. What do you think, Owen?"

He sat down close to her on the sofa. "I may not be the best person to ask, since I've never been to your river house, and I've never met your soon-to-be ex-husband. But you've said repeatedly that you're happier than you've been in years. I interpret that to mean you're making decisions that are right for you now, whereas decisions you made in the past didn't turn out as you'd hoped. My advice would be for you to trust your gut. If something feels right, go for it. That's always worked for me."

She smiled. "I shudder to think of the heartache I would've saved myself if I'd learned to trust my gut years ago." As she stood, she leaned over and kissed his cheek. "Thank you, Owen. You've been a good friend these past couple of months."

He touched his fingertips to the spot on his cheek where she'd kissed him. "I'd like to be more than friends, if you'll let me."

"I respect your feelings, Owen. I truly do. It's just that everything is happening so fast. The divorce. Moving to Charleston. Buying a business."

Closing his eyes, he gave a solemn nod. "I understand. And I want you to take all the time you need. I'm not going anywhere."

"You're the dearest man." She kissed his other cheek before retreating to her room.

Lena decided on the most daring of the outfits she'd brought with her—a red velvet long-sleeved top that showed an ample amount of cleavage, black satin pants, and black booties with a reasonable heel.

When she emerged from her room, Owen let out a low whistle. "You look sensational."

"You don't look so bad yourself," she said of his camel-hair sport coat and gray wool slacks.

The door was flung open, and Kayla and Zack tumbled into the room, their arms laden with shopping bags. Kayla's hand shot up, palm out. "I know. Don't say it. We're late. We were downstairs in the bar having a drink with Josh and Mike and Mike's new girlfriend, Emily. Mom, wait until you meet her. She's adorable. We'll change in a hurry and be back down in twenty minutes."

Owen held his elbow out to Lena. "What're we waiting for? It's New Year's Eve in New York. Let the party begin."

Alistair had booked a table in a private alcove at Tuscany Steakhouse. The evening was festive, the food and wine over the top. Everyone was in a celebratory mood, with the exception of Alistair. On the outside, he seemed fine. He laughed at jokes and participated in conversation. But he couldn't hide his feelings from Lena. She knew him too well. His smile fell short of reaching his eyes, and he refused to meet her gaze.

The youngsters left together around ten to join the circuit of parties being hosted by Mike's and Josh's friends.

Kayla kissed Lena's cheek as she got up from the table. "Happy New Year, Mom. Don't wait up for us."

"Don't worry," Lena said. "And don't wake me up when you come in."

Everyone at the table laughed.

The older crowd lingered over tiramisu for dessert. Lena and Olivia talked at length about their blog, while Alistair and Owen discovered hobbies they shared in common like fishing and golf. It was past eleven when they finally left the restaurant.

The weather was mild, and the foursome opted to walk the short distance back to the hotel. Lena grabbed Alistair by the elbow. "Let's you and I have a little talk." She held him back while Olivia and Owen walked ahead of them. "I get the feeling you're upset with me for selling my cottage."

"I'm not upset with you, Lena. I just think you're making a mistake. You've had so many changes lately. Why not wait awhile to be sure this is what you want? I can loan you the money to buy your business until you're absolutely sure about selling the cottage."

When doubt nagged at her conscience, she remembered Owen's words. *If something feels right, go for it.* "I am positively sure about this, Alistair. Worrying about the maintenance of the cottage is like a ball and chain, holding me back. I'm entering a new phase in my life. Be happy for me."

When they reached a street corner, they waited for the signal to cross. Lena was grateful that Olivia and Owen were too engrossed in conversation to pay attention to them.

"You're moving to New York, anyway," Lena said. "Why does it even matter to you if I sell my cottage?"

"We may not be moving. I haven't accepted the job yet."

Lena stopped in her tracks. "But you've been here for a week. I assumed you were looking for a place to live."

"We've looked at a few apartments. We even liked a couple of them. I don't know, Lena. I'm just so torn. I love it here. But I love it there too."

"Come on, Alistair. You're the least indecisive person I know. You made all the decisions when we were kids. What games we were going to play. Where we were going to fish on any given day. Whether we would ski or wakeboard."

"That's why this is so frustrating for me. All my life, I've known exactly what I wanted. Until now."

"But you're in your element here. You live for power lunches and closing multimillion-dollar deals."

Alistair stared at his feet. "I'm not getting any younger, you know. What if I lose my edge?"

Lena laughed out loud. "You? Alistair Hoffman? You'll take your edge with you to the grave. You worked a deal back in October. How did that go?"

His face lit up. "I crushed it. You should've seen it, Lena. I had them eating out of my hand."

"See! That's the Alistair Hoffman I know."

Noticing that Olivia and Owen were way ahead of them, they started walking again. Alistair said, "You say I'm in my element here, but I'm in my element in Irvington as well. I've enjoyed working in the café these past couple of months."

Lena shook her head. "You're not a barista. It's only a matter of time before you get bored with the café. Irvington's great for summers and long weekends. And retirement. You may think you're ready for retirement, but believe me, you're not. Empty nesting feels like early retirement, and I hated every minute of it. We thrive on challenges, you and me. Remember how action packed our days were as children? We dared each other to do the impossible."

He nodded. "I'd forgotten that about you. I never realized just how lost you've been."

"Slowly and surely, I'm finding myself. But this isn't about me. This is about you." They continued on for a minute in silence. "She's not coming back, you know." He looked confused, and she added, "Mary Anne. She's not coming back. You can safely sell the house, because the memories will always remain in your heart."

Alistair raked his fingers through his hair. "Maybe you're right. I've been telling myself this isn't about Mary Anne, but maybe it is. Don't get me wrong. I'm crazy in love with Olivia. Our relationship is exciting and adventurous and so very different from my relationship with my wife. Mary Anne was my soul mate. She was my home, inasmuch as a person can be a home."

"And that's why you can't bring yourself to sell that home. You spent your last days together in that house. What does Olivia think about moving to New York?"

"She says she'll support me whichever way I decide. Truthfully, she just wants me to make a decision. We agreed not to talk about it this week, if that tells you anything."

Lena's eyebrows shot up. "I don't understand. How did you look at apartments without discussing the move?"

He snickered. "It wasn't easy."

When they reached the hotel, Lena grabbed his elbow and spun him around to face her. "Don't make the same mistake I did. Don't lose yourself, Alistair. Accept this job offer. Rent out your house in the Northern Neck if you can't bring yourself to sell it. Like a wise man told me only hours ago—if something feels right, go for it. What's the worst thing that could happen?"

He thought about it a minute. "I could get fired."

"That's not going to happen, but if it does, you'll still have the boys and Olivia. And me. You'll pick up the pieces and find another challenge somewhere else."

Alistair lifted her off her feet and twirled her around. When he set her back down, he kissed her on both cheeks. "Thank you. I needed to hear the things you said. Wherever we end up, I'd like for us to promise to see each other as much as possible."

"That's a promise I definitely intend to keep."

They entered the building and found Olivia and Owen waiting for them in front of the hotel lounge. "Anybody up for a nightcap to ring in the New Year?" Owen asked without much enthusiasm.

When Lena's eyes met Owen's, something shifted inside her. *If something feels right, go for it.*

"I'm pretty tired from our trip," Lena said, faking a yawn.

Alistair and Olivia were quick to agree. Calling it an early night sounded like a good idea.

"Did you straighten him out?" Olivia asked when Lena hugged her good night.

"I certainly hope so."

As they rode up in the elevator, they made plans to have dinner together the following evening. When the elevator deposited Lena and Owen on the eleventh floor, the foursome bid each other a happy New Year.

Lena and Owen strolled hand in hand to their room. She turned to him just inside the door of their suite. "About what you said earlier. I want to be more than friends with you as well, but . . ." She looked away, and he tilted her chin toward him.

"But what?"

"But frankly, I'm terrified. And inexperienced, despite having been married for twenty-seven years."

His lips parted in a soft smile. "You're no more terrified and inexperienced than me. Actually, let me rephrase that. My wife and I had a great sex life. But there has been no one since her death six years ago." He reached over and flipped the switch, turning out the overhead fixture and leaving the room aglow from the city lights glimmering beyond the window. "We'll take things slow." He removed a bottle of red wine from the minibar and poured two glasses. "We won't do anything until we're both ready." He led her over to the love seat in front of the window. "We'll start by sipping wine and holding hands while we watch the fireworks."

Wrapping her arm around his neck, she drew his lips to hers and kissed him with a passion she didn't know she possessed. "And see where that takes us."

CHAPTER THIRTY-SEVEN

ALISTAIR

As Alistair was unlocking the door to their suite, Olivia's phone rang with a call from her daughter. "Darling! This is a surprise. Happy New Year."

Surprise? Alistair thought. She'd spoken to her daughter nearly every day since Christmas. Olivia had confided to Alistair that she sensed her daughter was uneasy about something, as though she was on the verge of making a major change.

At the makeshift bar, he poured bourbon over ice in a glass and went to the window beside Olivia. Laura was talking loud enough over what sounded like a party in the background for Alistair to hear what she said.

"I've got the most fab news, Mom. I've known about it all week, but I couldn't tell you until it was definite. I got a promotion, and my company is transferring me to our New York office. Isn't that incredible?"

Olivia locked eyes with Alistair. *So there had been a big change in the works.* "But I thought you love Seattle?"

"I do love Seattle. But I prefer to be on the East Coast closer to you. And if you and Alistair move to New York, we'll be in the same city."

"That's wonderful news, sweetheart. When will you move?"

"Right away. They want me to start in the New York office mid-January."

Alistair tuned out the conversation as he thought back over the week since Christmas. He'd managed to put all thoughts of Henry's job offer aside, and the days had passed in a blissful flurry of activity. They'd dined in the trendiest restaurants, attended Broadway shows, and ice-skated in Central Park. And they'd kept their promise not to discuss the move when they'd met with the Realtor on Friday. Olivia had fallen in love with the last of the six apartments they'd looked at—a two-thousand-square-foot two-bedroom on Central Park West with a stunning view of the park.

She'd teased, "If we can't live at The Ritz, this will do just fine."

His talk with Lena had hit on a sore subject, one he'd been subconsciously aware of but afraid to admit, even to himself. He was holding back, terrified of severing the strings that bound him to Mary Anne. But it wasn't just that. He truly loved his house on Carters Creek. He'd grown up there as a boy. The Northern Neck was in his blood. But Lena had been right on another count as well. He wasn't a barista. He thrived on the challenges of a high-pressure career.

Olivia ended her call with her daughter. "Guess what! Laura's moving to New York."

"So I heard. That's wonderful news. I know you're excited."

"Very." Looping her arm through his, she laid her head on his shoulder as the first fireworks boomed above the New York skyline. "It's time, Alistair. The new year is here. You have to make your decision. Your lunch with Henry is only hours away. What's it gonna be? New York or the Northern Neck?"

He let out a sigh. He could no longer put off the decision. "Laura moving to New York is a game changer for you."

"I admit the prospect of us living in the same city is appealing, but I don't want that to persuade your decision. This is about *your* career, Alistair. Not mine."

They stood watching the fireworks for a few minutes in silence.

"We've talked about you selling the house in Irvington and moving here or not selling the house and staying there," Olivia said. "What I don't understand is why we can't have it both ways. Let's move here and keep your river house as a second home. You did it before, when you and Mary Anne lived in Connecticut."

Alistair shook his head. "That was different. My parents owned the house back then, and they went down nearly every weekend to check on things. There's a lot of work involved in maintaining the place."

"I'm aware of that. For the past three months, I've watched you slave over the yard. But that doesn't mean you have to do it all. I'm sure we can hire a lawn service and a cleaning lady to come every couple of weeks. If it's an issue of money . . ."

"It's not about money," Alistair said. "We can afford both."

"It's simple, then. When you negotiate your contract with Henry, you make sure to ask for plenty of vacation time."

Alistair didn't have to negotiate. Henry had already promised him all the vacation time he wanted. "What about the café? I can't just abandon my crew."

"Puh-lease! Your *crew* will get along just fine without you. If things don't work out, you can always sell it."

"But I've already tried to find a buyer. It's not that easy."

With hands on hips, she glared at him. "Tell me the truth, Alistair. How hard did you really try?"

"Not that hard, actually," he said with a sheepish grin. "This would mean an awful lot of traveling back and forth. Would you be willing to spend holidays and long weekends down there?"

"Of course. I love the Northern Neck." She took his face in her hands. "We're making a bigger deal out of this than it has to be. Let's just do it. See how it goes. If living in the big city gets to be too much, we'll move back to Virginia. If not, we'll move back when you retire. In the meantime, we'll get to spend quality time with our children."

"I definitely love the thought of that." He would take his own advice. He wouldn't make a rash decision. He would give it some time and see if they could manage to keep the house.

He removed his phone from his pocket, and his thumbs flew across the screen.

"Who are you texting at this hour?" Olivia asked.

"The Realtor. First thing in the morning, we'll make an offer on the apartment you love so much on Central Park West."

She clasped her hands to her chest. "Do you mean it? Can I put my writing desk by the window next to the gas fireplace?"

"You can do anything you want with the apartment." He set his empty glass down and pulled her close. In a voice thick with lust, he said, "As long as you promise to keep my bed warm at night."

She touched the tip of her finger to his lips. "There's no place I'd rather be, Alistair Hoffman."

A NOTE FROM THE AUTHOR

Hands up if you've ever felt like running away. I know I have. More times than I care to admit, actually. In fact, one of those times provided inspiration for this book. We often feel trapped in our lives, desperate for escape. It's easy for women to get stuck in a rut. We are constantly putting the needs of our family members—our children, our spouses, our aging parents—ahead of our own. If you're like me, and Lena, you let frustration and anger build until you reach the boiling point. And that's not healthy. Lena would never have had the courage to run away from home if she hadn't acted on impulse. Seize the moment! I'm not suggesting you abandon your professional and personal responsibilities and take off on a self-indulgent, soul-searching journey. There are other ways to get out of a rut. Rekindle a forgotten passion. Take up a new hobby. Make a new friend. Audit a class. Start an exercise program.

To find happiness in your life, believe in yourself, be kind to yourself, constantly remind yourself of your worthiness. I recently saw an eccentric young man's audition on *American Idol*. His words struck me: "I'm living my best life."

Are *you* living *your* best life? You owe it to yourself to put your best foot forward every single day, to be the best that you can be. Don't wait until your children have left the nest to focus on *you*. Discover your passion now! I know what you're thinking—easier said than done. Boy, don't I know it. It's constant trial and error. But you're on your journey, and if something isn't working, try something new. Record only positive thoughts on your self-talk tape, and play it over and over in your mind. *I can. I will. I'm worth it.* And never, ever give up on *you*.

ACKNOWLEDGMENTS

I'm grateful to the many people who helped make this novel possible. First and foremost, to my editor, Patricia Peters, for her commitment to excellence and for making my work stronger without changing my voice. To my agent, Andrea Hurst, for her guidance, her sound advice, and her friendship. To Danielle Marshall, editorial director at Lake Union Publishing; Gabriella Dumpit, author relations manager extraordinaire; and the amazing Amazon marketing team. To Nicole Pomeroy, my production manager, for polishing the manuscript for publication, and to Tara Quigley Whitaker and Kellie Osborne, my very skilled copyeditors.

A great big heartfelt thank-you to Kathy Sinclair, criminal investigator with the Bartow County Sheriff's Office, for her expert advice on matters relating to Lena's arrest. A special thank-you to those who patiently answered my many questions regarding locale: Johanna Carrington and Karen Stephens for an inside look at the Northern Neck, and Alison Fauls as well as Cheryl and Jack Fockler for logistical information regarding New York City. Also to Alison for giving me honest and constructive feedback on this work while in progress.

I am blessed to have many supportive people in my life who offer the encouragement I need. Thank you to my behind-the-scenes team—Geneva Agnos and Kate Rock—for all the many things they do in managing my social media so effectively, and to my advanced review team, the lovely ladies of Georgia's Porch, for their enthusiasm for and commitment to my work. To Leslie at Levy's and the staff at Grove Avenue Pharmacy for helping my books make it into the hands of local readers. Love and thanks to my family—my mother, Joanne; my husband, Ted; and the best children in the world, Cameron and Ned.

Most of all, I'm grateful to my wonderful readers for their love of women's fiction. I love hearing from you. Feel free to shoot me an email at ashleyhfarley@gmail.com or stop by my website at www.ashleyfarley.com for more information about my characters and upcoming releases. Don't forget to sign up for my newsletter. Your subscription will grant you exclusive content, sneak previews, and special giveaways.

ABOUT THE AUTHOR

Ashley Farley is the bestselling author of the Sweeney Sisters series, as well as *Sweet Tea Tuesdays*, *Magnolia Nights*, *Beyond the Garden*, *Nell and Lady*, *Only One Life*, and other books about women for women. Her characters are mothers, daughters, sisters, and wives facing real-life situations, and her goal is to keep readers turning pages with stories that resonate long after the last word.

In addition to writing, she is an amateur photographer, an exercise junkie, and a wife and mother. While she has lived in Richmond, Virginia, for more than two decades, part of her heart remains in the salty marshes of the South Carolina Lowcountry, where she grew up. Through the eyes of her characters, she captures the moss-draped trees, delectable cuisine, and kindhearted folk with lazy drawls that make the area so unique. For more information, visit www.ashleyfarley.com.